P9-DGL-050

BEASTS OF A LITTLE LAND

BEASTS OF A LITTLE LAND

A Novel

JUHEA KIM

ecco
An Imprint of HarperCollins*Publishers*

This is a work of fiction. Names, characters, places, and incidents are products of the author's imagination or are used fictitiously and are not to be construed as real. Any resemblance to actual events, locales, organizations, or persons, living or dead, is entirely coincidental.

FIRST EDITION

Designed by Michelle Crowe

Title page and Part opener art by Sergey Pekar and khan3145 / Shutterstock, Inc.

Library of Congress Cataloging-in-Publication

Names: Kim, Juhea, author.
Title: Beasts of a little land: a novel / Juhea Kim.
Identifiers: LCCN 2021002241 (print) | LCCN 2021002242 (ebook) | ISBN 9780063093577 (hardcover) | ISBN 9780063093591 (ebook)
Subjects: LCSH: Courtesans—Fiction. | Korean resistance movements, 1905–1945—Fiction. | GSAFD: Historical fiction. | Love stories.
Classification: LCC PS3611.I454535 B43 2021 (print) | LCC PS3611.I454535 (ebook) | DDC 813/.6—dc23
LC record available at https://lccn.loc.gov/2021002241
LC ebook record available at https://lccn.loc.gov/2021002242

21 22 23 24 25 FB 10 9 8 7 6 5 4 3 2 1

For my mother, Inja Kim, and my father, Hackmoo Kim

어머니와 아버지께 드립니다

BEASTS OF A LITTLE LAND

PROLOGUE

THE HUNTER

1917

THE SKY WAS WHITE AND THE EARTH WAS BLACK, LIKE AT THE BEGINning of time before the first sunrise. Clouds left their realm and descended so low that they seemed to touch the ground. Giant pines loomed in and out of the ether. Nothing stirred or made a sound.

Hardly distinguishable in this obscure world, a speck of a man was walking alone. A hunter. Crouching over a raw paw print, still soft and almost warm, he sniffed in the direction of his prey. The sharp smell of snow filled his lungs, and he smiled. Soon, a light dusting would make it easier for him to track the animal—a large leopard, he guessed, from the size of the print.

He rose quietly like a shade among the trees. The animals moved without a sound, here in their own domain, but the mountains belonged to him also—or rather, he, like the animals, belonged to the mountains. Not because they were generous or comforting, for nowhere in these woods was safe for man or beast. But he knew how to *be* when he was on a hill, to breathe, walk, think, and kill, just as a leopard knows how to be a leopard.

The ground was mostly covered with red-brown pine needles, and the footprints came few and far between. Instead, he looked for scratchings on tree trunks or places where the thickets were left almost imperceptibly disturbed, perhaps just a few wispy hairs caught at the ends of a broken branch. He was closing the gap between them, but he still hadn't caught sight of his prey in the past two days. He had long ago run out of his provision, coarse barley balls flavored only with salt. He'd spent the previous night in the split-open trunk of a red pine, looking up at the white sickle moon to keep himself from falling asleep. But his hunger and fatigue made his feet lighter and head clearer, and he decided he would stop moving when he fell dead, but not before then.

There were no killings left behind thus far. Rabbits, deer, and other small beasts were dried up in winter, and it was just as hard for a leopard as it was for people. At some point it would have to stop, and that was how he was going to kill it. They both needed food and rest, but he was determined that he would go on longer than his prey, as long as necessary.

He came upon a glade, a circle of young pines huddling away from a rocky ridge. He walked up to the overhang and looked around the surrounding mountains in their wintry down of charcoal and ash green. The sheets of clouds, blown by the wind, were caught at the throats of hills and billowed like torn silk. Beneath his feet, there was a fall into the wild white abyss. He was glad to have been led to this place. Leopards loved rocky cliffs, and it was more than likely there was a den here.

Something soft and cold gently touched his face. He looked up at the sky and saw the first sprinkling of snow. Now he'd have more footprints to track, but he would also have to find the animal quickly and descend the mountain before the snow thickened. He tightened the grip on his bow.

If his instincts were true, and the leopard was just below him in its den on the side of the cliff, he wouldn't have to struggle to find it any longer. But he would have to wait at that spot until it came wandering out again, which might be in another hour, or three days hence. By then, the snow would go over the top of his head while standing. He would become snow and rock and wind, his insides would feed the leopard and his blood would nourish the young pines, so that he may as well have never had a life down below as a human among other humans.

In that life, he'd been a soldier in the Imperial Army, handpicked from the best archers in the country. No one could surpass him with a rifle or a bow. They called him PyongAhn Tiger, after an old saying about the personalities of each province. Of course, there were ferocious beasts in every mountain and forest in the little land that even the ancient Chinese had called the Country of Tigers, but the name suited him more than the farmers from the South. His people were born hunters, who survived where the land was too steep and unforgiving for tilling.

His father had also been a soldier under the PyongYang magistrate. Whenever they skipped paying the army, his father had gone into the mountains. Most often he'd brought back small game—deer, hares, foxes, and pheasants—though sometimes boars, black bears, leopards, and wolves.

When he was a child, his father had killed a tiger by himself, and six of the village's strongest men had to come help him carry the beast down the mountain. The rest of the villagers surrounded them in solidarity while the children ran ahead of the crowd, cheering. A tiger skin was worth more than a soldier's yearly wage. Its massive body was laid to rest in the village square under the ginkgo tree, and somehow the women prepared a feast out of nothing—that was their talent—and everyone drank their fill of the milky rice wine.

But later that night, sitting cross-legged on their hot-stone floor, his father turned grave. Never kill a tiger unless you have to, his father said sternly.

But Father, we are rich now. We'll be able to buy all the rice we need, he said. The stub candle was flickering modestly, without defying the darkness that protected them all like a thick winter quilt. His mother and younger sisters were either sewing or asleep in the other room, and there was only the murmurous sound of owls on their hunt.

His father just looked at him and said, You've been shooting hares and pheasants since you were a child.

Yes, Father.

You can take down a pheasant flying a hundred yards away.

Yes, Father, he said proudly. Already there was no better archer than him in the entire village, except for his father.

You can shoot an arrow into a tree from a hundred and twenty yards away, and shoot another one right on top of it.

Yes, Father.

So do you think you can kill a tiger? his father asked. He wanted to say Yes, and he did think he could. But his father's voice as he asked the question already foretold him that the only right answer was silence.

Show me your bow, his father said. He got up and brought his bow and laid it on the floor between them.

You can't kill a tiger with this bow no matter how good of a marksman you are, his father said. It's not powerful enough at a long distance, and a tiger is no pheasant. This bow can only carry enough force to wound a tiger if you shoot from twenty yards or under. To fatally wound, fifteen yards or less. Do you know how quickly a tiger can cross fifteen yards?

He admitted his ignorance with silence.

A tiger is three yards from nose to the tip of its tail, and can jump over the village tree if it wants to. To a tiger, leaping over this cottage is like skipping over a puddle to you and me.

If you take a shot at the tiger too soon, you'll only injure it lightly and make it more ferocious. Take a shot too late or miss, the tiger will be upon you before you finish blinking your eyes. A tiger can cross fifteen yards in a second.

But, Father, he said. You killed a tiger today.

I told you, kill a tiger if you have no other choice. And that's only when the tiger tries to kill you first. Never go after a tiger otherwise, do you understand?

• • •

THE HUNTER'S MEMORIES GATHERED SOFTLY like the snow falling around him. He hid himself behind a rock, facing out toward the ledge. His senses were dulled by the snow, which was swirling into his eyes and nose and crusting over his bare hands. It was coming down heavier than he'd thought—and from this height, with the clear view of the clouds blowing in from the east, he could see it wouldn't stop. He realized that he should have gone down the mountain the moment he first smelled the snow coming, when he stopped over that wet paw print.

He hated seeing his children staying so still and quiet inside the cottage, drained of the strength to even chatter. He had promised them that he would come back with something to eat. If only he'd caught a deer or a rabbit, he would have gone home to them and seen their small happy faces lit brightly like lanterns. Instead, he found only the leopard's footprint and was tempted by the possibility of its hide, worth more than half of a year's harvest.

Is this the day I die? he wondered. Suddenly he became very tired, losing all tension that had held him upright. Then he imagined that the snow looked like a steaming bowl of white rice, which he'd only eaten less than five times in his entire life. He didn't become angry—he laughed, as if the laughter were just a wind passing through his thin body. He wanted to think a bit more about foods he would've liked to eat before dying, like braised ribs with soy sauce and scallions, and oxtail broth so rich with melted marrow it sticks to the inside of your mouth. He'd had those things once at a holiday feast. But these fantasies were not as strong or seductive as other memories that now overwhelmed him.

When he first saw Sooni, walking arm in arm with her sisters, on her way to collect wormwood and fiddleheads in the valley. She was thirteen, and he was fifteen.

Sooni, wearing a green silk jacket and a red silk skirt, all embroidered with flowers, and a jeweled headdress—the court dress for royal princesses, which the common folk were allowed to wear only once in their lives for their wedding. A marriage was so sacred in the eyes of gods and men that a lowly tenant farmer's daughter, born and raised in undyed white hemp every day of her entire life, was permitted to play the part of the most noble of women just for a day. He himself was dressed in the official court uniform of a minister, a blue robe with a belt and a hat made of black horsehair. The villagers loudly teased him, How he stares at the bride! He doesn't look like he'll get any sleep tonight. Sooni kept her pretty eyes downcast even while she was walking. Two matrons attended her on either side so she could shuffle slowly under her heavy robes. They faced each other at the altar, took turns offering each other a cup of clear wine, drank from it, and then they were bound to each other forever.

When night fell and they were left alone in their marital chamber, he carefully removed the many silk layers of her princess outfit, which had been worn by every bride in their village for generations. Sooni was shy, unlike her usual cheerful self, and he himself was very nervous. But after he blew the candle out, and caressed her smooth shoulders and kissed her moonlight skin, she wrapped her legs around his waist and raised her hips. He was shocked and grateful that she desired him too. The joy in being one with her was unimaginable. It was the opposite of standing high in the mountains, which had been the most intense happiness he'd known until then. Whereas that was an ecstasy of height, coolness, and solitude, this was an ecstasy of depth, warmth, and union. He wrapped an arm around her and she nestled her head on the nook between his shoulder and chest. Are you happy? he'd asked. I wish we could be like this forever, she'd whispered. But I'm also so happy that I wouldn't have any regrets if I died right now. Like I wouldn't even be mad.

Me too, he'd said. That's exactly how I feel too.

The hunter felt himself fall into a soft, cloudy mound of memories. It was so sweet to let go of his grip on the present and dwell among the shadows of the past. Slipping into death really wasn't so bad—it was rather like passing through a door to a world of dreams. He closed his eyes. He could almost see Sooni gently calling out to him, My husband, my darling, I've been waiting for you. Come home.

Why did you leave me, he said. Do you know how hard it's been for me?

I was always next to you, Sooni said. You and the kids.

I want to go with you, he said, and waited for her to take him away.

Not yet, but soon, she said.

His eyes snapped open as he realized he really was hearing a sound. A soft breathing sound that came from the edge of the cliff, whence an icy fog was emanating like incense. Instinctively he readied his bow, knowing that even if he got his prey, he likely wouldn't make it down the mountain. He just didn't want to end up as a leopard's meal.

He felt, rather than saw, the leopard climb up onto the ledge, its silhouette weaving through the brume. He gasped and lowered his bow when it finally revealed itself, just yards away from him.

It wasn't a leopard at all, but a tigerling.

From nose to the tip of the tail, it was as long as his arms stretched wide apart—just the size of a full-grown leopard. It was too big to be called a cub, though still too young to hunt on its own. The tigerling looked at the hunter with curious eyes, twitching its circles of ears padded with white fur. Its calm yellow irises were neither threatened nor threatening. It had almost certainly never seen a human being before, and looked mildly puzzled by the strange apparition. The hunter gripped his bow tighter. It was, he realized, the first time he'd spotted a tiger within range.

Hunted by the Japanese in every hill and valley, tigers had been driven deep into the wildest mountains. The prices had gone up accordingly for their skin, bone, and even meat, which had never before been the reason they were hunted, but had become a fashionable delicacy on the tables of wealthy Japanese. They believed that eating tiger flesh gave you its valor, and held banquets where officers decked with epaulettes and medals and upper-class ladies in European dresses sat down to taste courses made entirely of tiger parts.

With this kill, he would be able to buy enough food to last three years. Perhaps even a plot of land. His children would be safe.

But the wind howled into his ear, and he lowered his bow and arrow. *Never kill a tiger unless it decides to kill you first.*

He got up to standing, which sent the tigerling scampering backward like a village pup. Before it even disappeared back into the fog, the hunter turned around and started his descent through the thickening snow. Within a span of a few hours, the snow had already gathered halfway up his calf. The hollowness that had made his feet lighter was now dragging him closer to the earth with every step. A gray, colorless dusk was draped over the shivering trees. He started praying to the god of the mountain, I've let go of your attendant creature, please let me make it down.

The blizzard stopped at nightfall. He came halfway down the mountain before his legs buckled and he fell knee first into snow. He was on fours like an animal; when even his elbows gave out he curled into the powder, sparkling white in the moonlight. Then he thought, I should be facing the sky, so he heaved himself over onto his back. The moon was gently smiling down on him: it was the closest thing in nature to mercy.

• • •

"WE'VE BEEN GOING IN CIRCLES," Captain Yamada said. The others around him looked frightened, not just because what he was saying was true, but also because he dared to voice this calamity in the presence of his superior.

"These trees are all growing thicker on this side—so that way must be south. But you see how we have been heading the opposite way for the past hour!" Captain Yamada exclaimed, barely concealing his contempt. At twenty-one, he already had the manner of someone used to giving orders and opinions without once being challenged, which was a habit born out of his highly influential family. The Yamadas were a cadet branch of an ancient samurai clan, and his father, Baron Yamada, was a close friend of Governor-General Hasegawa himself. The Hasegawas and the Yamadas both hired Englishmen to educate their sons, and Genzo had toured Europe and America with a Hasegawa cousin before returning to take the commission. That was how he'd been made a captain at such a young age, and why even his superior Major Hayashi was careful not to offend him.

"We can't keep going around like this, sir." Captain Yamada finally directed his comment at Major Hayashi, and the whole group came to a halt. These were four sergeants, the local police chief Fukuda and two of his men, and a Korean guide.

"So what do you think we should do then, Captain?" Major Hayashi said, slowly and deliberately, as though they were back in the barracks and not in the snowy mountains, the night fast closing down on them.

"It's getting darker by the minute, and we won't find the right way at night if we lost it by day. We should make camp for tonight.

As long as we can avoid freezing to death, we'll be able to make our way down tomorrow at first light."

The group fell even quieter, anxiously anticipating Major Hayashi's reaction. He had never before become impatient with Captain Yamada's impertinence, but this time, in such a dire state, the conflict had an air of mutiny. Major Hayashi regarded his subordinate's face with cool indifference, wearing the kind of expression he had when considering a new pair of boots or the best way to skin a rabbit. In spite of his pure and profound brutality, Hayashi was not a man given to uncalculated outbursts. At last, he turned to a sergeant and started giving orders for making camp. The group, visibly relieved, dispersed to collect firewood, or such as could be had when it was snowy and wet.

"Not you—you stay here with me," Major Hayashi said when the Korean guide, a timid creature named Baek, tried to scurry away. "Do you think I'd let you out of my sight?" Baek wrung his hands and whimpered, staring down at his feet bound in rags and shod in wet leather shoes.

Shortly after being assigned to the prefecture, Major Hayashi had asked Police Chief Fukuda where he could find game in these parts. Fukuda, who had made a detailed report and census of every Korean within fifty miles, had recommended three locals for the task of guiding their hunting party. The other two were potato farmers whom even other Koreans deemed quite savage, cloistered in the deep mountains, mating among themselves, and living off the land, only coming out to join the rest of the world a handful of times a year on market days. They both knew every stick and stone in the mountains—but Baek, a traveling silk merchant, was the only one who could speak Japanese. Major Hayashi had considered that to be a more important qualification, much to the regret of all, not least Baek himself.

• • •

IT WOULD BECOME ONE OF the images that would flash in front of Captain Yamada's eyes, just before the end of his life. The bearded man lying under the moonlight. When he'd gone about twenty feet into the woods to collect firewood, he nearly stumbled over the body sprawled out on the snow. After the initial shock, what struck Captain Yamada was how the man was spread calmly on his back, both hands over his heart—as if he hadn't frozen to death, but had fallen asleep in a moment of rapture. The second thing that struck him was how poorly clad this small man was. The quilted jacket he wore was so thin that the sharp angles of his shoulder blades showed clearly through.

Captain Yamada circled around the body. Then, for reasons he himself couldn't understand in retrospect, he lowered his ear to the bluish face.

"Hey, hey! Wake up!" he shouted, realizing that there was a trace of breath still flowing from the man's nostrils. When there was no response, Captain Yamada took the man's face in his hands and slapped it lightly. The man began to moan almost inaudibly.

Captain Yamada placed the man's head back on the snow. There was no reason he needed to help this nearly dead Josenjing, more of a vermin than a person. Captain Yamada started heading back toward the camp, but after a few steps he turned around, without understanding why. Sometimes the human heart was like a dark forest, and even a man as rational as Yamada had mysteries within. He picked up Josenjing in his arms, almost as easily as if he were a child.

"What the hell is this?" barked Major Hayashi when he returned.

"I found him in the woods," Captain Yamada said as he laid the man down on the ground.

"What do you want to do with a dead Josenjing? Unless you mean to burn him for fuel—and he'd make an awful fire—you should've left him where you found him."

"The man's still alive. He was hunting alone in these parts, which means he knows the mountains well. He might be able to find the way down," Captain Yamada explained coolly, unfazed by the veiled accusation of softheartedness; after all, that compassion had never been in the library of Yamada's motives and emotions was something both men knew well.

The rest of the group came back, and Captain Yamada ordered Baek to move the unconscious man next to the fire and shout to him in Korean. When he started coming to, Baek called out, smiling like a lunatic, "Sir! Sir! He's waking up!" Captain Yamada had Baek feed the man some crackers and dried persimmon from his own provisions.

"Make sure you stick the cracker in the snow to wet it a bit. He might choke otherwise," Captain Yamada said, and Baek promptly obeyed, holding the man's head on his lap and cooing something softly in Korean.

"Do they know each other?" Major Hayashi asked. He was eating his own supper of stiffly frozen *onigiri* and some pickled plum. There was even a bottle of sake that the sergeants were now passing around, suddenly merry and heartened.

"I don't think so. Baek didn't seem to recognize him," Captain Yamada said. Police Chief Fukuda also didn't know the man. But one of his officers thought that he might be a certain tenant farmer Nam, whose only distinction from all the other miserable peasants of the area was having once been in the Korean Imperial Army, and thus came to the police's attention.

"A dangerous man then. A viper," Major Hayashi said.

"He might prove himself useful. I would think it well worth keeping him alive for one night, if he can get us down this accursed mountain at dawn," Captain Yamada replied as calmly as ever. He himself ate just a few crackers and a dried persimmon, and prepared to take the first watch.

• • •

THE DAWN CAME without a sunrise, and illumined by the cinereal light the woods materialized around them once more. The absence of sun and shadows made everything seem weightless, as if the trees, rocks, and snow were all made out of soft silver air. It seemed a halfway world, a world between other worlds.

Upon waking to such a morning, Captain Yamada wondered if he was still dreaming and hoped that he would open his eyes to find himself in the warmth of his own bed. Then he realized the next moment where he truly was and felt almost sick to his stomach with disappointment. But by both nature and education, he'd been led to prize rationality and distrust emotions. He held love or even friendship in contempt as delusions of the lower classes, women, and unfit men. The biggest problem with emotions was that they were reactions to externalities rather than one's innate will and deliberate consciousness. Accordingly, he chastised himself for indulging in self-pity and shrugged his blanket off without delay.

Yamada got up and walked away to relieve himself; and there, just yards from where he was sleeping, he discovered huge paw prints, circling around the camp many times. He woke up Baek and the hunter, who had fallen asleep embracing each other for warmth. Baek jumped up instantly when he mentioned the tracks, and started explaining feverishly to the hunter in Korean. The latter man looked ill and weak, though his eyes were astonishingly sharp for someone who had nearly died just the previous night. He whispered something, then Baek helped pull him upright.

"What's he saying?" Captain Yamada asked as the hunter looked down at the tracks and mumbled in Korean.

"He's saying it must be a tiger. There's no other animal that has a footprint as big as a pot lid. Everyone knows that," Baek said.

"Now he's saying, we need to go down now. The tiger was here all night watching us, and it's not happy."

"Why didn't anyone on watch see this tiger?" Captain Yamada asked, feeling irritated at the ones who had taken over after him. Baek relayed this to the hunter and then translated his answer.

"He says the tiger didn't want to be seen. You see tigers when they want to be seen, not a moment before. We're in their home, their land, so it's best we leave it alone and go quietly."

"Nonsense. If I see that beast before we make it down, I will kill it—and present the skin and the meat to the governor-general," Captain Yamada said. "You cowardly Josenjing slaves know nothing of bravery."

Baek hung his head low in acceptance. Nonetheless it was clear to all, especially Captain Yamada, that the sooner they could find their way out of the mountain, the better. The hunter led the way with surprising agility, given that he'd only broken his fast with a bit of rice crackers, seaweed, and pickles: it seemed that he was used to surviving on very little food. Captain Yamada had confiscated his bow and arrows, but the hunter appeared to take that as a matter of course and briskly slipped through the trees, neither resentful nor pleading.

"Be sure to shoot him if he tries to run," Major Hayashi said, and the captain replied, "Yes, sir."

The sun stayed hidden on this gray day, and the world became gradually brighter without any visible light. The wind pricked their skin like a thousand points of ice, colder and less forgiving than on the previous day. Every step they made turned into deep, clear impressions on the snow, and the hunter turned around from time to time as if worried. He whispered to Baek, who delivered the message to Captain Yamada.

"Please, we must move more quickly, he says," Baek pleaded. "He's certain the tiger is tracking us, and quite likely right at our heels."

"You Josenjing are truly pathetic, cowardly worms," Captain Yamada said scornfully. "Tell him we have guns, not bows and arrows. The officers in the Japanese Imperial Army do not flee from animals—we hunt them."

Baek fell silent and shuffled back to his place in the group, behind the hunter. The others smiled and nodded assent to the captain's speech, and boasted about this or that hunting party they had been on, and animals that they'd killed since coming to Joseon: white leopard cubs with ice-blue eyes, black bears with a pale crescent moon mark on their chest, stags, and wolves. But none claimed to have hunted a tiger which, though supposedly omnipresent, was the most clever creature of them all.

Even their boasts died down as time passed. With the sun moving across the sky unseen, they couldn't guess what time it was except through hunger and a creeping frustration. They hadn't planned on being lost for almost an entire day, and after a scanty-enough dinner, most of them had finished off their last provisions at breakfast. They marched in silence, until the hunter stopped in his tracks and held out his hand to the rest of the group. He pointed at a tree that was still swinging slightly, shedding snow as fine and white as sea spray.

"What is it?" Captain Yamada asked Baek. But before he could answer, they heard a deep, haunting sound, like thunder during the Long Rain season. They all felt an indescribable gaze of an unknown power; it was coming from the flash of orange and black between the trees just ahead of them—less than twenty yards away. It was watching them boldly, unmoving save for the twitching of its shaggy, frosted mane. Its bright yellow eyes dotted with jet-black pupils were the only things so vivid and alive in this world of only white.

Within a second, the soldiers all drew out their rifles and aimed at the tiger, which remained as still as a statue. Captain Yamada gave a nod to his officers, then fired the first shot of the many bullets that flew almost simultaneously from the squad. Triggered by the attack, the tiger took to its feet and started bounding toward them as if flying. It covered the yards between them in the blink of an eye as the soldiers froze in their places. Captain Yamada felt his heart turn to ice just as someone started moving across his field of vision. The hunter was rushing forward, holding both his hands up in the air.

"Don't!" His shout rang out in the glade and the trees trembled. "No!"

Without slowing down, the tiger spun and turned toward him.

"No! No!" the hunter repeated, until just a yard away from him, the tiger stopped in its tracks. It locked its yellow eyes with him for a moment, then circled and ran away just as quickly as it had come. When the soldiers started shooting again, it had already disappeared into the thicket—leaving a trail of bright red blood that dotted every third footprint, on its left hind leg.

"What are you all standing like that for?" Major Hayashi shouted. "We're going to follow it—it can't go very quickly. We'll kill it before nightfall."

The hunter said something rapidly to Baek. The old merchant pleaded, "This man thinks we have to let this tiger go. An injured tiger is far more dangerous than a healthy one, he says. Tigers are vengeful creatures. They remember wrongs and rights, and if it's injured, it will attack to kill.

"Even if we kill the tiger, that will be the end of us if we get stuck in the mountain for another night, and it being already colder than the night before . . . so says this man, sir."

Major Hayashi looked around at his men, who looked defeated and unwilling to go deeper into the mountain after the enormous beast. It had shown no sign of slowing down even with the wound.

Hayashi had led not only hunting parties such as this one, but also combat on the field, most recently in Manchuria against the

Russians, and then of course the control of unrest and rebellions in Korea. He had never turned back from a fight but not out of bravery, which he equated to foolishness. He only believed in success, and even his bloodthirst was only secondarily for his own pleasure—primarily it was to assert his superiority to his peers and to intimidate his subordinates. Since success, to Hayashi, was of practical rather than virtuous nature, he again decided on the course that would serve him best. He ordered the Josenjing hunter to lead the descent.

Even as they made their way down and away from the beast, they felt as though a pair of yellow eyes were fixed on their necks the entire time. But at last they found themselves on a trail, recognizable even under a foot of snow. A few hours later, they came out of the deep woods and onto the overlook where they could see the village down below. The straw-thatched roofs were glowing amber with an unexpected flash of the sun, finally breaking through the clouds just above the horizon.

If they hadn't been officers, they would have run down the slippery, snowy slope like children, overjoyed as they were by that sight. But tempered by the presence of their leader, they marched only a little faster. It took another half an hour before the men finally reached the foot of the hill where the village farms met the border of wilderness. The fallow fields under a blanket of snow were stamped with the footprints of birds and of children.

Major Hayashi ordered a halt and discussed something with the police chief, an oily and gluttonous man to whom a few days of hardship had given a temporarily gaunt appearance. The other officers laid down their packs and began smoking, chatting lightheartedly. They had already forgotten the terror, and were exhilarated by the prospect of warming themselves with food and fire, laughing over it all.

"You," Captain Yamada called out to the hunter, who cautiously stepped closer to Baek. "Your name."

"My name is Nam KyungSoo," the hunter said in halting Japanese.

"You were in the Korean Imperial Army?"

Baek translated for Nam, who nodded.

"You know it's illegal for Josenjings to possess weapons of any kind? I could have you arrested right now."

Baek looked mortified as he whispered in Korean to Nam, who merely glared back at Captain Yamada. The officer frowned back at the hunter. The two men couldn't have been more different: one, dressed in a warm officer's outfit and a fur-trimmed hat, handsome and lithe and bursting with energy even after three hard days in the forest; and the other, shorter man, sharp cheekbones casting dark shadows on his face, hair with more gray than black, looking as ancient, weathered, and bony as a rock.

But even so, Yamada momentarily saw something in the other man's eyes. Soldiers on opposing sides are much more alike than different, often resembling one another more closely than they do their respective civilians. Despite his mangy appearance, Nam looked like he would kill his enemies and protect his allies; Yamada respected that.

"I'm confiscating your weapons. If I ever hear you've been hunting again, I will arrest you personally. Consider that your reward for leading us back down."

Baek relayed the message while bowing deeply at the young officer. Yamada gave a curt nod in acknowledgment, but Nam only glared back for a moment before turning away.

"Hey, Baek!" Major Hayashi called out, and the old merchant shuffled forward.

"Yes, sir."

"You led us astray, you stupid worm," Major Hayashi said, almost lazily. Baek cowered and kept his head bowed low.

"I'm sorry sir, the snow covered the trails and made it impossible to find them, I've gone up and down these mountains hundreds of times, but . . ."

"You ruined our hunt, and almost got us killed," Major Hayashi said. "Go. I'd run fast if I were you."

Baek trembled, dipped his head multiple times, and turned on his heels to run as quickly as his old body would allow. When he had nearly crossed the length of the rice field, Major Hayashi slung his rifle over his shoulder—and fired.

Baek fell forward as if he'd tripped on a rock, his arms splayed wide. He didn't make any noise—or perhaps it was too far for the sound to carry, muffled by the icy ether. The blood spread slowly from the center of his back and soaked through his pack filled with silk.

"That made up for the lack of real sport, what do you think, Chief Fukuda?" Major Hayashi asked, and Fukuda agreed obsequiously.

"And as for that man Nam, I'll turn him over to you, since this is your jurisdiction."

"Ah yes, of course. We will make a very good example out of him," Fukuda said. "After we are done with him, no one will dare pick up a weapon again in these parts."

"That doesn't seem called for, Chief." Captain Yamada stepped forward. "This Josenjing led us down from the mountain. We wouldn't have made it otherwise."

"You also saved his life, so I'd consider that even. But add to that his poaching—seems the scale is tilted against him," Fukuda said, smiling as if satisfied by his own cleverness.

"But he also saved us from that tiger," Yamada replied coolly. "It appears to me that squares the score back to even." He looked from Fukuda to Major Hayashi, then back to Fukuda. "I have no love of filthy Josenjings, and have no doubt that I have killed enough of them on the field. But if you harm this man, you would be owing him a debt of life, and nothing is more dishonorable than owing something to an inferior. As he also saved my life, I can't allow that to happen and be shamed. Let him go free."

"You really speak out of turn, Captain," Fukuda said, turning red in the face. He looked at Major Hayashi to back him up.

Hayashi looked almost expressionless, which was when he was at his most dangerous. He licked his lips, a serpentine habit.

"It doesn't seem necessary, after all, to kill every Josenjing who knows these parts. He was indeed useful, unlike that worthless old man Baek," Hayashi said.

At that, Fukuda quickly gave up and they decided to head to the police station.

When he was sure of not being noticed, Yamada breathed out with a sense of genuine relief. He had never wished anything for or from others, which gave him a secret satisfaction all his life. He felt complete in his independence, and never longed for warmth even from his mother—a quiet, elegant lady with cold white hands—or for the love of a woman. But the possibility of losing his face because of Fukuda's brutishness had roused Yamada more than he'd even expected. He was irritated by this sense of attachment to another's fate. The less he could be certain of Nam's safety, the longer this attachment would last. So he pulled Nam aside, who had been frozen silent, staring at Baek's body ahead. Crows were already gathered on it, cawing excitedly.

"If you get into trouble, come find me," Yamada said quietly, out of hearing of the others. "My name is Yamada Genzo."

Nam stared back. Yamada didn't know whether he'd understood, so he pulled out a silver cigarette case from the inside pocket of his coat and pressed it onto Nam's hand. Yamada ran his finger along its side, where his name was engraved. Then he pulled away with the rest of the officers; and now that Nam's fate was decided, at least temporarily, no one paid him any mind as he limped away on his own.

PART I

1918–1919

1

SECRET LETTERS

1918

ON A DAY HOVERING BETWEEN WINTER AND SPRING, THE CUSP OF warmth just visible on the glistening ice, a woman and a girl walked ten miles of country road where tender green shoots were coming up like eyelashes. They had started their journey before dawn and did not stop until they arrived in front of a walled mansion in Pyong-Yang.

The woman heaved a sigh and smoothed down the stray hairs clinging to the sides of her face. She looked more unkempt in contrast to her daughter, who had her shiny black tresses braided behind each ear and joined in one long rope down the center of her back. Jade had been made to work around the house and care for her siblings almost as soon as she could walk, but her mother had always combed and braided her hair every night. Her mother gave more food to her brothers because they were sons, but served her first because she was the oldest. These were the only acts of love Jade had received in the first ten years of her life. Now, she saw that even these had come to an end.

Jade tugged at her mother's sleeve.

"Can I go back home with you?" she said, her voice punctuated by tears.

"Stop crying like a child. Listen to me," her mother scolded her. "You'll be able to come visit for a half day, once every moon. Don't you want to help your mother and father?"

Jade nodded, mopping her face with little red hands like maple leaves. The weight of being a firstborn already hung heavily over her frame.

A servant greeted them at the side entrance and made them wait in the courtyard. There were several tile-roofed villas facing them on three sides, emanating that otherworldly air of fine and old mansions. Even without any wind, Jade was enveloped by a cool draft that seemed to be the house's exhalation. Where the wooden floor of the porch was rubbed smooth and dipped low, she could envision the countless guests taking off their shoes before entering: men seeking pleasure, solace, some jolting reminder of their virility or perhaps their first passion. Though Jade was young, it was easy to see what the men wanted here. Their motivations were simple—to feel alive. It was the women who remained outside of her understanding. Did they ever feel alive, the way they made the men feel?

One of the doors of the villa opened and a woman emerged. Even before she turned around, Jade could immediately tell that she was extremely beautiful just from the shape of her back and the particularly graceful distance between her nape and her shoulders. When she showed her face and even deigned to flash a small smile in their direction, Jade felt her insides clamp with yearning. Instead of the more common kind of female beauty that elicited jealousy in other women, this stranger had the much rarer kind that drew them in with a promise of something that might also rub off on them. But underneath an air of general benevolence, she was not easygoing. She seemed to toy with people's attraction to her, raising their hopes and then watching them cower.

Jade's mother gave a stiff bow, impervious to the woman's charms. Even though they were tenant farmers throwing themselves to a tiny plot of land, they were technically of a higher class than the *giseng*—who belonged to the same ignoble rung as butchers and tanners. Those who made their money in the filth.

"So this is the child?" the courtesan said mildly, and her mother mumbled in response. A cousin's friend was a servant in this house, which was how Jade was arranged to be taken in as a laundry maid earning two won a month, plus her room and board.

"It's a long way to be walking in the mud and the snow," the woman said to her mother but kept her gaze fixed on Jade. Then she sighed, as if seeing something regrettable that could not be helped. Jade imagined that those slender eyes were accustomed to judging the value of finer things, and that her own dry, chapped face was so beneath the mark as to incite pity, like a three-legged dog.

"Auntie, I'm sorry to tell you this. But there's been a mistake. I didn't hear anything from you for a fortnight and so I went ahead and hired another girl to help around the house. But since you've made this trip, please go and have a meal in the kitchen. Rest a while before heading back," she said, shaking her beautiful head wreathed in a braided chignon.

"No, how can that be, Madame Silver? We had sent word." Jade's mother pressed her hands together in front of her chest. The gesture struck Jade as rustic and off-putting, especially in contrast to Silver's cool elegance. "Wouldn't you need another helper in such a big household? My Jade has been taking care of chores since she was four years old. She's bound to be useful."

"I have plenty of help as is," Silver said impatiently. Nevertheless, Jade sensed that the courtesan continued to stare at her with a curious expression in that calm oval face. It was a look of someone who didn't always deign to respond to others and spoke only when it pleased her to say something.

"But if you want, I can take Jade as an apprentice." Silver turned to her mother with an air of finality. "One-time payment of fifty won—as much as she would have earned as a maid in two years. Plus her room, board, training, and clothes. After she starts working in a few years and pays me back the fifty won plus interest, she'll be free to send you whatever she likes."

Jade's mother drew a tight line with her mouth. "I didn't come here to sell my daughter to become a *courtesan*," she managed to spit out, overpronouncing the last word in lieu of saying: whore. "What kind of a mother do you think I am?"

"As you wish." Silver didn't seem perturbed, but Jade noticed that the corner of her mouth twisted with the tail end of a scornful smile. "At any rate, please help yourself to some soup in the kitchen," she said, turning around.

"Wait, Madame." Jade was surprised to hear herself speak. Her mother tapped her shoulder to silence her, but she continued. "I will stay here as an apprentice . . . It's okay, Mama. I'll do it."

"Shush. You don't know anything about what this is," her mother said. Had they been alone, she would have poured out salty diatribes about women who made their keep between their legs. In Silver's presence, she only smacked Jade between her sharp shoulder blades like the folded wings of an unfledged bird.

Silver smiled, as if hearing the unspoken thoughts. "It's true, this isn't for everyone. Do you know what we do?"

Jade brightly blushed and nodded. Her friends whose sisters had been married at fourteen or fifteen had told her what had happened on their wedding night. It seemed unpleasant but the thought also made her clutch her thighs. All things considered, whether it happened for free with one man or for money with many men seemed to be of little consequence, physically speaking. Jade would have been married off in a few years anyway to whoever offered the highest price, like the village doctor, who had been tirelessly seeking a bride for his sick son. In spite of her pity, Jade felt anything was preferable to marrying that simple boy with his clawlike hands. She wouldn't really be his wife, but his sister and then later his mother.

Fifty won was more than twice as much as even that doctor would give, and the money could go a long way—a small plot of land from their landlord, a young rooster and healthy hens for a chicken run. They would never again go to bed without dinner. They could send the boys to school, and the younger girl could make a match with a respectable, landowning family. But only if no one in the village knew that Jade had been sold to a courtesan's house.

Jade could almost see the same vision reflected in her mother's dark eyes, too exhausted even for tears. Silver reached out and held her mother's hand, and she didn't pull away.

"In my experience, even a girl kept in a convent can grow up to be a courtesan if she's meant to become one. The reverse is also true, and more often too. If Jade isn't meant for this, she'll find another path, even if she's raised in a *gibang*." Silver smiled gently. "I almost have no hand in it."

• • •

JADE HAD NEVER SEEN HERSELF in a mirror before arriving at Silver's house. The muted reflections she did glimpse on washing basins had not been a source of special vanity. She had a matte, smooth skin with a candle-wax yellow tinge. Her eyes were small but very bright under a pair of fluffy eyebrows like black feathers. By looking very closely, one could see that her left iris was positioned ever so slightly off-center, pointing outward—a fishlike tendency. Her lips were round and red, even without rouge. Her smile—twinkly, with an undertone of mischief—would have been considered charming had it not framed a few undeniably crooked upper teeth. There were other peculiarities to her physique that a more exceptional girl certainly would not have had. All told, Jade was the kind of young girl who stood exactly at the midpoint between plain and pretty. She hadn't minded, since her mother was suspicious of beauty in general.

Her mother had also viewed too much schooling as poisonous to young girls. Jade had been allowed just a year of classes at the one-room school for all the village students ranging from ages five to twenty. Even amid that chaos, she'd learned more than just simple sums and rudimentary letters, which was all that her mother would have preferred. Because of school, Jade had stopped feeling like a dutiful part of the household like the furnace or the hoe. She both shrank and expanded with knowledge, and was startled by her own, hazy discontent. This was, of course, why learning was deemed so dangerous in the first place. If she'd said aloud what swirled inside her head, her mother would have pinched and slapped her far more often. This fear even subdued her tears at their farewell, for she didn't know whether crying would please or anger her mother.

Jade remained silent and docile as she followed Silver along the first-floor porch. But the house called out to her in secret, and she longed to touch the columns made of fifty-year-old pines and painted red with cinnabar. When she passed by, silk lanterns danced under the eaves, somehow evoking both stillness and movement, artificiality and naturalness. That heady atmosphere could be felt all throughout the house, Jade thought as Silver led her down the hallway; but it was most noticeable in Silver herself. Jade had never seen anyone who glided so much as did Madame Silver—she looked barely capable of having such lowly body parts as feet and toes. And yet, Jade thought there was no one who better exemplified the naturalness of a woman. Silver smiled and spoke with the complete ease of someone who was born to be a female and knew it. She stopped gliding a few feet ahead of Jade and slid open a rice-papered door.

"This is the music classroom," Silver said. All four walls of the large hall were decorated with lavishly painted screens. On one side of the room, there were a dozen very young girls learning a traditional song, repeating line by line after an older courtesan; on the opposite side, eleven- or twelve-year-old girls were practicing the *gayageum*.

"The girls who are singing are in the first year. In the second year, you begin learning the *gayageum*, *daegeum*, and different types of drums. So these are two of the five arts that a courtesan must master—song and instrument," Silver explained. As she spoke, one of the singing girls jumped up from her seat and scampered toward them. Jade could almost hear Silver knit her brows in disapproval.

"Mama, who is this?" the little girl asked Silver, and Jade tried to hide her surprise. With a round face and undistinguished features, the girl looked nothing like her elegant mother.

"You should never leave class without your teacher's permission," Silver said sternly, and Jade was reminded of her own mother. She wondered whether there were any mothers in the world who didn't greet their daughters with anger.

"The class will be over in just a few minutes," the girl persisted. "Is she new? Can I take her around?"

Silver hesitated for a second, as though remembering important tasks much more worthy of her time, then dismissed them both with a flick of her hand. The girl took Jade by the elbow and led her along the hallway.

"I'm Lotus. Thanks for getting me out of class." She giggled. "What's your name?"

"Jade."

"That's a nice name. You probably won't need to change it," Lotus said, opening another sliding door. In this room, slightly smaller than the first room, a set of students were practicing watercolor paintings on one side and calligraphy on the other.

"Did Mama tell you about the five arts of a courtesan? Here are three and four: painting and poetry . . . We also take Korean, Japanese, and arithmetics here. You get tested on every subject once a month, and if you don't get everything correct, you have to repeat that month."

"Even Japanese and arithmetics?" Jade asked, feeling troubled.

"Aye, *especially* those two." Lotus nodded gravely. "I've been held back from moving on to second year for a while now. But that means we can be in the same class!"

Lotus giggled and ran up the flight of stairs to the second floor, and Jade followed her, breathless with laughter. Here, Lotus pulled Jade into the biggest classroom she had seen yet. This room was empty, its polished wooden floor shiny with wear. There were masks and colorful robes hanging on the walls; in one corner, stretched-leather drums and other instruments were neatly stacked one on top of the other.

"This room is for the fifth art of a courtesan—dance. You start learning it in the second year," Lotus said. "So this is it for our school building. Let me show you where you'll sleep."

The girls' dormitory was a single-story villa behind the school. They were crossing the courtyard toward the first years' bedroom when a dazzlingly beautiful girl came out of the kitchen wing. Jade could see that she was not a servant, however, from her costly outfit and the haughty way she was nibbling on a piece of rice taffy. She caught sight of them and started heading in their direction.

"My older sister Luna," Lotus whispered. Luna was unmistakably her mother's daughter. She resembled Silver the way the moon's reflection on the river mirrored its source.

"You're the new girl," Luna said, playing with the end of her braid, which was as thick and fluffy as a leopard's tail. Her face was so radiant that Jade could only steal glances in bits and pieces, a nose here and a mouth there.

"Yes, I'm Jade," she answered with a timid smile, and Luna broke into a splendid laughter.

"You'd be pretty if your teeth weren't so bad. They look like tombstones," the older girl taunted.

"And you have a brain like tombstones," Lotus said without missing a beat. But even the flush of rage did nothing to mar Luna's face and only made her look more like an adolescent empress. Despite her physical resemblance to Silver, Luna was more lively and cruel, with none of Silver's statuesque graciousness toward the less fortunate.

"You unruly girl. This is why no one loves you, even Mama,"

Luna said. Her younger sister just held her gaze until she swept away in contempt.

That night, Jade lay awake in her cot, wondering how she would last a month at the school, let alone graduate and become a courtesan. If she failed her exams, perhaps Silver would turn her into a servant after all. Even now, she was not far ahead of a servant in the household's hierarchy, and making an enemy of Luna was an inauspicious beginning. Complete obedience to the older students and courtesans was surely the most basic tenet at the school. Jade could tell that there were numerous other unspoken rules and expectations at play, and Silver was the undisputed judge who presided over them all.

Nevertheless, Jade soon learned that the mistress didn't take her position for granted. Nor was she a mystical being who never raised her voice except to pronounce platitudes. She exacted punishment on young apprentices who defied older courtesans, and older courtesans who spread gossip or hid their earnings from the house. Bedspreads soiled with menstrual blood, a filched hairpin, even a pot of honey from which a few spoonfuls kept disappearing—nothing escaped her notice. Although she became involved in the pettiest issues, her face remained gravely detached with the impassive attitude of a pale-faced beauty in a seventeenth-century painting. Jade saw that in all aspects Silver cultivated an antique aura, by both natural disposition and conscious decision. Her huge braided crown—a mix of her own hair and wig—would have been old-fashioned and fattening on many women. On her, it spoke to a romantic attachment to the past, a poetic sensibility.

The mistress of the house rarely complimented or took notice of Jade during the first few months. The only one who took any interest in her was Lotus, who was herself not a favorite in the house. Whenever she fought with her older sister, Silver always favored the latter. In their mother's eyes, Lotus was lazy, sneaky, and impetuous, and Luna could do no wrong. Knowing this didn't stop Lotus from trying to swipe back at her sister with tenacity and cunning, like a cat hiding behind a wall to spring out and attack. But with Jade, she readily retracted her claws. She could talk for hours about things of which she had only the faintest idea: the latest fashions, gossip circulating around PyongYang and Seoul, types of men, types of women, and what went on behind certain doors of the establishment where they were forbidden to go. Jade found her flagrant interest in male company shocking, not because she was young but because she was not pretty. Lotus had a bland moonfaced look that was more common in the South—not the oval delicacy of her mother, an archetypal PyongYang beauty. Until then, Jade had supposed that attractive women and girls had greater sensual appetites, and she now saw that this was not necessarily true.

Once they became better friends, Jade thought of this surplus of desire as not a peculiarity but just a quality. She no longer saw her friend's face as plain, but intriguing. Jade came to appreciate Lotus's gift of gab, the way she could make anything sound like shooting stars—unexpected and marvelous phenomena of which they were the only two witnesses. They were the perfect complements, because Jade liked to think endlessly and Lotus liked to talk constantly, and between the two the right balance was struck. Lotus also had a talent for transgressions: one afternoon, she stacked pillows, climbed to the top of the wardrobe, and nonchalantly pulled down the jar where Silver kept her personal stash of honey. Jade watched in amazement, until Silver came in and caught Lotus in the act. Even while being punished—made to stand on one foot or kneel with her arms high over her head—Lotus would cross her eyes and stick out her tongue behind her mother's back, making Jade laugh.

Shortly after their first monthly exam—which Jade had passed despite her worst fears, even Japanese—Lotus answered the question Jade had been too delicate to ask: why she and her sister were so unalike.

"The only man Mama has ever loved is Luna's father. They met when she was nineteen. She still wears the ring that he gave her. Even though she's had other patrons, she has never taken off that silver ring in years and years," Lotus told her. Jade remembered seeing the shimmering band, not as expensive or ornate as Silver's other jewels but noticeable for its heavy, rounded elegance.

Whereas Luna was born out of tragic love, Lotus was simply an accident left behind by a careless patron. Jade secretly believed that this was why Silver treated her younger daughter with such indifference; Lotus was the only thing in her life that had happened completely against her wishes. If a woman like Silver couldn't end up happy, Jade thought it was unlikely she herself would wind up better. Courtesans were considered past their prime by twenty-five and geriatric by thirty. If they didn't manage to become a concubine or a madame before then, they could end up no different from a common prostitute. Naturally, the senior courtesans in Silver's house excelled in the art of falling in love with wizened landlords and decrepit bankers. This was a game at which the men and the women participated in harmonious complicity.

Jade—a few years away from becoming a provincial courtesan of middling looks—still couldn't imagine bedding some landowner with gold teeth and terrible breath. Instead, she dreamed of handsome young aristocrats with a weakness for poetry. According to Silver, the best and most admired courtesans in history could agitate the noblest gentlemen just through poetic correspondences. They often fell deeply in love without even seeing each other's faces, so intensely heightened were their epistolary skills. Sometimes these passions were consummated; other times they tragically went on their whole lives burning with longing. Jade daydreamed often about these romances, sighing as offerings to these thwarted loves. Perhaps this was why her mother had warned against the corruptive power of education—even without any man in sight, language itself seduced her. She fluttered with the knowledge that certain words in a certain order could rearrange her on the inside, like moving furniture. Words changed and remade her constantly, and no one else could even sense a difference. So after their lessons, while other girls busied themselves with strolling in the garden or steaming their skin with rice water, Jade practiced her letters alone.

WHEN SPRING ARRIVED, SILVER MOVED the afternoon literature class to the folly in the garden. Each day, she assigned a girl to recite classical poetry by heart. For her turn Jade chose a poem by Hwang Jini, a sixteenth-century courtesan who made conquests of royals, monks, scholars, penniless artists, and rich philanderers alike. She was said to have had no equal in poetry, calligraphy, literature, painting, dance, and music, and her reputation for beauty spread throughout the kingdom and even reached China. But what Jade admired the most about her was that she freely chose her lovers and left them without tears.

Silver called Jade to the front of the class, and she began:

"Floating on the river, that little boat of pine tree,
How many years has it been moored by the shore?
If the next one asks who has crossed the river first,
I shall say it was a man both learned and gallant."

When she'd first read it, the poem had jolted her with both pain and pleasure. But the other girls seemed utterly unmoved. Only Lotus's face was distorted from suppressing a yawn.

"Very well—one of my favorites," Silver said approvingly. "Now who can tell me what this means?"

The girls looked around at one another furtively, shifting in their seats. Lotus piped, "Is it about going boating, Mama?" and the others twittered and giggled in unison.

"No, of course not. I really despair of teaching you lot any poetry." Silver shook her head gravely. Jade was about to raise her hand when Stoney appeared, bowed to his mistress, and rapped the wooden floor with his knuckles.

"The silk merchant is here? A new one then?" Silver asked. She could make out Stoney's hand-tapped messages no matter how complicated they were; no one else could understand the deaf-mute servant. Silver sighed and rose to standing in one graceful movement.

"I must go look at the fabrics. You may play now," she decreed, and the girls bowed their heads low.

"I could've sworn it was about boating. What do you think it means?" Lotus asked Jade as they slipped on their shoes. Jade had known what the poem meant and even the reason Silver liked it so much. That was why she'd chosen it in the first place.

"It's about a woman who is remembering her first love," she replied.

Among all the courtesans and apprentices, Jade felt that she was the only person who understood this secret language taught by her mistress. Regarding the things her best friend couldn't understand, Jade spoke to books instead. She wondered if she would one day find someone who would speak it back to her.

• • •

IN HER BEDCHAMBER, SILVER SAT down on her silk cot and waited for the merchant, one hand mindlessly twirling the ring on her finger. Through her latticed doors decked with gemstone tassels, she could hear the girls shrieking and laughing in their play.

"Madame Silver, this is Merchant Chun, at your service," the silk merchant announced himself outside her door.

"Please come in."

The merchant opened the sliding door and entered, carrying his pack full of fabrics and trinkets. He bowed low at Silver, who gestured at the burden on his back.

"Do put down that heavy pack and take a seat. And please make yourself comfortable. I've already asked my servant to bring in some refreshments."

"Thank you, Madame, your kindness is unwarranted," Chun said, and then took the pack off his back and laid it down on the floor. He himself sat cross-legged on the silk cushion she'd already set out for him, as Stoney brought over a tray of clear wine and squash fritters—delicacies that only a wealthy courtesan could afford these days.

"I was truly devastated to hear about Old Man Baek," Silver said. "You're a member of his guild—so you must know he's been bringing his wares to this house since even before my time."

Instead of an answer, Chun simply bowed his head.

"Were you close with him, Master Chun?"

"Madame, he was my family. My mother's brother."

"So have you inherited all of his territory?" Silver asked, suddenly keen. Chun considered her face for a moment before answering quietly.

"Yes, Madame. He'd lost his sons long ago and I was his closest kin, heir, and confidant."

"Show me your wares, then," Silver said.

Chun unwound the white fabric that wrapped around his pack. Inside there was a wooden crate that held bolts of silk in summer colors—lightest blue, celadon gray, azalea pink, forsythia yellow, willow green, elegant navy blue for the senior women like Silver, and exuberant camellia red for young girls just beginning to bloom. He pulled out jewelry as well: the silk tassels with coral and jade that dangle provocatively from just below a woman's cropped, unlined jacket; *garakji* double rings, worn stacked in pairs and made of enameled silver, amber, and green or white jade; a gold *binyuh* used to fix a chignon. Then there were jars of fragrant powder from England, cold cream from Japan, rouge for lips and cheeks, camellia oil for smooth and shiny hair, and a silk pouch with real musk, said to have aphrodisiac powers.

Silver picked out a number of fabrics and makeup, lightening his load considerably. When she finished, she turned to look at him.

"This is all great, but have you anything else?" she asked searchingly.

Though Chun and Baek were supposedly close relations, there was very little in the way of resemblance between the two men. Silver had known Baek for years; behind his frail frame and subservient demeanor concealed an immense physical strength that allowed him to make trips from the East Sea to PyongYang, then all the way to Uiju every year into his old age. In his younger years he had traveled to both Shanghai and Vladivostok, though he'd long given much of his former responsibilities to the younger men of his guild. By contrast, Chun's tawny face with shrewd, almost reptilian eyes gave Silver no immediate impulse to trust.

The merchant pulled out a sheet of folded paper from inside his sleeve and offered it to her with two hands. Silver drew a sharp breath and broke open the seal.

As always happened when she saw the general's writing, her hands holding the edges of the paper trembled lightly. She read the letter quickly, drinking his words with her eyes. He thanked her for the money she'd sent last summer and told of the victories and losses in the Siberian hills. His troops followed him into any battle, cold and unequipped as they were in contrast to their enemy. Some of them had brought their wives and children over to Vladivostok, and their happy reunions made him long to see her and Luna's faces. "She must be beautiful if she takes after you. But I fear I'll never see our daughter again before I die," he wrote.

She carefully folded the letter and hid it inside a book on her table. She would reread it again, slowly, when alone and free to dwell on every character.

"Thank you, Master Chun. When I heard Master Baek was killed, I thought this letter would have been found and all would be lost . . . our own lives and those of our men in Vladivostok. I waited all the rest of winter, expecting the worst . . . I slept with a knife by my bed, prepared to end my own life if they came, and yet they didn't."

"Those bastards left his body without searching it—if they had, everything surely would have gone the way you feared," Chun said. "My uncle was planning on luring them to our forces in the mountains, and killing a police chief and high-ranking officers would have been an immense victory . . . But either he truly lost his way in the snow, or our men weren't at their meeting place." Neither Chun nor Silver voiced what they both knew—that if the independence fighters didn't take advantage of trapping a group of lost Japanese soldiers, they may well have been killed off themselves in another unrecorded battle.

"And your uncle's body was untouched until you got to it?"

"No, Madame. I was myself ignorant of what had happened, as I was all the way South at the time. But there was a villager who picked up his body and prepared it for burial. A poor widower with three small children, on the brink of starving to death but an honest man nonetheless. He kept all my uncle's belongings for me until I got there for the funeral, and nothing was missing or tampered with, even his coins."

"What good fortune that was," Silver muttered. She opened her vanity chest and took out two drawstring pouches—one white and the other red, both heavy with solid gold ingots.

"The white one is for your troubles," she said, handing the pouches. "The red one is for the cause. Do you trust the man who will carry this across the border?"

"Madame, it will be no different than when my uncle was living," Chun said. "We lowly merchants love gold as much as any others, but even we have honor."

"I know that well, Master Chun. You should know too that what

I give you now isn't just from me, but from almost all PyongYang courtesans. It's the money we made pouring drinks and lying with men, and the jewelry we've hoarded for our retirement."

Master Chun bowed his head curtly in lieu of a response.

"How long will you stay in town? And when will you come back?" Silver asked.

"I will leave tomorrow at first light. I may be back by fall if I am lucky."

"You should spend the night here, it will be far more comfortable than the inn."

"Thank you, Madame, but that would attract undue attention. And there are my guild brothers waiting for me at the inn . . ." Chun said, already rising. "I should get going."

"Wait, I almost forgot," Silver said. "That poor man who recovered Master Baek's body . . . If you pass by his village on your way out of the city, would you give him something from me?" Silver opened her chest again and picked up this or that trinket. She'd sold her best jewelry and turned them into gold, which the merchant had already tucked safely into his pack. Finally, she pulled off her silver ring and gave it to Chun, smiling wanly.

"Please tell him that it's not very expensive, but that it was my favorite," she said, her lovely voice hesitating only slightly. Master Chun bowed his head once more before taking his leave.

All of her most expensive trinkets combined had meant far less to her than giving up this silver ring. But life had to be kept in balance: she had to do what actually felt like a sacrifice. She would gladly trade her life itself for the safety of the people she loved—the general, Luna, and Lotus. If those three were trapped in a burning house, she would pour a bucket of water over her head and jump into the fire to carry them out. That was the meaning of her love, she declared in her head. But her hand grieved, even as Chun went out the city gates the next morning to deliver the ring to the house of the hunter.

2

LUNA

1918

THE MOST EXTRAORDINARY TURN OF EVENTS BEGAN WITH A DROP OF a pin, an aberration stealing by no more dramatically than a stray dog. One morning, Jade woke up and discovered that all classes had been canceled. She ran outside to greet the air, like a new bee emerging from its cocoon in warm weather. The day was full of early-June vigor. The trees were singing their notes of green, and their freshness could be heard by the eyes. The girls were let loose in the garden like calves, and even Jade wasn't sorry about taking a break from books. When she plopped down to play cat's cradle with Lotus, the reason for such leniency became clear: Silver and Luna, both dressed in their loveliest outfits, were heading out for the day. As they crossed the courtyard, little girls with envious round faces crowded around, all silently yearning for an outing of their own. Jade alone pulled back, unwilling to annoy Silver with neediness. But Lotus came forward and ventured to say, "Mama, I want to come too," in the sad voice of a child knowingly playing up her childishness.

Silver glanced at her younger daughter as if organizing her jewelry box and discovering a memento of an uncertain vintage—amused and slightly embarrassed, but ultimately indifferent. After a moment she said, "Luna is herself only getting her photo taken at fifteen. I will take you too when you're older." She ignored Lotus's crestfallen face with her customary hauteur and climbed onto the rickshaw after Luna, her silk skirt billowing lavishly out of her seat.

An outing was a rare treat for even Luna, who kept sticking her head dangerously far out of the rickshaw and hovering at the edge of her seat. As they moved farther away from their house, Luna gradually lost sight of the things which were familiar to her, until everything around her was new and strange. Passing this or that landmark, her mother explained to her, "That's the new rubber shoe factory that Mr. Hong set up this year. He's already had sales of two thousand won," and "that's the secondary school—you'd see the boys later, but now they must all be in class," or "that sharp pointy thing there is where the Christians worship. They sing too, though not like we do."

"Mama, do you know any Christians? I heard that they were all secretly loyal to the Yankees," Luna said.

"I don't know any Christian who would be patron or friend to us courtesans," Silver said, frowning. "But how can you not become servants to Yankees when you believe in their God? It's not natural."

The rickshaw stopped in front of the studio and the women descended from the carriage, using their fans to shield their pale faces from the sun. The studio door jingled cheerfully as they walked in. The photographer greeted them and led them to the shooting area, which had velvet-upholstered chairs against a plain gray backdrop.

According to the photographer's directions, Silver sat on an armchair and Luna stood with her hands on her mother's shoulder. The photographer lit a lamp to one side of the camera and instructed them not to blink. He counted to three, then a bright flash went off, causing Luna to briefly go blind; then the faded Western-style chairs and props in the studio came back into focus, crowding her world once more. She had a very strange sensation like waking up after a long nap and not knowing whether it's dusk or dawn. It was a little lapse in her one long, continuous, uneventful existence—a skipped heartbeat, the meaning of which was as yet unclear.

As they prepared to leave, the doorbell jingled again and a pair of Japanese officers came in.

"Welcome back, sir," the photographer said loudly in Japanese. "Your photos are ready." At the same time Silver slipped by quickly, leading Luna by the hand. The officers cast a long look at the women as they rushed out and drove away in the rickshaw.

"Here they are. The photos turned out very nicely. I hope you'll be pleased, Major Hayashi," the photographer said, offering an envelope containing some photos of the officers, which he had been called to take after the town's Japanese photographer suddenly died of tuberculosis the previous year. But Major Hayashi barely even looked at the photos, asking instead, "Who were those two women?"

"My old friend and her daughter," the photographer replied nervously, looking over Hayashi's shoulder at his associate who, though dressed in a Japanese officer's uniform, was undoubtedly Korean.

"Sir, that was a famous courtesan named Silver, known as the most beautiful in PyongYang," the Korean man said in perfectly manicured Japanese. Then, with an eagerness that these spontaneous encounters effect in even the most coldhearted, he added, "I hadn't seen her in many years but recognized her immediately."

• • •

WHEN SILVER SENT STONEY to pick up the prints from the photographer, Luna was disappointed that they wouldn't go out again themselves. The drive had been most refreshing, and she liked seeing new sights. Most of all, she'd felt a secret thrill at the look that the officers had given her. It made her want to dress up in fine clothes and ride around town all day; she giggled, imagining how tiresome that would be for the poor rickshaw driver. Then she thought that she didn't want to sleep in her mother's chamber anymore, and was guilty for feeling that way because she knew how much her mother loved her.

Soon, it became so hot that the women took to sleeping out on the cool wooden floor of the covered porch. Luna gave the heat as an excuse and also joined in with the others. The women laid out their cots together so that they made one long bedding on the floor. To ward off mosquitoes they burned sweet-scented wormwood incense that snaked up to the pitch-black sky. The younger girls, excited by this changing of routine, whispered all night, lying in a row like a string of chatty pearls.

One night in bed, Luna said, "Hey, Lotus, I'm dying for some cold, sweet watermelon. Go cut up the one in the kitchen."

"Why should I? I'm not your maid," Lotus said, tucked in her place far away from her sister.

"Because I'm your older sister, you brat. Go do it now, or I'll tell Mama."

Sensing Lotus was about to get into another hopeless fight with Luna, Jade quickly got up.

"I'll go get it," she said, pulling on her slippers. She went round the back courtyard to the kitchen. Inside, there was a large wooden bucket filled with cold water, where the maid had put the watermelon to keep it cool. Jade placed it on the chopping block and stood examining it with a knife in her hand, like an executioner. A creeping sense of malaise came over her.

Jade held the sharp edge of the knife against the dark green skin of the watermelon, and pressed down hard. With a crisp crack, the knife slid down and revealed the deep pink flesh speckled with black seeds. She was cutting the halves into quarters when she felt something bite her hand. She looked down at her left palm and saw a deep gash, from which dark orbs of blood like pomegranate seeds were welling up rapidly. She held her hand away from the watermelon, letting the blood fall onto the floor instead. Without any rags to bind the wound, she balled up her bare left hand into a tight fist, and struggled to clean up the mess and wash up the cutting board and knife with one hand.

Jade wobbled back to the portico, carrying the watermelon wedges in a basket with her right arm. She heard them before she saw them: deep, unfamiliar voices speaking in a mix of Korean and Japanese. Rounding the corner, she saw the girls in their petticoats, standing in a row next to their cots. Walking around in the courtyard in front of them were four men, and next to them in her fine silk outfit, Silver. Jade found Stoney in the corner of her eye and breathed a sigh of relief.

"These are all the girls you have at this school?" asked a Korean man in Western civilian dress.

"Yes," Silver answered quietly. Her eyes were bloodshot even in the moonlight. Jade thought of the knife in the kitchen and backed away quietly—but her feet crunched lightly on the sand, and the Korean officer whipped his head around like a hound.

"You weren't trying to hide this one?" he said, grabbing Jade by the shoulders and making her stand in front of him.

"No, of course not. I didn't even realize she was out of bed," Silver said.

The other three men were dressed in uniform. One of them said something to the plainclothes officer in Japanese, stepping onto the portico without taking off his boots.

"Are you aware that all courtesans' establishments, brothels, and the like must be licensed and operated by the government?" the Korean man asked.

"This house has been in operation for more than a century, passed down from daughter to daughter," Silver said. "We've always paid our taxes. We've done nothing out of tradition."

"Don't pretend to be a fool, you whore. I'd be more careful with my words, if I were you—I know very well what you've been up to," he snapped, and she fell into silence. "You should be thankful that Major Hayashi hasn't shut this place down already," he added, glancing at the uniformed officer on the portico.

With his square head and muscular neck barely contained by his collar, Jade thought that the man called Hayashi looked like a khaki-clad bull. He walked slowly up and down the portico, looking at the girls with keen interest. They kept their faces bowed, and he paused in front of a girl, held up her face in his hand, and turned it left and right, before moving on to the next one. He stopped when he reached Luna and smiled, then shouted jovially in Japanese to his officers. They laughed.

Major Hayashi lifted up Luna's chin, studying her face closely. She kept her eyes downcast, her arms folded tightly over her chest. The major let go of her face and forcefully uncrossed her arms, letting them fall limply to her sides. Then he ran his finger across her collarbone, and then down to her chest, bound tightly by her petticoat. He cupped her breast in his hand and roughly squeezed, until she let out a distressed moan.

"Please." Silver turned to the Korean officer, suddenly more deferential. "I raised that one with more care than if she'd been born to a noble family. From birth she's only been treated like a young lady. This girl is not a courtesan. She's not even registered in the guild." Then she added, "He can have anyone but her."

"Among the young ones, she is clearly the best, and you yourself are too old. Better shut up about it rather than risk lives," the officer said. "If you don't want him to take her here in front of everyone, you may as well give him a room."

"No, I won't," Silver said defiantly. It only took one look from her, and suddenly Stoney leaped out of the corner and threw himself between Luna and the major, pushing the man away. The major's men all picked up their rifles and aimed at Stoney, causing the girls to scream. Hayashi himself staggered a little, then regained his composure with a smile. He threw a punch at Stoney's face, which he blocked with one arm. But immediately two of the officers grabbed hold of Stoney's arms, twisted them against his back, and forced him down to the floor, kicking and struggling silently. When Stoney was finally pinned down on his belly, the major lit up a cigarette and took a long drag, putting a booted foot on top of Stoney's neck.

Jade didn't know if the high-pitched shriek was coming from her own mouth or the other women's. Hearing the commotion, Hayashi laughed, digging in the heel firmly with all his bullish weight; Stoney, unable to scream out, panted like a dog. Some of the young girls were openly crying, and the older ones were frozen in terror, biting their lips. Jade felt her knees wobble and the edges of her consciousness fraying.

Hayashi muttered in Japanese, of which Jade could only catch the words for Joseon filth. He breathed out a white column of smoke and stepped even harder onto Stoney's neck. Sweat was streaming down the mute man's back, and his face was turning blue.

"Stop, please!" Silver rushed onto the portico and knelt next to Stoney. "Don't kill this man, he meant no harm." She too was crying—something she'd never done in front of the others. "He's only a simpleton and a mute, please have mercy."

It didn't matter that the major didn't understand Korean. He took his foot off and kicked Stoney's head hard—there was a loud cracking sound like a watermelon bursting. The officers then let go of their grasp, but Stoney was long past the point of struggling and lay limply in place.

Without waiting any longer, Hayashi grabbed Luna by her arm and dragged her to the floor. She screamed, kicking him away, and he hit her so hard across her head that her long hair flew out of its braid, covering her face. After he punched her several more times she stopped resisting and lay still and silent beneath him. Jade shut her eyes but she couldn't stop herself from hearing his mechanical grunts.

When it was over, Hayashi pulled up his pants as if nothing had happened and walked away, followed by his men. Silver threw herself down next to Luna's discarded figure, and some girls rushed to get rags to bind Stoney's head together. The sound of their crying faded in and out of Jade's ears. She realized she'd been carrying the basket of watermelon all along, which she set down carefully—although no one would eat it, no one would eat anything for a while. It didn't seem possible they could ever go back to playing games and reading poetry in that courtyard. The edges of her vision seemed to come unstitched, and her weak knees finally gave out. Jade passed out unnoticed by anyone, a pool of black-red blood drenching the ground beneath her hand.

3

SOMETHING TO REMEMBER WHEN YOU'RE DOWN

1918

AFTER THAT NIGHT, JADE HAD TO KEEP HER LEFT HAND BOUND IN LINEN for close to a month. When the dressing was removed, nothing was different in her except a long, dark-red line on her left palm that eventually faded to white. But Luna was changed. She could no longer torment anyone, and inspired no fear, only pity. She didn't come out of her room for any reason. Silver herself carried in trays piled with Luna's favorite dishes or fresh melons, and brought them back out a few hours later, mostly untouched. Jade lurked outside the chamber and offered to watch over Luna, but Silver refused all help and continued her vigil alone.

During this time, everyone said Luna would be fine and that Stoney would die. Luna was young, and though she was injured, it wouldn't kill her. But Stoney's head had split, and he'd gone into a stupor. The old herbalist said he probably wouldn't wake up again at his age, and that if he by chance regained consciousness, he would be an even more useless creature, unable to walk or even relieve himself without help. At that, Silver tossed a coin at the herbalist and told him to never set foot in her house again. She took to caring for Stoney herself, changing his clothes and bathing him with towels.

Then one day when Silver went to see him, he was awake, waiting for her. Within a week he could sit up, and then the following week he stood up and went to the outhouse by himself, though later they found him immobile on the ground, halfway to his room. The women carried him back, and he lay still for days.

The story of what happened had gotten around town, and some people said that it was a shame Stoney failed to protect his young mistress, that between the two of them it would be better losing a deaf servant than a young beauty just beginning to bloom. But Stoney, not being able to hear these opinions, eventually recovered most of his strength.

LYING IN HER BED for such a long time, Luna drifted in and out of sleep until she stopped distinguishing between her thoughts and her dreams. She remembered a story her mother used to tell her: a long time ago, there lived in the mountains a bear and a tiger. Both wanted to become human, so they prayed to the heavens and were told that they would transform if they stayed in a cave for one hundred days, eating only a bundle of wormwood and twenty cloves of garlic. The tiger eventually gave up and ran out of the cave—becoming so near to humans in intelligence and emotion, though still a beast in form. The bear persevered alone and turned into a beautiful woman on the hundred and first day. But the bear-woman wanted, most of all, to have a child. So she prayed again, and this time the son of heaven himself came down and lay with her. The child that the bear-woman bore became the first king of Korea.

As long as she could remember, Luna had heard dozens of stories like these about women who desperately longed for children. Such tales never told of women who didn't want to become mothers, although there were plenty of these among courtesans, servants, unmarried girls, widows, and matrons who already had too many mouths to feed. These women also had to pray and eat bitter herbs to get their wish.

A while back, a fourteen-year-old girl who did their washing had become pregnant and begged Silver for help. She didn't have any money to go to an herbalist, and at any rate she couldn't be caught buying something that would ruin her chances of marriage forever. Courtesans, of course, had the "medicine" in stock at all times. Luna had watched carefully as the maid prepared the bitter-smelling brew. Thick curls of cloudy steam overflowed from the bowl that the girl gulped down—almost greedily, Luna had thought at the time. This was what she now had to re-create.

Once she made up her mind, she rose from her bed quietly so as to not wake Silver. Her legs were weak and spindly under her weight, but she made it to the kitchen somehow. The herbs were still tucked in a bronze pot in the corner. Luna boiled water in a clay pot and let the herbs simmer until the liquid turned dark brown and thick. It tasted like woodsy bile.

Luna lay back down in her cot and waited for the medicine to take hold. She had only missed one period, but she could already feel something sharp and pointy in her womb that was never there before. That this seed was like an evil nail didn't surprise her in the least; it was to be expected from a man like Hayashi. The air was beginning to feel unbearably hot. And instead of flushing the nail out, the medicine seemed to make it grow larger, tearing her from the inside. Her mother was awake now, holding her hand and taking her temperature. She wanted to feel the blood rush out between her legs, but the nail was stuck inside her. If she could have spoken out loud, she would have asked someone to please scratch it out of her body, but she couldn't utter a word, as if caught in a bad dream.

When Luna woke up, it was nighttime—she had been in a fever for a whole day. Silver was sitting up next to her, and the darkness under her eyes showed she hadn't slept at all.

"You're too young to remember this. I also didn't want Lotus, and the brew didn't work for me either," Silver said.

"I was livid the entire time I was pregnant. Even after she was born I could hardly stand her. But before she was even two months old, she looked right into my eyes and smiled. Even though I was sure she knew in my womb how much I hated her." She paused, and saw that Luna was too silent and tense to be asleep.

"And at that moment, I held her tightly to my chest and cried like I would flood the world. Such a little body, still red from being inside mine. I kept saying like a madwoman, 'Please forgive me.' I'd tried to get rid of her but her soul had clung to me by a thread. It's an uncanny thing—*inyeon*. If it's not meant to be, you can't hold on to people no matter how hard you try. Some people you love deeply will turn into a stranger in an instant, if the *inyeon* has run its course. And sometimes people will be attached to you forever despite all likelihood. Lotus and I, our *inyeon* is deep and goes back further than this life.

"I will do anything for Lotus just as I'll do anything for you. You're both my daughters. So I promise you, you don't know yet how you'll feel later."

DESPITE THE BLAZING SUN and resinous air, Silver went out all the way across town to send a telegram to Seoul. The reason for her errand became clear when a visitor appeared at their door—a courtesan as beautiful as Silver, but dressed in simpler and more expensive clothes. Her inky black hair was scalloped around her forehead and coiled on her nape in the Western style. Instead of silk-and-leather slippers embroidered with flowers, she had on heeled pumps with straps over dainty silk stockings that only white women wore. Silver's first cousin was named YeDan, although friends and admirers called her Dani. She would take Luna to Seoul, ostensibly so she could have a fresh start. But everyone knew the real reason she was being sent away was to keep Hayashi from discovering her condition.

Lotus was being sent to Seoul as well, but she refused to leave unless she could take her closest friend with her. Silver had arranged to pay for the board of her two daughters so that they would be exempt from paying back the mistress of the establishment, as was customary. Jade, on the other hand, was an investment for which Silver had already paid a substantial sum, and her transfer was therefore a more delicate matter. Still, Dani agreed to take a look at the child, who was summoned after dinnertime.

"How old are you?" Dani asked, her sharp and beautiful eyes tracing the girl from the head to the hem of her skirt.

"I'm ten, Madame," Jade answered softly, focusing her gaze on Dani's freshly painted, scarlet lips. Silver and other courtesans wore rouge too, but Dani was the only woman she'd ever seen whose makeup was not just an ornament, but an effect; the color of her lips alone could make you feel as if she were tenderly caressing you, or—if she wanted—as if she were slapping your face. She pulled out a cigarette from an enameled case and rested it between gently parted lips while lighting it with one hand in a single fluid motion. Her manners and diction were impeccable, but an air of subversion trailed her like perfume. Dani defied simple categorization like no one else—and that was her most attractive quality.

"Let me see your eyes," Dani said, removing the cigarette from her lips. A soft white smoke curled around her mouth before departing into the air. Jade lifted her gaze and met Dani's irises, nearly black and foiled with flashes of golden brown.

"She is pretty, and quite bright, too," Silver said. "She won't be able to work for a while yet, but she'll still be useful to have around."

Dani turned toward her friend. Even the way she cocked her head to the side and opened up her elbow was languorously elegant, Jade thought.

"She looks like she would be a quick learner, as you say. Her eyes are not half bad. She is prettier than your Lotus, to be honest," Dani said with frankness, as if Jade weren't standing right in front of her.

"Lotus doesn't really take after me," Silver said, wounded.

"No question about it. Luna, that poor thing, is your exact copy though. This girl isn't a standout like Luna, but she has fine features, I'll admit. Intelligent eyebrows, full lips . . . But I don't think I'll take her, after all. She's too delicate. Weak, and I don't mean just in the physical sense. Worse than that, she doesn't have any personality—and you know how I dislike bland girls from the country." Dani shook her head.

"Jade has personality!" Silver exclaimed, looking earnestly at the girl, as if saying, Go ahead and show her your appealing side. The command didn't produce the desired effect; under the glare of two imperious women, Jade felt about as animated as a millstone.

"These are some bad times, Sister. There's no grain in the countryside, you know that. Every week I get at least five girls at my door. Their parents beg me to take them for nothing more than a small sack of rice. Even in their mud-stained rags, some are much prettier than this Jade. I refuse them all." Dani leaned back and crossed her arms, as though signaling the discussion was over.

"She's the best girl in class for poetry—recites classic verses like a little oriole. You should see her when she's playing with her mates in the courtyard. Very charming," Silver soldiered on.

"Forgive me, but little charming acts don't impress me as a proof of any originality. This child, I'm sure, is adorable when she plays, but I'm not just looking for liveliness. Now your second daughter, she has spirit! She does take after you, just not in looks . . ." Dani laughed, but Silver's face remained somber.

"I think you're being too harsh, Dani. Jade is only ten, after all. Children completely change a dozen times a year when they're growing," Silver said. "All I can say is, she is a good one. I've also seen my share of people to know what I'm talking about."

Dani cocked her beautiful face and made a slight noise that

sounded like *hrumph* to Jade. She tried to project that special quality that Dani was looking for, perhaps an air of effortless joy that Lotus so easily radiated. But while Jade wasn't prideful, she couldn't force a smile while being dressed down like this. A tiny tear was threatening to escape out of her right eye and she focused on putting it back in its place.

"Well, my dear sister," Dani sighed. "Honestly, I don't know if she has what it takes to make a living as a courtesan. She doesn't have sensuality, and what else do men want, really? On the other hand, she's too refined to make a great washing girl. She's a little in-between, don't you agree? But you're my cousin and my oldest friend. I will take her as an apprentice, if that would please you," she said, turning away from Jade and dismissing her with a cavalier wave.

Jade backed out of the room and ran to tell this news to Lotus. She didn't understand why Dani didn't care for her while valuing Lotus—or why the reverse was true of Silver. It was strange to think that her best friend had a special quality that she lacked, although she was prettier and understood literature. Instead of being crushed, she felt relief at the confirmation that they were perfect counterparts. She—observant, intelligent, and hardworking; her friend—spirited, disarming, and confident. They would never compete for the same hearts or the same happiness, as might happen to two friends who are too alike. Jade felt that they each would have only half of a life, a single wing, which would not be truly complete unless they stood together side by side.

WHEN THEY GOT ON THE TRAIN, Dani picked out a pair of seats facing one another at the end of the car. None of them spoke as the fields whipped past in a blur. A flock of sparrows seemed to follow them for a while, and then fell back as if exhausted.

"We are going faster than the birds!" Lotus half whispered, half exclaimed. Dani smiled indulgently. It was already clear to all that Dani doted on Lotus for her unflappable personality and Luna for her looks and tragedy. Jade felt less hurt than embarrassed to notice herself at the end of the line for her affections.

"You've never been on a train before, right? Wait till we get to Seoul, you'll see so many things you've never imagined even in your dreams," Dani said. "Hey, look outside for a second."

Dani paused, and the girls whipped their heads to the window, where the pearly sun was already halfway down the opaque, moist summer sky. "This railroad doesn't just go between PyongYang and Seoul. It stretches all the way south to the tip of the peninsula, and all the way north to Uiju, where you can take the western route to Beijing, then Shanghai; or go north to Manchuria, Siberia, and eventually Europe! Wouldn't that be a sight to see?"

"What would be the point of going so far? It's uncivilized," Lotus said, sounding unexpectedly like her mother. But Jade noticed how Luna's face briefly lightened at the mention of the West of the Ocean. Next to her, Dani was staring willfully at the horizon, as though she could fly through the window by the force of her beautiful, opinionated eyes.

As for herself, Jade didn't know whether she'd like going anywhere. The occasion to wonder this had never arisen before, and her mind always drew a blank when it came to uncertainties. Even worse, she was not even naturally curious: the books she liked best didn't teach her something new, they talked of things that she already understood just in a more beautiful way. Her imagination ran its circular course inside familiarities—a fountain rather than a river, particularly when it came to thinking about her own life. What else could she become besides what others wanted her to be? She was certain that Dani's imagination would have been an entire sea even as a young girl. Jade guessed that she would not grow up to be half as splendid as Dani—and worse, that Dani thought this too.

At sundown, the train slowly rolled into Seoul station like a tired horse returning to the stable. Once they walked out, the soupiness of the air suddenly intensified, glowing orange and violet over the sprawling unknown. Jade was struck most of all by the strangeness of the people crowding around her. Of course, people in PyongYang were also unfamiliar to her, but as a group she'd recognized their looks, sounds, and expressions on their faces; she'd felt safe in their company. The collective of strangers in Seoul had a different aura, more self-possessed, purposeful, and indifferent, not unlike Dani herself. They impatiently sidestepped the girls and flooded the large square in front of the station where street vendors and rickshaw drivers vied for attention. Beyond this, there was a huge, freestanding stone arch topped with a blue-black tiled roof. Small stores and odd buildings huddled on its sides like puppies.

"That's the Great South Gate," Dani pointed out, when they'd gotten on a rickshaw. "It was built more than five hundred years ago into the walls of the castle, which were still there when I first came to Seoul. It was a sight to behold, back then. The Japanese knocked off the walls long ago. And none of those unsightly electric poles used to be there, either."

The rickshaw driver started jogging, and the chaos of the station gradually receded.

"Are we going to go through the gate?" Jade asked, speaking up for the first time since leaving home.

"Why, of course we are," Dani said. "A gate doesn't cease to be a gate just because there are no walls around it. How else would you know you've arrived in Seoul?

"And besides, there's nothing like going through an arch to raise your spirits. Just remember that when you're down," she said gleefully. Her ability to find strangely uplifting things was another one of her peculiar talents. "Here we go—you'll see what I mean!"

And Jade did shiver with an inexplicable elation as the rickshaw passed under the arch and came out on the other side.

4

THE ORPHAN

1918

EARLIER ON THE SAME DAY WHEN THE GIRLS ENTERED THE CITY, A BOY had also gone through the Great South Gate. The night before, he'd parted ways with some traveling merchants who had taken him in for a few weeks in exchange for carrying a pack and running small errands. They had given him two pennies, enough for sleeping in a communal room at the inn and a bowl of broth. Instead, he headed to a ditch by the side of the road just outside the Gate, resolving to eat only when he no longer had any strength left. Once he found a rounded groove on the ground, he curled himself on his side and hugged his knees to the chest. As if they'd been waiting for him, soft strands of green foxtail gently bent over him like a coverlet. The boy looked sideways up at the sky, which was richly black and resplendent with stars.

His father had been a man of few words, but before he died, he'd said that looking at the sky could make you fearless against anything. He had been a formidable hunter, but toward the end of his life he couldn't walk out of his room. No matter what, take care of your sisters, he'd said, lying helplessly in his cot. Only the sprig of gray hair stood out from the rest of his body, which was as thin as a shadow. You're the head of the family now. If you need courage, just look at the sky.

When the stars went to bed, the boy awoke to the smell of the sun warming up the earth. He rubbed his eyes and crawled out from the ditch to get his first good look at the city, which was then drenched in liquid orange light. Summer dawn in Seoul was electrifying but short, almost nonexistent. The scorching sun hurled itself above the horizon, drying the dewdrops in seconds, and the city rose up as if obeying its commands. Already, there was a line of carts, travelers, and laborers entering and leaving the Great South Gate. The boy cautiously joined the crowd going into the city. No one questioned his presence or even looked at him. He safely snuck underneath the cool shade of the arch and came out on the other side, to a wide road buzzing with streetcars and lined with tall, stately buildings in Western style. And though weak with hunger, he couldn't help but smile. He reached for the drawstring pouch in his pocket and gave it a friendly squeeze, feeling the two pennies, a silver ring, and a cigarette case inside.

There were many mansions on both sides of the avenue that he thought were Christian houses, though in fact most belonged to government offices, consulates, and trading companies. On the streets, Koreans in white mixed with the Japanese in black. Then there were officers in uniform on horseback, around whom all the others swiveled past with discreet self-consciousness like schools of fish around patrolling sharks. The boy even caught sight of a couple of white men, their long, powerful legs sticking out of a rickshaw that was being pulled by a thin older man. Sweat dripped down from under his head scarf along his earthy face, and landed with a splash on the yellow dirt road or on top of his own feet. The image of his father came into the boy's mind, even as the rickshaw sped away from him and disappeared into the crowd.

The sun was beating down hard already, and his throat was dry to the point of closing up. He swallowed a few times, but barely a drop of spit went down his throat. Before he could do anything else, he would need to find water. In every country hamlet, there was a well near the village tree where the women came to fetch water for the day. One only had to look for the tallest tree or follow wherever girls were headed, balancing a large clay jug on their heads. Here, there were no trees anywhere, just endless streets filled with every type of human being except young girls fetching water. He spotted a matron carrying a basket nearby, and caught up to her.

"Excuse me, Aunt, where can I get some water?" His words came out dry and rusty as nails, and the woman went on her way without even slowing down for a moment. The next two people he approached also kept walking as though they hadn't heard him. He had thought that the latter, who looked like a university student, would surely stop and say something. When the youth also coldly passed him by, the boy felt all the blood rush down from his head, making it hard to stay on his feet. He found a piece of shade under the eaves of a building and plopped down on his bottom, making no effort to soften his landing—so drained was he of any energy. He pressed the heels of his hands into his eyes. One of the traveling merchants had done so when he was especially tired, and the gesture had impressed the boy as soothing, but not shameful or childish.

"You from the country?"

The boy put his hands down and looked up to see another boy around his age.

"I'm not," the boy instinctively lied.

"What's your name?"

"Nam JungHo."

"Ha, you're a country bumpkin all right. Who gives out his name to a stranger like that, except rustics who just passed through the gate that day?"

"How old are you, you little shit?" JungHo said. "You talk like you're itching for a beating." JungHo was only twelve, but he'd already had a reputation for being the best fighter among the village urchins back home. While small-boned, he was wiry and quick. Moreover, he wasn't at all afraid of pain and only cared about how much he could beat up his opponent, which was how he defeated boys bigger and older than he was.

"You crack me up. You look like you haven't eaten for days. You're so weak you can barely stand up," the city boy sneered.

In the blink of an eye, JungHo was standing with balled-up fists raised over his chin, ready to strike. The city boy was taller than JungHo, but only by a few inches.

"I was only joking," the city boy said, quickly changing his tone. "You don't need to get so riled up."

"Just leave me alone, you shitty dog," JungHo said quietly, with his fists still up. "Leave me in peace!"

"Hey, I'll leave you alone. But you look like you need some water or food, or something," the city boy said. "I'll show you where to get water, if you come with me."

"I bet you're lying," JungHo said.

"If it turns out I lied, you can always beat me up then, right?" the city boy said, smiling.

"What's your name?"

"They call me Loach."

"That's a stupid name," JungHo said sternly. But they started walking together, nevertheless. Loach was good at weaving through the crowd moving in all different directions, without ever stopping or losing his way—just like his namesake animal.

"How much farther?" JungHo couldn't help himself from asking.

"Just a little more," was all Loach would say.

At first, JungHo tried to remember the turns they took, as to be able to retrace his steps back to the Great South Gate; but he eventually gave up, as knowing his location only in relation to that one place was pointless. Whether or not he stayed on track, he still didn't know where anything was, and thus was essentially lost. The storefronts with their signs in Chinese characters, the *whoosh* of rickshaws, shouts of vendors, street performers, and even a streetcar threaded with an electric wire at the top and brimming with people crowded around him on all sides, exhausting his senses. To keep himself steady, he glued his eyes to Loach's slender back and the arrowhead-shaped sweat mark spreading slowly from its center.

"Here we are." Loach turned around and smirked, pointing forward.

"Hmm?"

They'd arrived at the edge of a canal—though it had nothing in common with the energetic, fresh streams around JungHo's village at the foot of the mountains. The swampy, shallow rivulet flowed about five yards below street level, its pebbled banks on either side lined with a levee of rocks and cement. Loach was pointing at a stone bridge just ahead, groaning under a heap of carts and pedestrians.

"What's this, stupid?" JungHo asked, not bothering to hide his frustration. "You said there would be water."

"It's under the bridge," Loach said, not missing a beat.

"That muddy water? You think I'm a dog?"

"Don't get so fiery all the time, it's fucking hot as it is. I live under the bridge," Loach responded. Then without waiting for more retorts, he said, "Either you follow me or just go back wherever you came from, country bumpkin." He crouched down, put his palms at the edge of the levee, then lightly swung his legs over the ledge and dropped down. JungHo hurried over and leaned out; Loach was already straightening himself up and dusting off his hands.

"Son of a bitch," JungHo whispered to himself, before dropping off the ledge.

"What took you so long? Not so brave now, are we?" Loach teased. "We're almost there."

Contrary to JungHo's hopes, the presence of water did nothing to cool the air as they walked together to the bridge. As they got closer, JungHo noticed a cluster of trash, which turned out to be makeshift tents. Several boys their age were sitting on large rocks nearby, talking among themselves, and then stood up to greet Loach. They were the kind of dirty that makes one's skin crawl and scalp itch just from looking.

JungHo tried to hide his unease as they made their way to the tents. The worst thing he could do at this point was to run away. He wouldn't make it up the levee, and they would swarm him in an instant. But if they thought he wasn't intimidated, he might still be fine.

"Who is this, Loach?" one of the boys asked. He was the tallest among them, and had the distinction of being the only one with a smattering of gray fuzz over his upper lip.

"A new guy, fresh from the country," Loach said. "Hey, he's dying of thirst. Get him some water." There was a brief squabble among the boys over who should get it, but eventually one of them fetched a bowl from a tent and handed it to JungHo.

"Drink it, country bumpkin," Loach said. "It's well water."

Once reassured, JungHo quickly lifted the bowl to his lips and gulped the water down, feeling their eyes on him the entire time.

"Feel better?" Loach asked, smirking, once JungHo lowered his bowl. He nodded.

"What's your name?" asked the tall one with the faint mustache.

"Nam JungHo. What's your name?" JungHo asked, calling him "you" in the familiar form, as if they were the same age.

"Mind your manners, you've just had our water . . . My name is YoungGu. But you're going to call me Older Brother."

JungHo didn't say anything, and YoungGu carried on.

"Which province are you from? And why did you come to Seoul?"

"I'm from PyongAhn province. And I came here for the same reason anyone comes to Seoul," JungHo said. "There is nothing to eat in the countryside anymore."

"What about your family?"

JungHo considered for a moment. After his father's death, a widower had come forward asking for his pretty older sister's hand in marriage. The man had offered to take in even JungHo's younger sister, but not himself. A five-year-old sister-in-law to feed was one thing, and a boy nearly all grown was quite another. Since his older sister would have refused the offer and starved together rather than abandon him, he had fled quietly in the middle of the night.

JungHo replied, "All dead."

"Then today is your lucky day," YoungGu said. "You become one of us, and you won't have to worry about starving to death. We eat little enough, but we share everything."

"We're all orphans like you," Loach chimed in helpfully.

"How do you find stuff to eat?" JungHo asked.

"We beg, we steal—don't worry, we only steal from the bad guys. You'll get the hang of it. But first things first," YoungGu said. "You have to swear an oath of loyalty, and surrender any money you've got."

"I don't have any . . ." JungHo started to protest, instinctively reaching for his drawstring pouch—and then panicked, realizing that it was gone.

"I have it, country bumpkin," Loach said, holding up the pouch. "You know, I could've just taken this and lost you in the crowd. Instead I brought you here, where we live. So don't look so fucking hurt, moron."

Loach tossed the pouch to YoungGu, who caught it with one hand. JungHo stood shaking in anger as the older boy opened the pouch and pulled out its contents. He immediately pocketed the two pennies, but held up the silver ring and the cigarette case in each hand.

"You can have the money. But not those two things," JungHo said. His heart was pounding. "Give them back to me."

"Do you think I'm crazy? Why would I give these back?" YoungGu snorted. "These are rich people's things. You stole them, didn't you?"

"My father gave me those before he died," JungHo said. Truthfully, he had found them under his father's pillow after he passed away, but he figured that was the same thing, since he was his father's only son and heir. They were his not because they were worth money, but because they were heirlooms.

"You don't get it, do you." YoungGu smirked. "Maybe you haven't felt real hunger yet, or maybe you're just that stupid, but these things won't keep you alive when you're lying in a ditch somewhere, waiting for death. On the other hand, if we sell these we could all eat until we're full." In spite of his swagger, YoungGu's last words tumbled out with a hint of genuine longing.

"I don't care if you all starve—I don't want to join you," JungHo said. "Now give it back!"

YoungGu laughed heartily, and then all the other boys joined in.

"You can leave, no one will stop you. But you're not getting these back. You really are a simpleton even to ask. Let this be your first lesson in Seoul," YoungGu said.

In a flash, JungHo raised his fists up to his chin, ready to fight. The other boys stopped laughing, and even YoungGu erased the smile from his face. He put the trinkets back inside the drawstring pouch and tossed it back to Loach for safekeeping.

The other boys, as if on cue, backed off one or two steps and widened the circle, as YoungGu and JungHo drew closer together. The air simmered with the hungry, gnawing energy of pubescent boys. Within that tension, there was a brief moment in which they both left the muddy canal strewn with rubbish, the dank shadow of the bridge, and the heartless city above them. YoungGu went to a mud hut where he was born and raised, less than half a mile from that spot. Disjointed memories of his mother's hand and the soft fur of his pet dog passed inexplicably through his mind, and he was filled with a sense of comfort. JungHo blocked out everything around him, even YoungGu, even his own physical body already beaten by exhaustion. In that split second before the first punches were thrown, he simply looked up at the sky, which glowed a violent yellow from the late afternoon sun. It offered him no comfort, nor courage, as his father had promised. But he thought that his father and mother were up there somewhere, that he didn't come into the world alone, and so was reminded why he must keep surviving as best he can as he sprang forward with a punch to YoungGu's head.

YoungGu easily dodged JungHo's fist and countered with his own attack, which the smaller boy sidestepped. For the next few minutes, they sized each other up, swiping and blocking, but from a safe distance. Then JungHo hurled himself forward with his fist aimed at YoungGu's stomach. Because JungHo had bent himself slightly at the waist, his head was now the perfect height for YoungGu to knock out with a punch. But just as the older boy confidently threw his fist, JungHo ducked under the arm and rammed his head as hard as he could into YoungGu's middle, felling him like a tree. JungHo knew that any advantage a taller boy has is eliminated once they're on the ground, and that whoever manages to pin the other down will almost always win no matter what size. The moment YoungGu was knocked out, more by surprise than anything else, JungHo straddled his chest and punched his head savagely and repeatedly with both fists. YoungGu quickly grabbed JungHo's scrawny wrists, shrieking in real anger this time: "You little shit! You little shit!" Just at that moment, JungHo pulled his head back, then rammed it with all his strength into YoungGu's forehead. YoungGu screamed out in pain, but JungHo—without even blinking—smashed his head against YoungGu's once more, even harder this time. The older boy let go of JungHo's wrists and lay limply, bleeding quietly. Only then did JungHo get up, wiping his own blood-smeared forehead with the back of his hand.

"Give me back my things," he said to Loach, who tossed the drawstring pouch back to him.

JungHo dug into YoungGu's pocket for the two pennies and added those to the pouch as the other boys silently watched. He started walking out from under the bridge, intending to find a crevice in the levee that would be easier to climb. But when he'd gone about a minute, there was a sound of footsteps running after him, and a shout.

"Hey! Stop there!" It was Loach's voice.

"What do you want?" JungHo snarled. "You want a beating as well?"

"Don't go," Loach said. "Don't you realize what's happened?" He took a moment to catch his breath, then blurted out, "You just beat up our chief. That means you're the chief now."

JungHo snorted. "I don't want to be your chief. Let YoungGu enjoy lording it over you and all his underlings. I want no part in it."

"That's not how it works!" Loach insisted. "Fine, you don't want to join us? How are you going to survive out there on your own? Do you think we're the only band of beggars in Seoul? There are many even in this one district, and then there are real gangs of grown-up criminals—do you think they'd let you live?"

"What's that to you?" JungHo shouted. "If I die, then I die. You don't get a say in it!"

"You are such a hothead. I'm only trying to help," Loach said. "If you want to live, you have to stick with a group. And if you're the chief, you can do anything you want. You can order the other boys to give you a big share and not even have to beg on the streets yourself."

"How can you say this, when just a few minutes ago you were YoungGu's right-hand man?" JungHo asked scornfully.

"I'm no one's right-hand man," Loach snorted. "I do what I can to survive. If you weren't such a bullheaded idiot, you'd do the same."

The two boys locked eyes for a moment. Loach had smiled while leading him to their den, and had smiled while stealing his money. He was one of those boys with small, tadpole-shaped eyes whose easy, cheap smiles for anyone and everyone made them inscrutable and loathsome. As JungHo's mind arrived at this conclusion, he suppressed an overwhelming urge to give Loach a nasty black eye. But it was undeniable that the city boy hadn't directly lied or intended him harm, and in this case, was telling the truth about the necessity of sticking together.

In the next instant, Loach extended his hand. JungHo took it without even knowing why—then surprised himself by shaking it up and down a few times, before they both dropped their hands as though embarrassed.

"Come on, let's go," Loach said. "Pretty soon, the kids who went out will come back. We have acrobats, pickpockets, straight-up beggars. Hopefully we'll have made enough today for some supper."

"What do you guys eat normally?" JungHo couldn't help but ask, filled with curiosity and hope.

"Stew, or potatoes if we're lucky. Old fish, things like that."

"I could really use some stew. I haven't eaten anything in more than a day," JungHo said, and even as he spoke he felt ashamed at revealing himself.

"Me neither. But you only really need to eat every other day. My mother used to tell me that," Loach said with another easy smile. This time, it didn't seem so contemptible in JungHo's eyes.

5

THE FRIEND FROM SHANGHAI

1918

EVERY HUMAN BEING FUNDAMENTALLY BELIEVES IN HIS OR HER UNIQUE and inherent significance, without which life would be unbearable; but in Kim SungSoo's psyche, that belief was not merely a foundation but the pièce de résistance. He himself was not conscious of that fact, of course, since such people are precisely the least likely to admit to selfishness. Being a well-educated, modern man, he had his own code of conduct and was sufficiently pleased with himself for meeting it without too many difficulties. That is to say, he was pro-independence but against any form of native activism (change could only come top-down through imploring the United States to free Korea, he believed). Among friends, he would say aptly vitriolic comments about the oppression, enjoying the eloquence of his own speech and the smooth taste of his Japanese cigarettes. He could carry on love affairs that were physically, financially, and sometimes even emotionally involving; but he wouldn't be so base as to flaunt them in front of his wife, subjecting her to needless humiliation. In short, his moral character was no worse than any other Korean male who is born the only son of a prominent landowning family with an annual income of nearly two hundred thousand won.

When Kim SungSoo was young, his father was known around

the entire province simply as "Rich Man Kim," and he himself was called "Little Master," not only by their own servants but also by peasants for miles around and in neighboring villages. Like all sons of wealthy landlords, he was sent away to Seoul for high school, followed by university. He was betrothed and married at twenty, to an official's daughter who had only recently graduated from a Christian women's college. They lived together for almost three years in the five-room guesthouse at his uncle's mansion, across the courtyard from the main building. SungSoo spent those days mingling with his friends, all young men of wealth and education, and carousing with courtesans at expensive restaurants. At night, he came home senselessly inebriated to his wife, and let her undress him and gently admonish him. She'd been educated by American missionaries at school, but at home she'd also been taught that an ideal wife embraces her husband's flaws with patience and self-sacrifice. But Kim SungSoo's uncle, a government official who would eventually become a count in the wake of the Annexation in 1910, determined that his nephew couldn't go on wasting away family fortune and his own talent, and had him sent to Japan for further studies.

SungSoo left his wife at home and arrived in Tokyo alone, and spent the next three years halfheartedly studying French, German, and Russian literature. When he wasn't reading Pushkin and Goethe he was in the company of other expat students, many of whom were as carefree as he was. The others who were earnest and occupied with political theories, sovereignty, and equality, he avoided without even being conscious of it; one was too tiresome, another was truculent, and still another was unsophisticated and had no appreciation for culture. Yet, SungSoo had unexpectedly become close with a student of the political circle, as one sometimes picks out and strikes up a friendship with only a single person out of a group that he otherwise scorns. This student had impressed SungSoo with his uncommon intelligence, illustrious family background, and—something that helped sort their relationship time and again—genuine humility. Such was the history between Kim SungSoo and his old friend Lee MyungBo.

After SungSoo returned to Seoul, MyungBo stayed in Tokyo for another year. He then moved on to Vladivostok, continued westward across Manchuria, and settled semipermanently in Shanghai. SungSoo had lost touch with his friend six or seven years previously, and had not thought of him even in his private unspoken thoughts for so long that it jolted him when out of the blue he received a letter from MyungBo asking him to meet. After the initial surprise, however, SungSoo regained his composure and warmed himself to the idea of reuniting with his friend, until he became genuinely excited.

On the appointed day, SungSoo woke up and washed his face with hot water, made ready for him by the old woman who served the family as a housekeeper. He shaved carefully, then put on a crisp white shirt that his wife had ironed and laid out for him. The smartly creased sleeves cracked open as he pushed his arms through them, a distinct sensation that he greatly enjoyed. When he was fully dressed, his wife appeared with his breakfast, consisting of a bowl of white rice, fried fish, soybean sprout soup, kimchi, and steamed eggs with fermented shrimp.

"Did you sleep well?" she asked in a friendly voice as she laid down the tray. He grunted in reply. She chattered about their son, who had again gotten himself in some sort of trouble at school, and their infant daughter, who she suspected might have contracted the chickenpox. To all of these domestic issues, SungSoo paid only the slightest attention. It often felt to him as though his children belonged more to his wife than to himself; he was disappointed by how little affection he naturally had for them, and suspected that his attitude toward them was an extension of how he felt about his wife, their mother. The other three got along imperfectly, but with perfectly natural, warm, and even passionate attachment to one another. It was as if SungSoo had been dropped into a picture of an actual, real family lacking just a father figure. He often felt as though he were playacting with someone else's wife and children.

"That's all great," SungSoo replied, only half aware that his wife was talking about their daughter's rash. "I better get going."

It was one of those October mornings when the sky is brilliantly blue and the air is wonderfully fresh. From the roofs of houses to walled gardens and the streets, everything was washed clean and anointed by the cool golden light of autumn. Alone, SungSoo became conscious of his own healthy, vigorous body, sharply dressed in a charcoal suit that was made precisely for this weather and delivered to his house by his tailor only the previous week. His tie, and the starched collar to which it was pinned, the silk-backed waistcoat, the brimmed wool hat, and the polished shoes—everything was delightful. The streets of Jongno were particularly beautiful too, and where he'd only have noticed the peasants and laborers during the summer, without any beauty and unpleasant in the extreme, he now saw that the trees aflame with foliage were casting watery shadows over the avenue.

His mood stayed bright as he reached his office and settled into his work. First, his secretary, a young man from the country, eager to prove himself but with an oily brown face and mannerisms that were too rustic to make him a man of letters, brought a stack of the morning's newspapers and deferentially laid them across his desk. SungSoo skimmed them, starting with the important news in order to feel that he did the right thing, but losing interest and moving on before reaching the conclusion. There was an editorial piece on the second page about the riot that had broken out due to the sky-rocketing price of rice, which had gone from fifteen won per eighty kilograms in January of the previous year to thirty-eight won this August. It was said that never before in Korea's five-thousand-year history had rice been so expensive, and the peasants and the laborers were starving en masse. On the day of the riot, a thousand men and women, young and old, had thrown mud and stones at the police armed with swords and rifles, right in the heart of Jongno, where SungSoo had just had such a nice walk in the morning. Finally, the military troops were deployed to disperse the crowd, and hundreds were arrested—and now the editorial was pleading for the release of these rioters.

After dutifully gathering the main points from the editorial, SungSoo moved on to a novel that was being serialized and read it with a great deal more interest. The protagonist of the story was an upper-class, modern-educated man in his thirties, just like SungSoo and the author himself. At this point, the protagonist was in the middle of falling in love with his late best friend's widow, despite numerous complications owing to their other loyalties. Though SungSoo laid down the newspaper muttering, "What garbage! Disgusting rubbish!" he secretly was engrossed in the story, could not help anticipating the next installment, and longed to write something in a similar style.

Over the next few hours, he worked on editing a manuscript for his quarterly literary journal, for which he was the editor in chief. There was a short meeting with his publisher, who had some troubling news about the printing press in the basement floor of the office, where they produced their own magazine as well as other publishers' works and even brochures. Kim SungSoo had only barely sent out the publisher when his secretary knocked on his door and let in his friend Lee MyungBo.

"How long has it been? How long?" The two friends clasped their hands and kept loudly exclaiming over one another. When they were done, SungSoo shouted at his secretary to bring in coffee immediately, and then they both sat down with glowing faces.

"Why haven't you let me know you were in Seoul? I thought you were still in Shanghai," SungSoo said reproachfully.

"I've only just arrived. And I will be going back in a month or two," MyungBo replied, smiling.

"Well, you look great. That country suits you!" SungSoo laughed good-naturedly. But in fact, as his eyes adjusted to the difference between his memory and the figure before him, he was beginning to see that MyungBo had aged faster than himself, that his cheeks and chin looked dark even though it wasn't yet evening, and that his coat hung loosely on his shoulders. And this made SungSoo feel truly sorry for his friend, which then had the bizarre effect of brightening his mood, and making him feel healthier and stronger than ever.

The secretary hurriedly brought in two cups of coffee on saucers, and they took a minute to settle themselves over the drinks.

"You shouldn't flatter me like that. You're the one who looks so hale and hearty. I guess that's the thing when one is married to a good woman. How is my sister-in-law, by the way?" MyungBo asked, and SungSoo smiled at his using the friendly term "sister-in-law" to describe his wife, whom MyungBo had never even met.

"She is good, she's never not good," SungSoo said.

"And the children? How old are they now?"

"The boy is fifteen, and the girl just turned one."

And in this way, they spent the next half hour catching up with all the details of their lives, each other's families, mutual friends and acquaintances, SungSoo's publishing house, and a side venture he'd just begun.

"A bicycle shop!" MyungBo exclaimed. "How ever did you come up with that?"

"I always loved riding it, it's a favorite hobby of mine," SungSoo said. "But enough about me. What brings you here? No, let's discuss that over lunch. Aren't you hungry? I'll take you to a new restaurant that's just opened, called MyungWol. They do palace-style cuisine, seven or nine courses; it's very splendid."

For the first time, MyungBo's face became subtly opaque, as if concealing some displeasure. He said, "No, thank you, I'm not very hungry, and besides, it's so comfortable here."

"Are you sure? Please, it will be my treat," SungSoo implored. "You embarrass me by not allowing me to buy you lunch after all these years."

At that, MyungBo smiled and the chilliness disappeared from his face. He explained, "You're still as generous as I remembered. Even at school, when some of the others talked about you as if you were a spoiled rich kid, I always defended you, because I knew you are far kinder than people make you out to be."

"Oh, MyungBo. I don't know," SungSoo said, suddenly feeling deflated. "I'm not that kind. I don't do anything to deserve such praise."

"But what if you had the chance?" MyungBo asked excitedly. "What if you had the chance to prove your goodness, wouldn't you take the right path?"

"What do you mean? I don't understand . . ."

"Surely you know. Don't you see? The people are dying, Sung-Soo. The good, hardworking peasants, who have never done anything bad in their lives, because every single waking minute is spent trying to put some food on the table . . .

"Just outside this office, here in Jongno, the beating heart of Seoul—thousands of people standing up against the oppression, fighting with their bare hands, and you haven't noticed?" MyungBo's eyes glittered in a strange way. "Why is there no rice for them? You tell me."

"Because the prices are rising," SungSoo answered reluctantly.

"No—well, that's not the full answer. The prices are rising because the Japanese have proclaimed a census and measured every inch of Korea, and all the miserable illiterate peasants, who have no proof of ownership except ancestral and oral rights, woke up one morning and found that their land was no longer theirs. Any so-called unclaimed land, the government takes for itself, or sells to the grand landlords and the Japanese trading company. So, they go from small landowners to tenants under the great landowners, and after they pay off the taxes to the government, the rent for the land, fees for the tools, irrigation water, et cetera, et cetera, they no longer have any money to buy even their own food, and have to borrow from their landlords against the following year's crop, just to be able to secure the seeds. The cycle gets worse every single year, and they're sucked dry, down to their bones. Then, of course, the landlord makes them sign a communal contract so that if one tenant runs away, the other tenants of the village will have to pay off the remaining debt, so no one may dare escape, making them struggle in the same spot until they all die. Meanwhile, the great landowners, who control the vast majority of rice, see that the more they hold on to it, the higher the prices rise; and the higher the prices rise, the richer they become, so they keep their warehouses full to the top with sacks of grain, while everyone else is starving to death. Now, can you tell me that you don't know what's wrong with this state of things!"

"It's not ideal, but what can I do? And besides," SungSoo said mildly, though not all in good faith, "you yourself are a son of a landowner. You have profited from your birth as much as I have. So what do you propose?"

"Great. I'm glad you asked me that," MyungBo said with a satisfied smile. "I can't, in good conscience, continue to benefit from a system that every part of my body and soul knows is immoral. When my father dies and the estate passes on to me, I will give half of it to the peasants who have always tended it, and sell the other half for the cause. Just now though, I'm not getting any money from my family, and it's been awfully difficult trying to sustain the movement in Shanghai on so little . . ."

"Goodness, is that why you came to visit me?" SungSoo asked. "Well, then, how much is needed?"

"You must first understand that this isn't for me. It is for the movement, feeding and clothing and training our brave young men in Manchuria, who would throw away their lives gladly for our country." MyungBo's face became red, and his eyes shined with tears. "I was thinking that a contribution of twenty thousand won would be most appropriate for a man of your stature."

"Twenty thousand won? My fellow, do you realize that's enough to buy twenty villas?" SungSoo exclaimed. "I know everyone thinks I'm so rich, but that's a lot of money even for me. I would have to think on it," he said, even though he already knew he would never give MyungBo that much, or even anything close; he had decided instantly, and only the reasoning was what he needed time to formulate.

"You are an artist, SungSoo . . . How can you close your heart to the rest of the world?" MyungBo muttered bitterly.

"On the contrary, it is *because* I am an artist that I must concern myself with art. Politics are the concern of politicians, like yourself," SungSoo replied. What was next? Was he supposed to feel sorry for the cows toiling in the fields? Each being had its place in the universe.

"Fine, then, I can't force you to do anything. Just think how much you spent setting up a house for that geisha in Tokyo, and what that money could have done for the young fighters who only ask for a gun and bullets to serve our country."

"Really, MyungBo, I need time to process all this." SungSoo suppressed his irritation as politely as he could. "It's too bad you didn't want to eat lunch, that we had to get into this talk without even a drop of liquor. But there, we had it all out, and now we can talk of something else."

"No, I see that I've made you uneasy. I'll get going now. But please, for all of our memories together, if you have even a bit of affection for me, would you think about it?"

"I promise, I promise," SungSoo said, and felt the most vivid relief as MyungBo put on his hat and walked out of the office.

• • •

DANI'S HOUSE WAS IN YEONGEON-DONG near the ChangGyeong Palace Zoo, where many old and noble families had their ancestral homes. There was an excess of space: Dani alone occupied the ground floor of the two-story building, and there was even a charming pavilion across the courtyard. Each of the girls was given her own room on the second floor of the main house, where the maid and the housekeeper also slept. It was the finest home Jade had ever seen, filled with leather sofas, velvet curtains, and even a Steinway piano; and ensconced in the courtyard garden were strange and lovely plants from faraway places. With her characteristic poetic whimsy, Dani assigned flowers to each of the girls based on their qualities. Lotus was given summer sunflowers because they were bright, wholesome, and happy. Luna got Dani's favorite flowers, fall cosmoses, which she claimed were not much to look at singly but sublime when bunched together in a bouquet.

Jade was matched with the winter camellia, a southern-flowering tree that she had never seen in the frigid North. Dani assured her, somewhat more warmly than usual, that the camellia was a very lucky flower for a woman. Its mate was the lovely, pale green camellia bird, which drank only its nectar and visited no other blossom. And at the end of its season, the camellia didn't brown or blow away petal by petal as other flowers do; it fell down unblemished and intact, bloodred and velvety like a heart. As beautiful on the ground as on the day it first opened. "What all women want—an unchanging love. It's what I see for you," Dani said with a curious smile. Jade thought that her foster aunt had an intuitive streak of a born creative, somewhere between the levels of an artist and a clairvoyant. Sometimes her aesthetic fancy could get carried away and take on the shape of a small prophecy. Whether or not Dani actually had a feeling for the future, her enthusiastic delivery was what made it feel real.

"But Aunt Dani, what kind of flower would *you* be?" Lotus asked.

"I know," Jade said before Dani could answer. "She could only be the regal spring rose." As if on cue, the two little girls linked hands and made a ring around Dani, and ran in a small circle shouting "Queen Rose! Queen Rose!" until she burst out laughing. But even in the height of their amusements, Jade felt guilty when she saw how Luna continued to stay quiet. Nothing seemed able to make her speak, smile, or even get angry and scold the little girls.

ONE GRAY DAY IN EARLY FALL, Luna finally broke her months of silence. The rain was falling softly, casting everything in indigo. The three girls crawled back into their cots after lunch and listened to the downpour in a state of melancholy. Jade begged their maid Hesoon to tell them stories of her childhood in Jejudo, the magical southern island where there were trees without any branches and wild horses running freely under a snowcapped mountain. Hesoon said her mother and her four sisters were all seawomen who dove in the water to harvest abalones, holding their breath for two minutes at a time.

"That's impossible, you're making it up!" Lotus giggled.

"It's all true. Jejudo women dive even when they're pregnant. My mother almost gave birth to me in the sea but she swam out just in time for me to be born on the beach. She caught me with her own hands and wiped me off with kelp," Hesoon said. She was always telling these unbelievable stories, about mountains breathing fire and ice and long-winged birds that nested in the waves. When Jade closed her eyes, she could see women who turned to fish in the sea and babies rocked to sleep in the shallows, anchored in place by seaweed ropes.

When they were about to pepper the maid with more questions, Dani appeared at the door and feigned shock at their laziness.

"I know it's rainy today, but you girls can't just lie around all afternoon. When I was your age, I was the smartest student at my school—I even learned English! Come downstairs, and I'll teach you something fun."

By the time the girls came down to the sitting room, the sofa was pushed against one wall and Dani was putting on a record—a paper-thin, polished black disc that shone deliciously in the candlelight. It started spinning slowly on the turntable, filling the room with the warm syncopation of strings and trumpets. Jade closed her eyes, willing the wave of sound to sweep her out to sea.

"Isn't it wonderful? This is called a foxtrot." Dani beamed. "I wish I knew how to dance this one, but I didn't learn it in school. Hold on, I'll put on a waltz and teach you that."

Before long, they were all standing on tiptoe—Dani, Luna, Jade, Lotus, and even Hesoon—and dancing in circles around the sitting room, roaring with laughter. Jade noticed that for the first time in months, Luna's face was lighting up with a smile.

"Come into my room, girls," Dani said. "You can try on my clothes." Her words had the desired effect of driving up the merriment—Jade and Lotus screamed in joy, and even Luna couldn't resist putting on a priceless embroidered dress and twirling around. After they had exhausted themselves dancing, they lay down on the floor together in a heap of colorful silk skirts. They were only roused by the sound of wheels parting the mud-flooded street. Hesoon ran to the front gates, came back shivering from the rain, and announced, "Madame, His Honor is here."

"Did he send word earlier?" Dani asked, frowning. She immediately rose and started straightening her dress, while Hesoon picked up around the room and the housekeeper corralled the girls and ushered them upstairs.

Jade lagged behind the others. Just before rounding the corner at the landing, she turned around and caught a glimpse of a gray-haired man being greeted by Dani. He had the proud bearing of a hale old age, but already seemed to show all the promises of the frailness to come in just five or six years. With his muddy complexion and soft voice, he was not someone Jade had imagined for her lovely and indomitable aunt, who seemed able to make any man fall obediently at her feet. So Dani was just as shrewd as the others in choosing money over feelings. Jade felt with a pang of disappointment that Dani was not, after all, a fantastical creature.

The following day, Dani began giving the girls lessons in music and dance. Lotus had struggled to pass the tests under her mother's tutelage; under Dani's guidance she gained enough confidence to discover, for the first time, a remarkable voice that seemed to emanate from her whole body rather than her throat. Luna was interested in learning English, which only upper-class women in the most modern families ever learned. Jade took to dance the way she did to poetry—she discovered that they both originated from the same unfathomable place. She could imitate any movement on the first try; on the second or third try, she made it her own by adding a slight twist of the torso, a tilt of her chin, or a simple breath where there was none. With those nearly imperceptible differences, other girls remained girls while she became a crane, a legendary heroine, a season, an idea. When this happened, Dani perched her chin on a cupped hand and narrowed her eyes severely—whether in approval or displeasure, Jade was never certain.

In October, Dani told the girls that they were to have a special outing. MyungWol, the new restaurant where she'd been booked almost every evening for a fortnight, had asked her and other courtesans in her guild to help advertise its opening in Jongno. She was bringing the two younger girls as well, though Luna couldn't go in her condition. New costumes were ordered for both Jade and Lotus, and they practiced their routine in their rooms every night before bed. Afterward, Jade felt the injustice of having to sleep when there was so much to do, so much to think about; only after being thoroughly tortured by excitement was she able to fall into a restless slumber.

The week leading up to the appointed day was gray and drizzly, which made Jade miserable with worry. That morning, however, the sun rose brilliantly against a cloudless sky. The girls helped Dani cut the cosmoses in the garden before getting dressed, sharing Hesoon between them. Before fixing the embroidered headdress over the crown of Jade's head, the maid twisted her long braid into a low chignon and fixed it with a silver *binyuh* for the very first time. A bridal regalia. The updo marked her as a nonvirgin in status, if not in body. But she was different from normal married women: her wrap skirt opening on the right side indicated her profession. The last step in getting ready was the makeup. When it was finished, Jade saw in the mirror a beautiful stranger—red lips stark against the powdered skin—and was startled to realize that she looked very much like Dani.

"Goodbye, I will miss you," Jade whispered in the garden as Hesoon opened the gates. She was coming back in a few hours, but nothing would be the same as before. After being seen like this, she could never go back to being a marriageable girl in people's eyes. She had come into the house as a child, and was now stepping out of its gates as a courtesan.

6

THE PARADE

1918

AFTER MYUNGBO LEFT, SUNGSOO WAITED TEN MINUTES IN HIS OFFICE before heading out himself. He did truly regret that the meeting with his old friend hadn't gone as he'd hoped; that instead of reminiscing about their old adventures over food and drink, and reveling in the discovery that someone else remembers you as you once were, and vice versa, they were each shocked at how different the other had become. It was far worse than meeting someone new and failing to like one another. Moreover, no one had called out SungSoo's faults to him in years. Everyone was eager to please him, his subordinates with deference, his peers with compliments, his wife with adoration. And this universal approval was so unconditional, and so much a part of his reality, that someone telling him to his face that he was wrong shook him to the core.

"Is he right? Am I wrong to not want to renounce my birthright, move to Shanghai, or some mountain village in Siberia, and spend my days target shooting and plotting assassinations?" SungSoo asked himself. He'd heard stories of how these young men—from wealthy and noble families, peasantry, or anywhere in between—gathered in safe houses in these places and swore an oath to give up their lives for the cause. They cut off the tip of their ring finger and signed the pledges in blood, and wore sharply tailored suits and hats in the highest style in order to look dignified when they died, which may be at any moment. It was also said that women fell passionately in love with them.

"But for what? It is all foolish—nothing will be gained from it. Not only that, assassination is murder." This train of thought was beginning to soothe his angst. "We say the Japanese are murdering our people, but is the right answer murdering them in return? It's all so barbaric, and no less wrong. No, I won't contribute to such reckless violence. I won't be bullied into it, no matter how MyungBo judges me."

Having thus arranged his reasoning, SungSoo was satisfied. He nearly smiled with the increase in self-respect as he headed out to the streets. The sun was high in the cerulean sky, and there was a cool invigorating breeze. Before long he ran into a friend, a playwright who had also studied in Japan. SungSoo shook hands with him and brought up MyungBo, whom the playwright knew.

"How strange it is to see you both in one day," SungSoo said. Then, he discreetly communicated that MyungBo wasn't in good shape physically or financially, that he was in Seoul for a while to ask friends for money, and that SungSoo himself couldn't agree to it immediately—though he was thinking about it still. All of this, SungSoo made sure to skillfully convey without saying anything directly.

"You did right to refuse him," the playwright said. "I never could stand him. Thanks for the heads-up—if he asks to meet me, I'll come up with some excuse."

As they were thus catching up and walking, they noticed a throng of people just ahead, loudly shouting something.

"Oh goodness, is this another protest? We should take a different road," SungSoo said.

"I don't think so, that sounds like laughing. Maybe it's some show?" The playwright, who liked spectacles, started heading in that direction. As they approached they could see that the crowd was whooping and clapping at something in the middle of the boulevard. They pushed their way to the front, and saw that it was a procession of about two dozen courtesans.

Each woman was dressed in a marvelous silk costume, tied together with a white sash that trailed behind them. On the sash was written the name of the courtesan and the name of the new restaurant MyungWol. Some of them carried baskets of flowers, and from time to time tossed a blossom at the adoring crowd.

"Incredible!" The playwright laughed. "How brilliant. MyungWol will be the talk of the town! We have to go there together soon."

SungSoo had always enjoyed the sight of beautiful women, and he watched the courtesans with great interest. Then, in surprise, he froze. In the middle of the procession was the familiar yet changed face of Dani.

At first, SungSoo could only process her appearance in comparison to the one in his memory. Her round face had thinned, and her features had become more prominent. Her powdered skin looked like polished marble, though it had once been as fresh and rosy as a spring dawn. Her black-lined eyes, sharp cheekbones, and painted red lips gave her a formidable air. It was undeniable that she no longer looked young. Only the lively expression of her eyes, which showed a glimpse of the mysterious garden within her and seemed capable of looking into anyone's soul, remained unchanged. But so, so unchanged! The moment he finally made that connection, he saw her as other people saw her: a resplendent woman against whom all other women simply paled.

How, in the seven years since coming back to Seoul, had he never seen her? The truth was that he'd long known she had become a courtesan, and a grand courtesan at that. In fact, it would have been impossible for him not to hear about her. In the capital, intellectuals, artists, writers, diplomats, and the like moved in just a few intricately connected circles, and they all loved beautiful courtesans, some more basely, and some more innocently. But, he admitted to himself, he had deliberately avoided running into her, and had stuck to parties where he knew she wouldn't be entertaining. In his mind he had thought that their relations were finished a long time ago, and that it was useless to dig up old bones and try to make a broth out of them, so to speak. The best thing about the past was that it was behind you. So he never once wondered about her or indulged in fantasies of meeting her. Yet, when she was before his eyes, he suddenly felt troubled and did not know how to react.

"Have you met that one, Dani?" the playwright asked with a knowing smile, noticing SungSoo's gaze.

"I knew her a long time ago," he said. "She was a student back then."

"A student?" The playwright raised his eyebrows in disbelief.

SungSoo explained how Dani's mother—a celebrated courtesan herself—had retired when she became the second wife of an influential official.

"So a stepchild in a distinguished house. But if they sent her to school, why become a courtesan?" the playwright persisted.

SungSoo shrugged rather than implicate himself further in the story. He knew that Dani had been raised as a normal girl and was innocent when they met by chance in front of her school—she was never meant to become a courtesan. SungSoo had seduced her with implied promises and slipped away when he was called to study abroad. This had not troubled him, since he hadn't explicitly said, I will marry you. He could never have chosen anyone other than a woman of unimpeachable birth and wealth—a woman with a certain aristocratic blandness, like his dutiful and contented wife. If Dani hadn't realized that, it wasn't his fault.

"She's being kept by a very powerful protector, you know." The playwright gave the name of a Japanese judge near the very pinnacle of law, who had evidently set her up in a two-story house and even given her diamonds. "So if you're interested in her, you should know she is a forbidden fruit." The playwright winked. "As they say, you can see it, but you can't touch it. The good ones are always like that!"

"Oh, I wouldn't, anyway," SungSoo said, turning his eyes away with difficulty from the back of Dani's red robes.

AT THE SAME MOMENT, several blocks away, Yamada Genzo was riding out from his regimental headquarters with a fellow officer, named Ito. Disgusted by Hayashi's brutality on the hunting trip, Yamada had easily succeeded in persuading his father that he should move away from PyongYang. Baron Yamada, as is typical of heads of powerful families, was unconditionally supportive of his children's ambitions as a rule. He reached into his considerable network of friends and useful connections, and by spring, Genzo had received a commission in Seoul as a major. The promotion elicited veiled hostility from nearly all Yamada's PyongYang comrades, especially Major Hayashi, and Yamada knew it and they knew that he knew. But they all hid their true feelings so well, and expressed and accepted congratulations without any hint of bitterness, that no one had a reason to confront anyone.

In Seoul, Yamada found that no single superior held unshakable power, as in PyongYang, but that several heads of the military balanced one another out in their vying for advancement and influence. Following his father's advice, he had aligned himself with a faction to which Major Ito also belonged. The two men were both near the same age, well-built, handsome, and from the highest society. Though not tall, Ito had a lithe waist and muscular calves that made him appear full of restrained energy. He was the heir to an earldom but wore his distinguished background lightly and was rather unpretentious. Insofar as friendship was possible in Yamada's soul, he liked Ito. They were often in each other's company outside the regiment, and were now headed to an off-site meeting on horseback.

"You see, the absorption of a weaker nation and/or peoples by a stronger nation and/or peoples is not only inevitable, but desirable," Ito said, running a finger along his shapely mustache. "Without Japan, how could Korea have modernized? Who brought the trains, roads, power lines, progress? We are benevolent, as much as it is possible to be while governing so unruly a country. And yet these bastards don't know what's good for them."

"No doubt that we brought progress here. And you are right that the law of nature applies in this instance. But I do wonder about the whole issue of rice," Yamada countered. "Why bleed them out? It makes them hostile and uncontrollable. Can't there be another way?"

"But that rice is needed in Japan, the mother country. It is as when the body routes nutrients and fresh blood to the heart at the expense of a limb. Japan is the heart, and Korea is an extremity. Also, these Josenjings are too well fed and energetic and full-blooded. They will be more docile once they are bled out." Ito was smiling. The rhythmic swaying of his body on the saddle put him in a particularly jaunty state of mind on this fine afternoon. "We bring them progress, in return they provide the rice, and exotic goods—the antique celadons, the tiger skins, and the like. It's the same way everywhere else in the world now. Look at Britain, France, Germany, the Netherlands, Belgium, how they divided up Africa and Asia and grow stronger. The United States in the Philippines and the South Pacific. It is the world order." He paused a moment, then noticing a crowd gathered along the boulevard, he pointed ahead and started off at a gallop. Yamada followed, picking up his pace.

"It's a parade of Joseon courtesans!" Ito exclaimed, beckoning him. Yamada brought his horse next to Ito's and saw over the heads of the crowd a line of beautifully dressed women, singing and chanting and strewing flowers. Ito was laughing so heartily that his handsome black stallion stepped in place uneasily beneath him.

"Ah, and I forgot about the women, of course. Rice, tigers, and women—that's what Joseon is good for." Ito smirked and joined in the clapping and cheering. Turning to Yamada again, he said, "I myself am quite fond of these girls. They have a different flavor than the geisha."

"What might that be?" Yamada asked.

"I find that they are more headstrong than our geisha, who are like water, soothing and yielding. These Joseon courtesans have fire—they will fight you with passion. But there is such a distinct pleasure to be had at overcoming their resistance. It's like cracking the shell of a walnut to get to the meat inside." Ito winked, making a lewd gesture with his hands.

Just then, a pair of very young apprentices walked past with linked arms, smiling winningly at the crowd, and Ito cried, "Look at those baby courtesans. Adorable, aren't they? Charming!"

AS THEY NEARED THE END of the parade, Jade suddenly felt overwhelmed by all the strangers so pointedly looking at her. The subtle weight of Lotus's right elbow resting on her left elbow reassured her, and she tried to suppress her anxieties. In her other arm Jade carried a basket of cosmoses and mums, cut just that morning from Dani's garden. Once in a while, Lotus reached over to the basket with her left hand and tossed the flowers at the crowd. Each time the petals rained down, people cheered and clapped.

"Now you try, it's really fun," Lotus whispered, taking the basket from Jade.

"I don't think I can throw far like you!" Jade said in a panic. Then they both giggled secretively.

"Don't be silly, they weigh nothing," Lotus coached. "Just don't think about it too much and don't throw them right at people's faces."

Jade took a handful of flowers in her hand and tossed them to her right. The petals were carried by a light blue breeze and floated for a moment before fluttering down, making pink, white, and violet patterns in the atmosphere. The crowd clapped, mesmerized. The city streets shot through with sunshine, the feeling of her shoes crunching on the packed sand—it all filled her lungs with something besides air. Here was something that Jade hadn't known was possible: a sense of being free. She nearly wanted to flap her arms like wings. Resisting the fancy, she instead laughed and carelessly tossed a flower, which soared through the air and hit a boy in the face.

JUNGHO HAD BEEN WATCHING the parade of courtesans with intense fascination, standing between Loach, YoungGu, and the dog. YoungGu and JungHo had become close friends as boys often do after a good fistfight. The dog was a new addition to the group: one day in September, YoungGu found it wandering underneath the bridge, dirty and emaciated but still energetic. JungHo and Loach had both wanted to sell it to the butcher, but YoungGu looked ready to get into another fight. JungHo finally relented and let YoungGu keep the dog, as long as he fed it from his own share of food. Thereafter, YoungGu split his own meager ration with the dog and tenderly picked its fur for fleas, which he squished between his fingers. The dog was always within a few feet of YoungGu, and proved to be surprisingly useful for finding crowded places to beg. They had been roaming aimlessly when the dog led them to the parade and sat down on its haunches in front of the spectators, as if it too wanted to enjoy the sight.

Until then, JungHo had never realized that women could be so beautiful. The courtesans were almost like a different kind of people from all the women he'd known previously. The sight was so overwhelming that his stomach felt sick, but he couldn't look away. He noticed at the end of the parade a pair of girls closer to his age. They were about the same medium height and build, and dressed in identical costumes of long bud-green robes over a pink skirt. Objectively they were both little girls with ordinary faces, too young for their approaching beauty to be discerned. But his eyes were immediately fastened on one of them, as if he'd been searching precisely for her. She had a round face—especially set off by the strict center part from the hairline to the crown of her head—a pair of bright eyes, and cheeks like apples, slightly reddened from the crisp fall air. That and not much more, but that was all that was needed.

As he stared at her, she grabbed a cosmos blossom from the basket and threw it directly at his face, smiling radiantly. He met the soft flower with terror at the thought that she was taunting him on purpose—and euphoria, for the same reason. Noticing his amazement, Loach and YoungGu broke into laughter and began teasing him mercilessly, but JungHo couldn't even find it in himself to be irritated. The consciousness of something wonderful had entered his heart, though he did not yet know what it was.

7

THE ESCAPE

1918

IT IS A CONDITION OF YOUTH TO HAVE AN UNQUESTIONING BELIEF that life is a steady progression. Jade took it for granted that one step must follow another, and that she had caught a certain forward momentum at the parade that would take her into adulthood. So she was surprised and disappointed when nothing changed in the smallness of their daily routine. Dani still didn't allow them to go beyond five houses in either direction. Jade obeyed as she always had, but dust began to settle over the loveliness of the house. She'd seen that just a little outside their neighborhood, there were shows, music, wealthy housewives imitating the fashions of courtesans, starry-eyed high school students in newsboy caps, gentlemen in high collars and monocles, stores selling all manner of delicacies. The world pulled at her, irresistible and real like the first hot day of summer. But she was cut off from everything, walled up in the middle of Seoul. As winter set in, Jade developed a habit of going out alone and sitting at the end of their street, the farthest point from the house that Dani would allow. It was on one of these afternoons that she noticed a strange boy around the neighborhood.

Later on, Jade wouldn't be able to recall exactly how he seemed when she first saw him. She realized his existence over the course of many days. He seemed to be a natural part of the surroundings like a tree or a hedge, so she became used to him before she even noticed him. He was about her age, small and skinny. His skin was nut-brown, and it was hard to tell whether that was because of the sun or from the lack of washing. The moment her eyes finally trained on him as something distinct, he smiled, as if he'd been waiting for her to do just that. He started walking toward her, a yellow dog with a curled tail following him at his heels. That was when she realized that something was off about his appearance. It was his clothes, so worn-out that they seemed to be turning themselves back into yarns. Some beggars wore more patches than the original fabric on their clothes, but his gashes were just gaping open and flapping vigorously in the piercing wind. She was torn by equal forces of pity and disgust.

"I've seen you here a lot. Do you live around here?" he asked her. She nodded reluctantly. Dani hadn't forbidden her from talking to other children, but she knew without being told. On the other hand, the force of her ennui was greater than the fear of Dani. And as dirty as the boy was, he was not so different from the village urchins she'd known growing up.

"Is that your dog?" she asked, pointing at the dog sniffing the ground behind him.

The boy whistled and the dog came bounding forward, joyfully wagging its tail.

"It's my friend's dog. You can pet him, he's gentle."

Jade squatted down and stroked the grateful dog from the head to the tail, behind the ears, and under the chin. "What's his name?" she asked.

"He doesn't have one. We just call him 'dog,'" the boy explained. "My name is JungHo, though."

Jade laughed. "Sorry. I should've asked your name first. I'm Jade." Then she added, "I should probably go home soon. I'm not allowed to go far."

"What's far?"

"Across this street."

JungHo shook his head in disbelief. "Don't you get sick of being cooped up? I've walked every street in Seoul, just to know what's out there. There's the river, the marketplace, a street where all the Yankees live . . . Not too far from here, there is a zoo. I can show you, if you want."

"Oh, I don't know." Jade paused. "What's a zoo?"

JungHo explained that that's where they kept all the animals of the world, that its most famous star was an elephant named Giant, and that they wouldn't need to pay money to see it. Jade bit her lips and considered her options. Dani had already gone out and wasn't coming back until late at night. If Jade let go of this chance, the next outing might come in a year or two, whenever the whim struck Dani's free spirit.

"Okay, but I have to be back as quickly as possible," she said, walking up to JungHo. Closer together, she saw that he was only her height or even a little shorter. But he didn't look weak. Beggars usually shuffled, whereas JungHo marched with his arms swinging high, unconcerned by the way people looked at him. He almost acted as though he dressed that way out of a sense of adventure, like a prince in disguise from old wives' tales. As they walked side by side JungHo pointed out the places of interest, as if all of Seoul belonged to him.

"That's the zoo. It used to be a palace," he said at last. There were dozens of people lined up outside its gates, even in the middle of winter. Sounds of music, shouts, and laughter wafted over the stone walls.

"Come on, this way." JungHo led her away from the entrance and rounded the corner. There were not so many passersby here; a zelkova tree was leaning its boughs over the zoo wall.

"Do you know how to climb?" JungHo asked, and she shook her head. He interlaced his hands together next to the tree and told her to step her right foot on top. Jade thought he would stumble under her weight, but he stayed in place until she found a groove in the trunk with her other foot and heaved herself up to a bough. Within seconds, he followed and crouched next to her under the leafless branches. The dog sat and whimpered below them.

"See, there is Giant." JungHo pointed. Over the wall, there were hundreds of people thronged around a dry moat; inside the moat, there was a raised island covered by chalky, bone-colored sand. Giant was standing in the dead center of it like a beached ship with gray sails. He was so large that even from afar, Jade could see him blinking his eyes as big as the palm of her hand. The crowd cheered and threw things into the enclosure to get his attention. Whether out of patience or stubbornness, the elephant gave no reaction, and soon the bored spectators left and were replaced by the next row. Some people cursed and spat into the moat, and others tossed him apple cores, but Giant still didn't stir.

Jade thought that the creature's suffering was all the greater for its strength and size; there was nothing tragic about a captive flea. She didn't want to keep looking, and at the same time couldn't turn around and leave it. She had been longing to see the world. Now that she saw what it was, she felt a creeping sense of nausea.

JungHo tugged at her sleeve. Someone was shouting in their direction.

About thirty yards away, a uniformed guard was waving his rifle at them and swearing. Jade struggled to hold her scream; JungHo had already scrambled down to the ground. The dog was barking and growling at the guard, baring all its white teeth.

"Jump!" JungHo shouted. The guard was making his way toward them, brandishing the butt of his rifle like a club. JungHo yelled, "I'll catch you!" and Jade shook her head.

Almost at the foot of the tree, the guard cursed and aimed his rifle at the dog. JungHo stayed still, unwilling to run away without her. Jade took a breath and jumped off, landing on her knees and palms in front of JungHo. The three of them fled without turning back to see whether the guard was following them—not stopping or slowing down until they'd reached her house.

"Are you okay? Let me see your hands," JungHo said, breathing hard.

"I'm okay, it's just a scrape," she protested as he took her hands in his and blew away the dirt. The dog thumped his tail, whimpered loudly, and flattened himself on the ground in exhaustion.

"That elephant," Jade began. "Do you know what it's thinking all day, standing so still and quiet?"

JungHo reflected for a moment. "It's probably just annoyed at having so many people around. Or it's thinking about food," he offered.

"No, it's thinking, How can I get out of here? You saw how it wasn't chained. It was very tall, but obviously it can't cross over that moat. So elephants can't jump. But don't you think there's a way it could get out?"

JungHo's face turned dark and serious as he mulled it over. "I don't know, I'm so sorry."

"Let's come up with ideas, next time we meet," Jade said.

When she came back inside the house, she announced to Lotus, "My new friend took me to the zoo and we saw the biggest animal in the world! What's strange is that I thought it would make me happy, but it made me sad."

"A new friend?" Lotus asked, closing her sewing kit. She'd just finished reattaching the *goreum* ribbon of her jacket.

"Yes, a boy our age with a yellow dog."

"Oh, I've seen him around the neighborhood," Lotus said, suddenly reopening the sewing kit. She began pointedly adding more stitches to the ribbon, which was already secured. "He's a dirty, pickpocketing street urchin. You should stay far away if you don't want to catch lice."

Jade was wounded. They had never disagreed about anything

before, and Jade tried to shake off the feeling that there was a change in their friendship as thin and inevitable as a hairline break in a frozen lake. She tried to reassure Lotus that no one would take her place, that they would always be the oldest and closest friends in the world. But still, no matter how many times Jade tried to get her to come out and meet JungHo, she refused. Instead, Lotus stayed in the house next to Luna, who was heading to late pregnancy in catatonic silence.

From then on, whenever Jade came out of the house to play, JungHo was waiting for her by the gates. Sometimes he brought the dog and they cuddled him or made him fetch sticks. Other times he came alone and they strategized the elephant's escape while walking around the block. By the time JungHo let her know he'd lost his entire family and slept outside in a tent, Jade didn't think there was anything wrong about her new friend.

"You know, we're not so different. I don't have parents either, although mine are still alive," Jade told him. "My mother told me I must never come back looking for them. They would be ruined if the other villagers found out I'd become a courtesan apprentice."

"Do you miss them?" JungHo asked. Jade tried to recall her mother combing and braiding her hair at night, and how she embraced Jade one last time while making her swear not to come back. Those memories were already becoming fainter, like stars at the approaching of dawn.

"I used to miss them, but now I feel like I've met my real family," Jade said.

One especially cold day, Jade snuck out one of the countless silk comforters from the paulownia-tree chest and gave it to JungHo. He seemed more shocked than pleased.

"Don't worry, take it," Jade said, pushing it into his arms. "We have dozens more inside."

JungHo wordlessly looked down at the comforter filled with

silk cocoons as light as air. Something seemed to stir in his mind, and he turned resolute.

"When I'm older I'll give you something a hundred times finer than this," he told her. Jade smiled and said of course, without expecting him to ever make good on his promise. This was why JungHo made such an impression on her, the way he said with total confidence that he would give her something worth more than he would probably earn in his life. JungHo had nothing compared to Jade, yet he seemed incapable of cowering. He never blamed his circumstances or thought regretfully about the past. He was like an empty vessel, but in the best way: it was true he didn't hold a lot of knowledge, but his mind was free to flow in whatever direction, and he didn't nurture pain. Whatever he did keep permanently, Jade was certain that he would protect firmly in the bottom of his *jangdok* pot. He might never fling himself far from where he'd landed, Jade thought, but he would nonetheless be happy for the simple reason that he refused to be caged.

8

I HAVE MET THE RIGHT PERSON, AT LAST

1919

THE SECRET TO DANI'S SUCCESS WAS THAT SHE LIKED NOT JUST TO BE busy, but to have *projects* to which she could apply her considerable mental and physical abilities. Her fame, her two-story house with its exquisite furnishings and rarefied garden, her powerful protector, even her unusual beauty and allure—none of these had resulted from chance, but from her imagination, planning, and execution.

Her most recent project was rearing her three young charges. They had come into her life unbidden, as a favor to her dearest cousin. But she had accepted them partly because she was at an age when wealthy, childless courtesans started to think of adopting foster daughters to care for them in retirement. She thought it would be amusing to teach everything she knew to worthy successors, the same way men of higher status tried to leave their legacies through bequests, writings, and descendants in general. Why not her?

But this project was turning out to be more complicated than she'd imagined. While the children, even Jade, were growing on her, she still didn't feel like a mother. This lack of instinct probably originated from an emptiness in her womb, she thought. Dani had never become pregnant, and now she wondered if she just wasn't meant for the job. All through her twenties, she had been terrified of falling prey to this malady, stuffing herself with silk cocoons beforehand and afterward taking the tea that would bring on her cycle earlier and more heavily than usual. But she couldn't always know when an encounter would take place; and sometimes when, in the middle of the act, she would whisper to her client that she wasn't properly protected, he would nonetheless go inside her. On such occasions, she lay very still, horrified by the stickiness between her legs, while the man rolled off, sighing contentedly and closing his eyes, as though he'd just accomplished a great deal. Though a grand courtesan, admired in vast circles of cultured and important men, all she could do in those situations was wait until he felt well enough to leave, wash off as thoroughly as possible with scalding hot water, and never see him again.

These events had happened often enough over the years that now, at an age when most married women had at least three or four children, Dani suspected that she was never able to conceive in the first place. On one hand, it mystified her to see Luna fall pregnant after just one unfortunate incident and endure such prolonged agony; on the other hand, she felt relieved that she'd never had to suffer that way.

Despite this lack of an inner compass for parenting, Dani was finally beginning to feel that she was prodding the girls in the right direction. Every day they were acting less like empty-headed little children; she'd once even caught Lotus with a book. But just as Dani was observing how all three girls were improving in looks, mind, and attitude, her commitment to the mothering project was shaken by a highly distracting incident. It was a letter addressed in a familiar hand, delivered at breakfast a few days after the parade.

Leaving her porridge barely touched, she went to her room to read its contents in peace. In it, SungSoo talked of how he'd obtained her address by inquiring at MyungWol, and that he'd been absorbed by the demands of his businesses and his family since returning from abroad. In such a life there was no room for romance, and indeed he had long given up hope of love beyond comfort; he had had no feelings in that regard for many years. (He did not say "since you," but that was the intended effect.) But seeing her again at the parade woke in him the blissful yearning he had always felt for her. "You looked as beautiful as when I first met you," he wrote. He had left her alone and gone to Japan, thinking they were both young and would eventually heal. (He didn't mention the part about his marrying his wife.) Only now that he was older, he saw how wrong it was to have gone away without her. He wished to offer her his penitence—in person.

Dani read and reread this letter, tossed it on her little desk, asked Hesoon to bring her some coffee, and clutched it back again with a cup in her other hand. The warm drink had the familiar effect of calming her emotions and at the same time, sharpening her mind, bringing back images that had been long buried. As painful as the memories were, the act of recollection was bittersweet and delicious. She saw herself watching clear-eyed over her life as from the ether, even as her body was huddled over her writing table. The letter proved that the love she once had for him wasn't just an illusion, a false memory. She had truly lived.

"All the same, I don't have any feelings left for him, only for his memories," she thought. Unconsciously, she unfolded her vanity mirror. When she saw her reflection, she admitted to herself that she was curious how she'd looked to him that day; she was hoping she didn't appear too old or changed. Satisfied with her appearance, she closed the mirror with a triumphant smile.

"No, I won't see him," she thought. "Or even write back to him. He doesn't even deserve a response. Ignoring him is the only dignified choice I have."

Though Dani believed she had made the right decision by not responding, in the days that followed, she suffered from an unexplained and relentless headache. She struggled to hide her irritability at parties and snapped at the children over the littlest things, even at Luna. At night, lying on her silk bedspread, she felt more alone than she'd been in years. "I will never fall in love again," she moaned, wiping her cheeks with the back of her hand. She was thirty-three, no one new was going to court her, and she had blown off the one man she'd passionately loved. When these thoughts kept her awake, Dani downed some glasses of soju alone and in her nightclothes—a practice she normally despised as untidy, but deemed medicinal under the present circumstances.

Just after the first snowfall, another letter came for Dani which, in spite of her pounding heart at seeing the envelope in the maid's hand, was not from SungSoo. It was from an activist who had recently returned from working in Shanghai, and though she did not know him, she had heard of his reputation. In addition, he'd been recommended to write to her by General _____, based in Vladivostok, who was being supported by her cousin Silver in PyongYang. He did not write either the general's name or her cousin's in fear of interception, but Dani immediately agreed to see him at an unassuming little teahouse where no one of any importance would ever go.

When she arrived at their meeting place, there was only one guest seated by himself at a corner table away from the door, deep in his own thoughts. He met her eyes immediately when she entered, and rose courteously as she walked toward him.

"I'm Lee MyungBo. It is so good of you to come," he said with a bow.

"You shouldn't say that, it is my honor." Dani returned the bow and settled on the chair across from him. They ordered tea and warmed into some small talk about the weather.

"It is so much colder here, of course. In Shanghai, it only ever gets as cool as autumn in our country, and it seldom snows," MyungBo said with a smile. Though not as handsome as SungSoo, MyungBo had a woodsy attractiveness in his umber eyes and baritone voice.

"Oh, how I should like to see Shanghai," Dani replied naturally, without thinking. She liked how he had said "our country," that he'd been everywhere in the wide-open world where she also longed to go, and that he was warm, simple, and unaffected in all his mannerisms. He was so modest that he nearly blushed as he struggled to bring up the true purpose of their meeting. She broached the subject first.

"With regards to that matter, which you could not specify in your letter for reasons of discretion, I am ready to lend you my support in whatever way I can." She gazed significantly at his warm, weary face.

"Thank you for such a clear pledge. It is so taxing to ask of a stranger, and a woman no less . . ." he muttered, looking down at the table as to avoid her dark and dazzling stare. Then he explained, in fits and starts, that there were several simultaneous "initiatives" being planned all at once, both in the peninsula and abroad. The leaders of separate activist groups and militias across Manchuria, Primorski, and even the United States and Hawaii were attempting to create a unified center in the form of a provisional government in Shanghai. Meanwhile, in Korea itself, there was an effort to bring together the various factions led by the Cheondoists, the Christians, the Buddhists, the Nationalists, and the Communists, in an unequivocal declaration of independence at a single moment.

"All of these efforts take a considerable amount of resources, to feed and arm our soldiers and activists, to have offices and safe houses, print the pamphlets and manifestos, transport the people across the border, bribe officials and get people out of jail, and for a hundred other reasons. I am constantly straining to discover new sources of funds," MyungBo said apologetically. His cheeks crimsoned like a child's, which was unexpected and touching in someone so grave and dignified.

"My friends have all but abandoned me, and even my younger brother refuses to see me. Among my family, only my wife and my son have stayed by my side." He smiled a bittersweet smile, and Dani felt herself smart just a little, as if she'd been jabbed with something sharp.

"Speak no more. I understand. But do you see, you've met just the right person." She smiled reassuringly. "The rich are ever so much more willing to spend their money on courtesans than on the cause. Luckily, the courtesans have more heart than they do. I can round up the five courtesan guilds in Seoul. I am the leader of one and know the heads of each of the others. No one is better suited to convince them than I am."

"Truly, I am overwhelmed." MyungBo looked up at her with a joyful expression, and she also felt her spirits soaring. "Yes, I have met the right person, at last."

On the way home, Dani reflected on these words and MyungBo's expression as he uttered them. She wondered anxiously whether they had a hidden meaning or were innocently spoken. In the deepest part of her heart, she sensed that there was some significance there besides the relief at finding a willing supporter. This thought came to her as a strange new delight after the onslaught of depression caused by SungSoo's letter. It occurred to her that SungSoo's moral laxity was what made him both available and less appealing; conversely, MyungBo's integrity kept him aloof and more worthy of admiration. As she reflected she took in the snow-covered streets, blue-gray in the shade and brilliant gold in the afternoon sun, and thought it was all more beautiful and alive than usual. She felt younger than she had in a long time—perhaps even years.

• • •

ONE AFTERNOON, there was a quiet knock on their gates and Jade went out, expecting to see JungHo's familiar face. Instead, she was greeted by a handsome gentleman who asked her politely whether her aunt was home. Jade went back inside to announce the visitor, and Dani put on her coat and went outside.

"You didn't reply to my letter," SungSoo said to her, without any superfluous greetings. He was wearing a fashionable hat with a medium brim and a new coat of the finest English wool. A fresh scent of cologne and good health emanated from his robust, well-fed body, but his face wore a sorrowful expression.

"I hope you know how sorry I am. I should never have left you here and gone to Japan . . ." he continued, feet firmly planted on the ground, as if demonstrating his steadfastness. Above his head, bits of snow were starting to float around like dandelion fluff. They were so weightless that their descent seemed to take forever.

"You do look very sorry judging by your expression," she replied. "But you know what gives you away? Your voice. It doesn't sound sorry at all."

She turned around and was about to walk away when he grabbed hold of her hand. He pulled her firmly, spinning her round to him and placing his other hand behind the small of her back. Then he kissed her.

At the moment right before he kissed her, when she realized what was going to happen, she thought that she would pull away, disgusted. But when his lips met hers, she wanted to keep kissing him. The fact that he craved her made her deliriously happy. When they let go of each other she sighed. "No, I don't hate you."

SungSoo looked with a sincere expression into her eyes, waiting for her to absolve him. He was aware that at that moment Dani thought him as handsome and attractive as when they first met. He was intoxicated by that distinct and palmy pleasure, the consciousness of one's own seductive power, which in so many people's lives is the closest thing to love that they experience. He reached for her hand, and she did not pull away.

"But it's too late for forgiveness. So leave me in peace." Her voice shook when she said those last words, and they both sensed how she didn't really mean them, and in fact meant just the opposite.

He didn't know what to do. He could just as well have left her then and there and not pursued her further, not because of her wishes or because he was a proud man, but because he was fundamentally unable to truly lose himself for another person. Not only was it distasteful to him intellectually, his soul was also incapable of it. But at that moment, he noticed how Dani was shivering and was moved by the sight of her fragility. He leaned in and enveloped her in his arms. As soon as he did so, a tear loosened from Dani's eyes and she melted into his embrace.

When they came apart, she wordlessly led him through the gates. They both suppressed the urge to run to her room, walking calmly as if they weren't burning with the need to tear off the layers of wool and wrap their legs around each other's waists. Once inside, they made love not knowing or caring about anything else except how their bodies felt together.

It was close to midnight when they were finished and lying side by side in the candlelight. Dani thought to herself, This is the happiest time of my entire life. There could be nothing that would follow that would be better than this evening spent with him alone, away from the rest of the world. Though it would feel much longer in her memory, it was no more than a few hours in reality. Like all such moments, it ended before she was ready—with a knock on her door.

"There is a gentleman at the front gates, asking for you," Hesoon whispered in her ear. "I tried to tell him that you were not home, but then he said he would wait for you, and then I didn't know what to do."

"Well, who is it?" Dani bristled, stepping out into the hallway. "It's not the police? Or someone that the judge may have sent?"

"I don't think so. He said he goes by Lee—and didn't tell me his given name, but said you'll know who he is."

"Oh!" Dani drew a sharp breath. "I do know who that is. I wonder why he's here? At any rate, I can't have him waiting outside in this cold for hours, thinking I'll be on my way home. I'll have to receive him. Show him into the sitting room."

Dani went back inside her room and began putting on her clothes. She asked SungSoo to stay quiet in the room while she dealt with a visitor in the sitting room. At this, SungSoo let his irritation show: he wasn't going to hide from this mysterious stranger, who Dani insisted was not her lover and yet was visiting her in the dead of the night. No, he would rather leave than hide in the room like a thief.

"Fine then, do as you wish," Dani said, exasperated beyond her control, a deep flush rising to her cheeks. She stormed out of the room and hurried into the sitting room, where Lee MyungBo was standing uncertainly in his coat, holding his hat in two hands.

"Miss Dani, I apologize for barging in on you like this . . ." He started to explain, and Dani noticed with hidden pleasure the subtle brightness of his eyes and a hint of color on his face. "I know how inappropriate it is, but I've come to tell you . . ."

"Yes?" Dani approached him with a light step, excited and also ashamed to feel so drawn. MyungBo took a step toward her too, almost involuntarily. As he appeared to reach his hand toward her upper arm, she heard the door of her room creak open, and SungSoo walked through the hallway and into the sitting room.

What happened next was as deep a confusion as any three people had ever experienced. SungSoo and MyungBo started saying at the same time, "What are you doing here?" while Dani looked rapidly between both men and exclaimed, "How do you two know each other?" An embarrassed silence followed for a minute. SungSoo, the quickest to recover, said to Dani:

"MyungBo and I are old friends from our student days in Tokyo."

"I see," Dani said, and then the room was plunged into silence once more.

"I came to tell you something important," MyungBo said, but

this time his eyes no longer had the brilliance she'd seen before. "His Majesty, Emperor Gojong, has passed away."

Drawing a sharp breath, Dani clutched a hand to her chest. Both men sprang forward instinctively as to steady her, but MyungBo checked himself while SungSoo laid a protective hand on Dani's waist. MyungBo continued.

"It happened just a few hours ago. One of our informers, a lady of the bedchamber, sent a message as soon as it happened. He was having a bowl of sweet rice water when suddenly, he started choking and crying out, coughing up blood. The lady said his dead body was covered in hives."

A horrified moan escaped Dani's lips, and she sank onto the floor. SungSoo sat down next to her, keeping a hand on her back, while MyungBo remained standing in his place.

"But why poison him? He's already been deposed many years, and his son is a mere puppet," SungSoo said.

"Who knows? But I think, most likely, to let us know that they can kill our sovereign without consequences, just as they assassinated his wife, the empress . . ." MyungBo paused, glancing at Dani, who looked alarmingly pale. "Miss Dani is ill. The news is so shocking . . ."

"I'm all right. I'll feel better if I have a little drink," she replied, and ordered Hesoon to bring her a bottle of soju and three glasses. The maid soon returned with the drink, a bowl of refreshing white kimchi and other snacks, and set the tray down in front of Dani. At her urging, MyungBo sat down as well. Dani first poured for the two men, and then SungSoo poured for her, and they raised their glasses at the same time, murmuring, "To His Majesty."

Once the soju had circulated through their bodies, each began to feel more comfortable—not about the emperor's death, but the situation among themselves. It is always excruciating to discover that one's distinct connections, who ought to belong firmly and chastely in separate spheres of one's life, are somehow acquainted, and perhaps more intimately than one would like. Each of them keenly suffered from this, though SungSoo in particular took this as an insult and a betrayal. His good breeding and the soothing effects of soju were the only things that kept him from succumbing to the jealousy that burned deeply in his chest.

"So what happens now?" Dani asked MyungBo, revived a bit from the soju.

"You know that we've been preparing for the demonstration . . ." he began carefully, wondering whether he could be more forthcoming in SungSoo's presence. Then, making up his mind to be direct, he said, "It probably means we will gather our forces earlier than we'd planned. In about a month, around His Majesty's funeral, when the crowds gather in Seoul to pay their respects."

"But are you ready? Can everything come together before then?" Dani questioned while pouring another round for the two men. This time, MyungBo took the bottle from Dani and poured her drink for her. The gesture was customary, as one must never pour one's own drink, but nonetheless it roiled SungSoo with its intimacy.

"That's also why I came to see you. I immediately realized that things will start to move very quickly, and I didn't know whom I may possibly trust, except you."

After he finished, MyungBo downed his soju without meeting the eyes of either of his companions.

"Please, tell me how I can be of any help," Dani pleaded. "What is needed?"

MyungBo's face crimsoned at once. Already wounded by the death of the emperor, he was shocked once more at finding SungSoo at Dani's house, and somehow strangely hurt as well. Now he was humiliated by having to ask again for favors in plain view of the man who had already refused him so coldly. He focused on the candlelight dancing inside his cup of soju in order to avoid looking at either of the lovers in the eyes.

"We plan on making the demonstration peaceful. For that we would need to prepare only the manifestos, and as many Korean flags as we can manage. But without a doubt, we will need to be ready for whatever comes after the demonstration. That means guns, safe houses, transportation for countless activists and messengers . . . And then again, that's not even including the preparation for the outbreak of direct military combat. Not just in Manchuria, where most of our remaining troops are, but in Korea itself. If we succeed in gathering enough force, there will be a definite war within our borders, for the first time in more than twenty years."

"I understand." Dani nodded. "I haven't been idle since our meeting. I've personally met with each of the guild leaders. You'll be heartened to know that they've all pledged a third of their earnings this month, to begin with." She smiled, her cheeks flushing beautifully. The presence of the two men had put her in a feverish—yet not wholly unpleasant—state of mind. For one, MyungBo's visible discomfort confirmed to her that he was jealous of SungSoo. Even with grave issues at stake, she couldn't help but feel rather delighted.

"When the five courtesan guilds of Seoul pool their money together, you'll see that it's not an insignificant sum, even when we're talking about war. You see, people look down on us for how we make our living, but we have our honor. Actually, I've never been so glad as I am now to be able to help in my own small way . . ." Dani's voice trailed away and her eyes welled up. She was quite overcome with emotion, although it was unclear even to her whether that gladness was purely from contributing to the movement, or from other, less selfless causes.

She sipped on her soju, and explained when and how she may be able to transfer the money to him in the coming weeks. As MyungBo thanked her in the most effusive but dignified manner, Dani turned to SungSoo and innocently asked, "Well, isn't there something you could do as well?"

SungSoo, blindsided by this question, blurted out, "Me?"

"You must surely be able to contribute something, you of all people," Dani persisted.

"That's all my family's money, don't you see . . . I myself don't make very much," SungSoo protested rapidly. "As it is, I'm spending endlessly on my publishing house and the bicycle shop, neither of which have ever been profitable." Dani's face lit up unexpectedly.

"Oh! But you *can* help! How could we have missed it!" She clasped her hands around SungSoo's arm. "Didn't you hear what Mr. MyungBo just said? We will need thousands of copies of manifestos and flags. You have your own printing press, don't you?"

"I do, but . . ." SungSoo muttered with a sinking heart. He couldn't protest that it was too dangerous, or try to get out of it in any other way. He addressed MyungBo directly, saying, "But is that what you need, my fellow?"

"If you're offering, I will take it very gladly," MyungBo replied, courteously and sincerely as ever. "But only if it's not a burden to you. And speak freely if it is, and I will never bring up any of this in front of you, ever again."

Seeing Dani's eyes intensely fixed on his face, SungSoo had no choice but to say, "Of course it's not a burden." And as these words left his lips, he already felt a little less in love with her.

9

THE MARCH

1919

IT WAS THE SECOND TIME MYUNGBO FOUND HIMSELF AT SUNGSOO'S publishing house, where he'd thought he would never return. When he arrived, he was told by the secretary—the same brown-faced young man from the country—to wait outside SungSoo's office; he wasn't asked if he'd like coffee.

MyungBo was not offended, however. Years of similar experiences had left him well conscious of the coldness that enters into amicable relationships when money becomes involved. He himself had never cared that much for possessions; even as a child, he was sometimes scolded for giving away his clothes and books to poorer classmates and servants' children. It had appeared to him then that no matter how much he gave, he would always have more than enough. As he grew older, he even relished the struggles brought on by his sacrifices. There was a soaring awareness that illuminated his soul whenever he did the right thing, which also cost him something.

This euphoria, however, was balanced by the utter terror he felt when he looked around and saw so many others to whom this consciousness was not only absent, but unknowable and abhorrent. Most people, MyungBo realized, were made of a different material than his; and it was not something that could shift, as from coldness to warmth, but an elemental and fundamental difference, like wood from metal. At a time like this, an apocalyptic time if it ever was—his people dying under the Japanese bayonet, everywhere in the world bloodshed and rape, and the war in Europe, which had only just ended—people still thought about going to university, obtaining a lucrative post, or squeezing more profits out of their land, and churning ever greater wealth, as if the world itself weren't burning all around them. It was one thing for the starving peasants to not care about independence, and many of them did not mind whether their landlord was Japanese or Korean, as long as they got to keep some grain to feed their families. But the indifference and hostility from the educated class, who should know better and willingly take up their duty, cut MyungBo to the deepest core. Even his wife would have preferred that he had stayed in Korea to take a position or while away his years waiting to inherit his father's land. She never said this, but MyungBo knew her feelings. Regarding their marriage, he was profoundly disappointed at not being understood exactly where he felt most proud of himself.

This was surely the reason he had felt so taken in by Dani, who had shown such acute perception and genuine empathy for the cause. Turning his hat mindlessly in his hands, MyungBo recalled Dani's brilliant eyes and her eloquent, expressive lips. It was such a shame that people only ever saw sensuality in that lovely face, which was so clearly full of intelligence and purity. And more than that—there was something very touching about her, strong and proud yet simultaneously very tender and open. But at that moment, MyungBo abruptly stopped his musing and rose from his chair. The secretary had announced that SungSoo was ready for him.

"Have you been waiting a long time?" SungSoo asked him as he entered the office.

"No, not very long," MyungBo said, smiling weakly. "And I

would have waited even longer. I am indebted to you for the rest of my life."

Instead of protesting, SungSoo remained quiet and lit up a cigarette with downcast eyes. Leaning back and sinking into his deep-seated chair, he breathed out the smoke while crossing one long leg over the other.

"I won't say it hasn't been . . . troublesome," he replied at last.

"I understand that. I truly do, my friend." MyungBo blushed. "But you, with your intelligence and education, you must surely understand that with this contribution, you've gained your place in history. Don't you?"

"Ah, history! Ha!" SungSoo laughed a hollow laugh, scattering wisps of smoke. "Fine, MyungBo, let's discuss history then. You remember as I do the story of Koguryo? That martial kingdom of our ancestors ruled not just the entire northern part of the Korean peninsula, but far into Primorski and Manchuria, for seven hundred years beginning in the first century. Then after its demise, Balhae ruled another three hundred years in those same territories. Now though, those lands belong to Russia and China, and who do you see there? The Russians and the Chinese. Then what happened to the Koreans who used to live there for a thousand years? They've been wiped out, or they've moved to the south, or intermarried with the Russians and the Chinese. But the few ethnic Koreans, the descendants of Koguryo who remain, do they mourn the loss of their mother country? No, they have no longing or patriotism for the Korean peninsula. Their identity has been completely diluted in the past thousand years.

"The concept of a nation is a pure construct. It serves to hold up our reality, we need it for government et cetera, but it is neither self-evident nor natural, and becomes more meaningless when you think of it in historical context. For all of human history, nations have been destroyed, absorbed into others, reborn, or forgotten, and that makes no difference to the well-being of the posterity. Whether it's Koguryo, the Roman Empire, or ancient Persia, it's all the same. We were annexed by Japan nine years ago, now that's a fact. If nothing changes, then in a thousand years, there won't be a 'Korea' or the 'Korean people.' But people then will not care one bit that their country was once, a thousand years ago, independent."

The logic of his argument was clear to both of them. A self-satisfied smile appeared on SungSoo's handsome face as his friend struggled to collect his thoughts.

"What you're saying appears very rational," MyungBo said at last. "You may be right that all of this—all the struggle, death, and sacrifice—won't matter at all in the grand scheme of history. But what you're saying is like this: suppose there is a little boy who is playing on the train tracks. Suddenly you see the train approaching, and the boy is too young or too scared to know how to save himself. Then you say to yourself, 'Well, in the grand scheme of things, he will eventually die, whether it's now or sixty years down the road. So why should I bother saving him? Better to just go about my business.' That might be rational, but that doesn't make it *right*."

SungSoo was about to respond, "Who is to say what is right then? Is it always you?" But changing his mind, he quietly extinguished his cigarette while MyungBo sat up straighter and cleared his throat.

"Well, that's enough talking, I think. You wanted to check on the progress?" SungSoo rose from the chair, pulling down at the hem of his smart wool suit. "Come now, let's go downstairs."

The two men walked through a narrow hallway, and took the stairs to the basement level. At the landing, there was a locked door under a bare lightbulb; SungSoo opened it with a key and went inside first.

At a glance, it looked as though the cavernous space was completely unlit. As his eyes adjusted, however, MyungBo noticed a pair of tiny windows near the top of one wall, which peeked out onto the street at ankle level of the pedestrians. In the middle of the room, there were two men bent over some tables, busy at work, while nearby another man was operating the printing press. MyungBo walked over to the machine and picked up the top copy from a stack of broadsheet papers; the title THE GREAT REPUBLIC OF KOREA DECLARATION OF INDEPENDENCE was emblazoned boldly at the top like fresh footprints in snow.

"How many copies?" MyungBo asked.

"Two thousand thus far, ten thousand before March first," SungSoo replied.

"Ah, SungSoo," his friend exclaimed warmly. "You have done your part for your country. And the flags?"

SungSoo pointed at the two men at the tables, who were painting red, blue, and black ink onto wood blocks and stamping them onto sheets of muslin.

"I don't care what you say, it's your actions that count. SungSoo, you are a patriot indeed," MyungBo said quietly. SungSoo sighed, shaking his head.

"Listen, MyungBo, if you want my advice . . . If you want Korea to truly survive this storm, and not be obliterated without any trace in history, heed my words," he said, more sincerely than before. "I have no faith that this will work. What will a protest accomplish? What is a 'Declaration of Independence' without any true power? All this will cause is more clamping down from the Japanese, thousands of arrests and worse."

"We are expecting that, SungSoo," MyungBo said resolutely. "All the representatives have sworn to sign the Declaration together and then get arrested with no resistance. The religious leaders—Cheondoists, Christians, Buddhists—put their weight behind nonviolence, that we must first try to do this without force. None of us have any expectation of getting out of this alive, but we're going through with it anyway."

"No, hear me out. If you want Korea to actually overthrow Japanese rule, it's not going to come from rounding up the powerless people and marching, carrying nothing but flags. What you need is outside help—the United States, most likely. You know about President Wilson's Fourteen Points speech to reestablish the sovereignty of every colonized people in the world. He made that promise in front of all the nations, and will not ignore us, especially if we make an appeal to American interests in Asia. It doesn't benefit the U.S. to have a Japan that's too strong and too greedy in the Pacific, so he will listen," SungSoo said, revealing more of his inner thoughts than he'd ever had in all these years. For that at least, MyungBo felt grateful.

"I've heard this before, of course. Some people even believe that we are so behind the rest of the world that we need to ask America to govern us rather than fight for sovereignty." MyungBo smiled bitterly, lowering his eyes.

"Well, at least that way we won't be destroyed. What matters more, a titular independence, or actual prosperity? If you end up killing half the country in order to make it 'independent,' doesn't that defeat the purpose of fighting? You act like you don't care about death, but the whole point of this struggle is to live, isn't it?" SungSoo said, and MyungBo saw the truth, *his* truth, in his eyes. SungSoo was a man best suited to living—no one could do it better than he. MyungBo was only good at making life harder for himself, but he could see no other alternative. He sighed.

"You're right, I don't care about dying. But I don't think our resistance is all in vain, as you do. I accept your help with ineffable gratitude—truly. For me, however—and for many others like me . . . The purpose of our movement isn't simply to avoid extinction. Its purpose is to do what's right. And you see how we've come back to that point where neither of us can convince the other? It is truly outside the realm of logic to determine what is right or wrong. Without any expectations of making you see things the way I do, I can only tell you what my soul insists on." With that, MyungBo put on his hat again, signaling he was ready to leave.

• • •

ON THE MORNING OF THE FIRST DAY of March, JungHo woke up with a strange, unintelligible whisper in his ear.

His followers all believed that JungHo had an uncanny ability to sense things before they happened. He had explained that his father had been a tiger hunter in PyongAhn province, and so he'd inherited the same instinct that animals—and their hunters—have for survival. Secretly, he didn't know if that was true; but living on the streets, he had become attuned to reading people's faces, hearing their words, and interpreting their silence. Sometimes he really did feel he could simply smell a change in the air and run from danger, whether that was the police or another gang of older boys and grown-ups. In this way, he'd led his group out of trouble several times, and had earned their unshakable trust.

JungHo sat up from the pile of dirty straw mats that made up both the floor and the bed. To his left, Loach was asleep on his side; YoungGu was at the other end, and the dog was snuggling between the two boys at the most comfortable spot in the tent.

"Loach, wake up," JungHo whispered, shaking his friend's shoulder.

"Hm? Cut it out, I'm still sleepy."

"Wake up," JungHo repeated. "I think something's going to happen today."

"What are you talking about?" Loach asked, rubbing his eyes with his knuckles. "What's going to happen?"

"I don't know. Something pretty bad," JungHo said. It was only as these words left his lips that he realized what he was sensing.

"We have to be careful today. I don't think we should divide up as we normally do. Let's stick together."

Noticing JungHo's seriousness, Loach rounded his eyes and nodded. "Whatever you say, Chief."

When the pale pink sun rose like an eye over the quiet city, all fifteen boys and one dog left the camp together. Some of the boys wanted to do their usual routines and shows, but JungHo would not let them. Nothing was out of the ordinary beyond the swell of visitors from the countryside, waiting to attend the emperor's funeral, four days hence. The streets teemed with merchants, vendors, laborers, and students, and their shouts and footsteps made humming sounds on the roads packed brightly with snow. A tantalizing fragrance of roasted chestnuts wafted through the crisp, cold air. All the boys and the dog felt their mouths water and tried to forget their hunger as they wandered through the streets.

When the sun was past its highest point, they stumbled into a wide plaza, which was filled with hundreds of people, many of them students wearing uniforms.

"Hey, JungHo, look at this crowd! I bet we could make a lot of money if we did our act here," Loach shouted gleefully. But JungHo shook his head; his eyes were gazing far out to the pagoda at the edge of the plaza, where a student was standing, facing the crowd. He was wearing a black newsboy cap and a long winter coat, and looked to be eighteen at most. He raised a fist, and as one the crowd fell silent.

"Today, we declare that Korea is an independent nation and that Koreans are a free people," the student began, reading from a broadsheet in his hands. His voice should have been lost in the distance; instead, the cold air seemed to magnify it through the plaza, which was filled with an eerie silence.

"We seek to announce this to the whole world in order to illuminate the inviolable truth of human equality, and for our posterity to enjoy the rights of sovereignty and survival in perpetuity. This is in keeping with the conscience of the world, the ordinance of the heavens, and the ethos of our modern era; thus, no power in the world will be able to stop us.

"It has been ten years since we've been sacrificed to Imperialism, that dark legacy of the past, suffering immeasurable pain under the oppression of another people for the first time in our five-thousand-year history. All of our twenty million people hold freedom as our most sacred desire. The conscience of all humanity is on our side. Today, our army is Justice, and our spear and shield are Humanitarianism, and with these we shall never fail!" He threw his fist up as though punching the sky, and the crowd roared.

"Today we seek only to build ourselves, not to destroy another. We do not want vengeance. We only seek to right the wrongs of the Japanese Imperialists who oppress and plunder us, so we can live in a fair and humane way . . . A new world is coming. The era of Force is past, and the era of Righteousness is here. After a century of preparation, Humanitarianism has begun to shine its bright light all over the world, and a new spring is giving life to every being on earth. We have nothing to fear . . ."

JungHo didn't understand much of what was said, but he saw around him the rapturous faces, many wet with tears, and was surprised by the hotness welling up in his own eyes. JungHo had never had a day of schooling. What he now understood was that the world was a desperately dark place, not just for his family and for the beggar boys, but for everyone standing there. Their shared pain reverberated through his body like a common heartbeat.

Finished with the speech, the student held up a flag, white with a red and blue symbol in the center. "Korean Independence *manseh*!" he shouted, and after the first time the crowd also joined in.

"Manseh! Manseh!" It felt as though their voices could be heard all across Seoul, carried by that same cold wind. The crowd had more than tripled in the plaza by this point, and somehow they were each holding a flag over their heads. The thousands of white flags

waving and shimmering in the wind resembled a flock of cranes about to take flight.

Soon the crowd began to move, marchers standing shoulder to shoulder as they walked westward across the city. JungHo and his gang joined in, making their way down the entire length of Legation Street, from the American Consulate at number 10 to the French Legation at number 28. A slender female student walked up to the ornately carved front gates of the Legation and knocked as people shouted, "France! France! Friend of liberty! Liberty, equality, fraternity! Help us!" But it remained shut, and no sound or movement could be perceived from the curtained windows of the limestone mansion.

A whole minute had passed with enthusiastic chants of *manseh* before JungHo realized that the French would not open their doors. The strange whisper returned to his ear—a sound as soft as snow falling on snow. He turned to his right and left, and saw Loach, YoungGu, and all his blood brothers shouting with the crowd—and felt the stretching and slowing of time.

"Guys! We must leave. Now!" he yelled. The boys looked at him, mouths open.

He grabbed Loach and YoungGu by the arm and ran as fast as he could. The dog was barking madly, as though it had seen a ghost.

As JungHo slid into an alley, the chanting died down and turned into shouts on one end of the avenue. A Japanese squadron had arrived, led by cavalry officers. Within seconds, the marchers began running from that end, pushing the others farther into the avenue. Loud cracking noises erupted just ahead of piercing screams; the troops were firing into the backs of the people as they fled.

• • •

ON HORSEBACK, YAMADA GENZO WAS surveying this scene as coldly as he'd regarded any battle with Korean rebels. Yamada paid little mind to their anger, but he couldn't tolerate their abject ignorance. What did they think to achieve by this? Did they really believe they could survive the twentieth century under their own feeble-minded monarch and his cross-eyed, sterile son? Their colonization by a world power was inevitable, and better Japan with its shared Asian heritage than America, England, or France. Japan was the sun that would shine on the entire continent and lead it to the new age of enlightenment.

His chestnut charger was picking its way through the crowd as if wading through mud, while on all sides the Koreans scattered away, pushing and screaming. He felt nothing, inured to the indistinguishability of people in combat. Every battle was the same—there was your side and there were your enemies, and nothing more. Yamada watched indifferently as several young students in secondary school were shot in the back. It was only when they fell forward onto the snow and blood spread across their bodies that he suddenly felt something like a sharp jolt. It reminded him, he realized, of the old merchant who had lain facedown on the snow, his warm blood soaking through his silk package. Yamada had known viscerally even then that Hayashi's execution of the man was wrongly done. A shiver ran through his spine. He turned to his left and saw Major Ito astride his black stallion. At Ito's order, delivered with crisp alacrity, the troops aimed their guns and fired.

Yamada's eyes found one man who was standing his ground as the other marchers fled the shower of bullets. Raising the Korean flag high in his right hand, he started running toward the troops. His face was brown, weathered, and common like a day laborer's; it made a stark contrast against his carefully combed black hair and the snow-white gentleman's robe, which had the appearance of extra conscientiousness, as if he had known this would be his last day. In spite of himself, Yamada was arrested by this sight. Meanwhile, Ito effortlessly swung his legs over his horse and dismounted. The young officer's steps were calm and confident as he pulled out his sword and in one swift motion, struck down the protester's right arm. Severed above the elbow, it fell to the ground like a tree branch struck by lightning, still encased in a white sleeve.

The man screamed out in pain, but by an unaccountable strength of will, he remained standing. In the next moment, he bent down and picked up the flag with his remaining hand. Ito swung again without hesitation, and the left arm fell to the ground as well. The armless man tried to keep running, still shouting hoarsely, "*Manseh! Manseh*!" until Ito's sword plunged cleanly into the center of his back.

Yamada was still motionless on his horse while Ito wiped off his bloody sword on the dead man's white robes. Meanwhile, the marchers who saw this scene began rallying again. Somehow, they seemed to have regained their courage after witnessing the man's unbreakable will.

Another hailstorm rained upon the marchers, and this time, they took the bullets in the front. Piercing screams and smoke filled the avenue. Even Ito, now back on his stallion, was wiping the sweat on his brow and cursing. When the smoke cleared, Yamada saw that a group of women had made their way to the front with locked hands. With their elaborate braided crowns, expensive outfits, and fashionable makeup, it was clear to him that they were courtesans. The troops looked questioningly back at Ito, and even he was momentarily speechless. Yamada raised his hand, shouting, "Hold!"

At the same time, Ito ordered, "Fire!"

The troops hesitated, then started loading their guns again when Ito repeated his order. The courtesans still stood unflinchingly, only tightening their grip on one another. With their tear-stained, powder-streaked faces, hoarse voices, and bloated lips, they looked nothing like seductresses or even exactly like women. And yet, the very fact they were so undone made them feel so female to Yamada.

Guns were pointed at their chests when, farther along the avenue in front of number 10, a deafening cheer was heard.

"America! America! *America!*"

The cries filled the frosty white sky, and beneath it the sea of flags quivered.

"Hold!" Yamada shouted again, and the troops slowly lowered their guns, sensing an important shift in the situation. The gates of the American Consulate had just opened.

The crowd continued to chant as the consul-general walked out the gates, flanked by a red-haired deputy and a translator. A male student stepped forward and recited the Korean Declaration of Independence in English. "Help us. Please tell President Wilson what is happening here. Help us get justice," he said at the end, looking straight at the consul-general.

Yamada held his breath to see what the consul-general would do. If he closed the door of the consulate now, that would mean there would be no consequences from America—as well as the rest of the West.

"Yes, I will help you. I will tell President Wilson what I've seen," the consul-general said loudly in English, and the translator repeated it in Korean. "The world will hear your cries. America will not forsake you! I promise you that."

There rose a deafening cheer from the crowd. The red-haired young deputy sponged off his eyes with one hand and clasped the translator on the back with the other. With the shift in the crowd's energy, Yamada looked in the direction of Ito, who met his eyes and curled his lips in anger. They stood momentarily frozen, both knowing they could not attack in front of the consulate and risk American involvement. A silence enveloped them like volcanic ash. In the quiet, Yamada heard his arteries pulsing with no soldierly wrath, only a shameful hope that the carnage was over.

But after bowing and waving to the crowd several times, the consul-general stepped back inside the gates with his entourage.

As soon as they disappeared, Ito regained his composure. He was no longer sanguine, however—the unrest was far larger in scope than he'd first thought, and the Josenjings' unarmed resilience was unexpectedly draining. His troops still stood in awe of the courtesans with locked arms. Ito sighed, swinging his body around to dismount from his horse in one swift motion. It was not his habit to kill women, but he'd always been accepting of the fact that this may need to change. Holding his rifle, he walked toward the leader of the courtesans.

"Do you know who I am? I'm the consort of Judge ___," the woman screamed in Japanese. Her lead-white face was distorted in fear, and Ito felt only repulsion.

"Whore!" Ito whacked her head with the back of his rifle and she fell forward, slamming her knees into the dirt. A soldier rushed to tie her hands together behind her back and take her into custody, and at this signal, a breathtaking chaos broke out all around. Ito stepped back to watch the protesters flee amid screams and gunshots. The Americans' doors remained closed. Their show of solidarity seemed to have been just that—a show.

An hour passed, or perhaps two—Ito could no longer be sure. He was accustomed to being in control of his situation, including and most of all his mind, but it had run out from underneath him like a wayward horse. When he regained his full senses, he saw that the troops were walking around, impaling anyone who still squirmed underneath their boots. Ito also looked down and saw a mangled heap of a man, more body parts than a whole human, whose only sign of life was blood-sputtering breath. Both arms were gone from his shoulders, making him look like a fish—and Ito realized that this was the same white-robed man he'd cut down earlier. In the nearly dead man's bloodshot eyes, there was still a pianissimo hope that he would somehow survive. It was like taking off a bee's wings and watching it crawl around—in Ito's experience, every single being did the exact same thing. Always clung, always chose suffering over death. Ito finished the man off with a thrust of his sword and then passed the hilt to his left hand. His right hand was cramping painfully; otherwise, he felt nothing.

The sun sank behind heavy black clouds, which looked as though they had been burned. In the semidarkness, Ito saw a flash of red some fifty yards away and recognized the flame-headed young deputy from earlier in the day. He was hunched over a corpse; there was another, shorter white man next to him, also bent over at the waist and holding something small and rectangular in his hand. When Ito started walking toward them with a drawn pistol, they raised their hands above their heads and shouted in Japanese, "Don't shoot! Americans!"

Closer up, Ito saw that the small rectangle in the shorter man's hand was a vest pocket camera. "Associated Press. Don't shoot," the man repeated slowly. It was amusing how, even until the moment a bullet entered their skin, people refused to believe that they could die—despite the fact that death was the only thing everyone could be certain of getting, sooner or later. That was what life amounted to—an absurd disbelief, Ito sighed to himself. He raised his pistol, aimed at the photographer's forehead, and pulled the trigger.

The gun clicked, and the man's lids fluttered like a dying moth. He was still standing, unharmed, but with a quickly spreading stain on his crotch. The smell of his piss attacked Ito's nostrils anew. Ito had run out of bullets.

He holstered his pistol and drew his sword out instead. The two white men were shaking like leaves, sweat dripping down their faces. The red-haired deputy was whispering something under his breath with closed eyes. When they finally seemed ready to die, Ito sighed and slid his sword back in its sheath. His right hand was cramping ferociously, and he wasn't a butcher who would just hack away with his left hand.

"Go," Ito said. It had truly been a long day and he was tired to the very ends of his lashes. He'd done his part well, and needed rest. Before he could change his mind, he made a gesture like flicking off an annoying fly. And the two Americans, streaming with sweat, tears, and urine, fled behind the walls of their sanctuary.

10

THE DARKEST SHADE OF BLUE

1919

ONCE HE'D SAFELY LED THE GANG BACK TO THEIR TENTS AFTER THE March, JungHo left again by himself. He knew something serious was happening to Jade by the way he was being pulled toward her house, as though they were connected by an invisible line that she was now tugging on for his help. But when he arrived, the gate was firmly shut. He knocked on the door, nervous about being met by her servants, or worse, her family.

The door cracked open an inch and a gasp was heard. "Oh, it's you!" Jade said, sliding away the bolt. "Come inside quickly."

"Are you okay? What's the matter?" JungHo slipped in and Jade bolted the door shut again. Her face was flushed and wet with what could have been either sweat or tears.

"Aunt Dani and our maid Hesoon went to the protest today. They haven't come back and Luna's really sick," Jade said. "She's going to have her baby. I don't know what to do."

JungHo didn't know anything about childbirth except the fact that his mother had died giving birth to his younger sister. He kept this to himself and asked, "Who else is here? And how can I help?"

"Lotus is next to Luna. She's even more scared than I am." Jade wiped her face. "I don't know where we could find a midwife and it's still dangerous out on the streets."

"Okay, I'll bring help. You stay here." JungHo tried to remember anything he'd heard from his mother's midwife. He shouted over his shoulder as he ran out: "Make sure Luna stays warm and give her water!"

It was the time of stillness just before night turned into dawn. The sky was painted in the darkest shade of blue; birds would start singing exactly an hour later. JungHo flew through the neighborhood, where he knew every store, building, and even the jujube tree house that drew pregnant visitors around the clock. That was where he found the old midwife in her bed. Out of everyone in Seoul, she alone didn't seem taken aback by JungHo's appearance. All the babies of the area had long been born into her wrinkled hands, whether on the earth floor of mud huts or silk cots in mansions.

When the midwife arrived, she took a look at Luna and ordered the girls to bring her a pair of shears, some yarn, clean linens, hot water, and cold water. A few hours passed without much progress. Despite the girls' panic, the midwife went outside to take a break and sat next to JungHo in front of the garden. He didn't understand why she seemed so relaxed. Just before daybreak she disappeared inside again and left him to watch the gradual graying of the world alone.

JungHo dozed off for a half hour, perhaps more. He was startled awake when Jade came out and said with a smile, "It's a girl."

"How are they doing? And are you feeling okay?" JungHo asked.

"They're both sleeping. The granny said the baby is the prettiest newborn she's ever delivered—and she's even been midwife to a royal princess," Jade said, beckoning him to follow her to the kitchen. "Here, you can take whatever you'd like."

"I didn't do this to get food," JungHo said, confused and disappointed. "I wanted to help *you*."

"I know, JungHo. Thank you." Jade reached out and grabbed his hand. Her fingertips sent blooming stars up and down the length of his arm. He wished he could stay standing there forever, holding hands with her. But then she let go and started wrapping food in a large kerchief.

"I'm sorry you can't stay . . . I have to go back to Luna now." She led him again by hand across the courtyard toward the gates, and suddenly stopped. "If you hadn't come, Luna might have died. It's strange how you showed up at that moment, because I was thinking about you. I didn't even know how you could help but you just came into my head."

He wanted to tell her that she was inside his head all the time, that she could very well be living there like it was her house, but a sudden wave of shyness stopped him. The morning sun was sparkling on the tips of her eyelashes; her wispy hair escaped from last night's braid and frizzed around her face like a cloud. She shone with the promise of something far greater than the eleven years of her life, and JungHo thought he could see and love even her future self.

"I'm going to tell Aunt Dani how you helped and she's going to reward you. She might even let you stay with us, in a spare room in the house. Then you wouldn't have to sleep outside in the cold. You'd always have plenty to eat here, and maybe you'd even get to go to school. JungHo, I'm so happy!" She smiled and let him pass through the gates.

• • •

ON HER THIRD MORNING IN JAIL, Dani woke up with a nauseating wetness on her lower body and realized that she'd urinated in her sleep. Since getting arrested at the March, she had held herself instead of pissing straight onto the floor like the others. There was no chamber pot in the women's cell. They weren't getting water either, but she'd nonetheless felt the poison building pressure and spreading throughout her body, turning her skin yellow. Before she fell asleep the previous night, she—an intelligent and courageous woman—could think of no greater wish or pleasure than pissing like a waterfall, utterly alone.

As Dani gained full consciousness, the sheer, dumb, bodily relief turned into shame, and she cried for the first time since her arrest. No other inmate remarked on her accident or her sobbing, but they didn't comfort her either. In prolonged destruction, there was no spirit of unity such as the one they had shared in face of a quick and heroic death.

The door at the end of the hallway clanked open, and a soldier approached with a bucket. Dani braced for him to throw the water into the cell, as he did so the past two days to dampen the putrefying smells. But he set the bucket down and called out.

"Kokoni Kimu Dani iru?"

She stood up, wobbling on her weakened legs. *"Watashiga Kimu Dani desu."*

The soldier wrinkled his nose and put a fat finger to his nostrils, as if he could sense her stench growing stronger with her movement. His wispy mustache, waxed and curled like the f-hole of a violin, shook lightly as he beckoned her with his other hand.

"Out," he said, opening the door.

No other explanation was given, but Dani knew who had saved her. She stumbled out of the cell before the guard could change his mind. As he locked the door once more, she didn't look back at the others still inside.

ALL DANI COULD DO in the first few hours of her release was wash herself and drink water. Then she fell onto the clean warmth of her bed and slept for an untold amount of time. She felt she never wanted to go outside her room or speak to anyone again. She wished to hole up in her cocoon and jealously guard her body, energy, and sanity. It took her days to summon Luna's baby, and even then she barely held her or told the girls that they'd all done such a good job. Jade tried to tell her about her friend who brought over the midwife, but Dani merely shrugged.

"But without him, Luna would never have made it," Jade persisted in a small voice. "She could've died."

"That's enough," Dani snapped. "Luna didn't die, did she? Many, many people did die and I almost did as well. Now leave me alone, I need to rest."

While she recuperated, Dani was absorbed only in waiting for the Judge. A week later when he finally came to her house, she was wearing her most becoming outfit, a dress from Paris decorated with jet beads. A necklace of diamonds glittered at her throat, and a single magnolia was pinned to her chest. Her skin gleamed like marble under the black velvet; her red lips had the look of suede.

"You look pale," the Judge said in Japanese upon seeing her. Dani smiled her most deferential smile, reaching out and taking his mottled hand. She raised it to her lips for a kiss, then pressed it against her décolletage.

"I haven't been myself lately, as you know . . ." she replied. "Still, I wouldn't be here if it weren't for you."

The Judge merely looked back at her, and Dani filled the void by pouring his sake. Next to the lacquered serving table, she'd put the rest of the earliest magnolias into a late eighteenth-century vase, knowing that would please her patron. With his cloudy eyes, the Judge saw and noticed everything and formed his conclusions quietly and precisely.

A faint yet voluptuous scent of the magnolias filled the room. But more than the flowers' beauty and fragrance, the Judge appreciated that the tree outside was stripped bare of its first blossoms for his sake—and that Dani knew exactly how his mind worked. That was what he had always found most attractive about Dani: he admired her looks and poise, but was seduced by her singular ability to communicate beneath the surface. It was an elegance of the mind.

"You see, I have two friends who are still in custody. They are just as innocent as I am," Dani began speaking again.

"One is my maid, Hesoon, who has served me faithfully over the years. She was only accompanying me on errands when we got caught up by the crowd. They put her in a different cell with all the commoners, so I don't know how she could be doing, the poor girl. She knows nothing, understands nothing, and can be guilty of nothing," Dani explained.

"The other is a cousin of mine. I don't know his whole story, why he was arrested . . . But I am sure he is also innocent, as he is not in the least political. As far as his family background goes, it is of the best: his father is a wealthy landowner down in the country, and his great-uncle is a former finance minister with a famous Jongno mansion that has ninety-nine rooms. He went to university in Tokyo, as well. His name is Lee MyungBo."

"Lee MyungBo? Your cousin?" the Judge asked with eyes lowered over his sake.

"Yes."

"I did not know you had Lee cousins. On your mother's side, I assume?"

Dani blushed slightly, before replying, "Yes. On my mother's side."

The Judge sighed. "Lee MyungBo is one of the thirty-three signers who were arrested at MyungWol. Even I can't just release him. But I can try to mitigate his sentence, and in the meantime, make him a bit more comfortable in jail. As for your maid, that should not be difficult."

Dani threw her bare arms around the Judge and pressed her soft body into his old, bony chest.

"Thank you . . . I will never forget your generosity," she whispered.

"Oh and one more thing, Dani," said the Judge. "I do like that diamond necklace on you. When I saw it, I knew you would be just the right woman for it. There is such a satisfaction to seeing something valuable find its rightful owner. That's why I bought it for you. And when I saw you for the first time, I thought the same thing about you belonging to me. I should like to think that you'd wear that necklace only for me. Don't put it on for other people . . . even cousins."

"Of course, I would never do anything to displease you," Dani said, smiling luminously and pretending to not understand. She wrapped both her hands around his and reverently brought them to her lips.

• • •

EACH TIME MYUNGBO LOST CONSCIOUSNESS, the blackness overtook him more completely than before. This time, he'd been lashed with a studded whip and then confined in a body-tight niche carved into a wall for three days. When he woke up, he was in a different cell with a barred window set high on the wall. Without turning his head, he scanned the room and noticed a chamber pot in the corner. Still moving only his eyes, he looked down at his body, which had been bandaged and given clean clothes. He was even lying on a thin mat, although any comfort that may have afforded was obliterated by the excruciating pain that exploded from every part of his body. He did not even have the mental clarity to process his improved situation before blacking out once more.

• • •

HE OFTEN OPENED HIS EYES to a bowl of water and some thin porridge next to him. Then without wondering how many days had passed, or what time of day it was, he gulped down the water first and spooned the porridge into his mouth. After that, he relieved himself and went back to sleep.

Time was a winter fog—gray, shapeless, indifferent to his existence. It passed on its own like a ship that sails without passengers. Or perhaps it was a ship that was carrying everyone else except MyungBo. Being left outside the world of time was a special kind of torture that said, You mean nothing. He was reminded he was still living only by feeling how much his beard had grown.

At some point, MyungBo was strong enough to stay awake for the arrival of his caretaker and to ask whether he could get some paper and a pencil. To his surprise, the guard brought those things the next day with the water and food. After drinking some water and leaving the porridge untouched, MyungBo crawled to his mat and began to work on a letter.

In the flashes of consciousness that were allowed him during his incarceration, MyungBo's thoughts had turned to his two mistakes. The first one was that he was wrong to resent his wife's pragmatism while falling for Dani. For months leading up to the protest, he'd longed to see Dani and to talk to her about almost anything that came to his mind. At first, he'd chalked this up to simple admiration for a beautiful and intelligent woman, but his jealousy upon seeing SungSoo by her side forced him to admit that he was in love with her. Since he had long looked down on his friend's womanizing, he had been all the more confused about his attraction to Dani. But it all felt so faded and tarnished now. Upon thinking of her for the first time since his arrest, he only felt ashamed. Love was defined by how much one could suffer for another, by what you were willing to do to protect this person. It was a question of choosing the person with whom you'd like to hold hands on your last train ride. Now he knew the one he truly loved.

"To my beloved son HyunWoo," he started writing.

How have you been? How is your mother? I hope that you two stayed warm and healthy over the winter. It's colder here, but thinking of you and your mother makes me feel better.

You just turned four, so you must be getting bigger now. I wish I could watch you grow up. I think often of the days when you were very little, and we three were together every night. You probably can't remember anything, but we were very happy back then. HyunWoo, listen to what your mother tells you. And when you're older, be the kind of person who is courageous in the face of the powerful, and generous toward the weak. That's all I wish for you.

I miss you both very much. I'm always watching over you.

—Your father

MyungBo had started writing in small letters, thinking that he would fill up the whole page. In the end, however, he could fill no more than a third of the paper—it was too hard to say all that was in his heart. The guard, who had been under new orders to attend to the inmate's needs, mailed the letter to MyungBo's father's house, where it was forwarded to Shanghai by his younger brother.

The second and worst mistake of MyungBo's life was that he had put his faith in unarmed resistance. Like the other signers, he'd believed that they would gladly die if that could bring them closer to independence. But he now saw that the death of so many people was wasted. With both the leadership and civilians annihilated, progress had not only stalled but even taken several steps backward. Nothing could change without force in the face of such inhumanity. MyungBo didn't know if he could get out of jail alive; in addition to his wounds, which kept reopening and festering, he had contracted tuberculosis. But if given another chance, MyungBo vowed he would win back their freedom at any cost—life for life, blood for blood.

When MyungBo's conditions stabilized against all odds, he was called into trial for treason and received a light sentence of two years. In prison, MyungBo was sometimes favored with a warm comforter or better food. He was even allowed to read a few books. Oblivious to the true reason for his special treatment, MyungBo now recalled Dani as he did SungSoo and his other schoolmates—infrequently and with a vague sense of embarrassment.

SUNGSOO ALSO DIDN'T SPEND MUCH time pining for his old friend after the March. He had been arrested in the late afternoon that day as he was taking coffee in his office with his publisher. He'd been arraigned on the charges of associating with MyungBo, but the raid into his publishing house had turned up no evidence. In fact, the deeper the investigators searched, the more evidence they found of his enduring friendship with the Japanese. The very next day, his father paid ten thousand won in cash for his bail and SungSoo was released, tired and in need of a bath but unharmed.

Neither SungSoo nor Dani reached out to the other afterward, and they both understood that their mutual silence was the end of their relationship. SungSoo was conscious that his intense desire for Dani had been fulfilled; there was something neat and deeply satisfying about its completion after all. Besides her splendid beauty, there was a passion and a mystery about her that would always entice him. He thought he may even miss her in the future. But for now, he was only glad of the natural end of their affair, which saved him the enormous headache of untangling feminine emotions. (And of apologizing when he didn't feel like it, just to appear to be a gentleman—women had such a desperation for apologies.) After all the chaos and uncertainties of winter, he felt as lighthearted as the parents of Gregor at the end of his favorite short story. His yearning for a woman was replaced by that for industry and progress, and he congratulated himself on this positive new direction. He decided that in the spring, he would look into expanding his bicycle shop and then go for a long ride down in the countryside.

• • •

ON AN UNUSUALLY COLD APRIL day, as Dani was cleaning the last remaining snow in the garden, the Judge's driver returned Hesoon to the house in a small wooden reliquary. The Judge hadn't found her in time. The two younger girls cried unceasingly for three days and nights. Luna, who had always been soothed by Hesoon's sturdy presence, named her daughter Hesook in her memory.

Dani, who looked down upon public tears, didn't grieve in front of the girls. It was all the more important to her that she stay resolute, because she believed that she was the reason Hesoon was dead. She'd brought her maid along to the March, and she'd failed to immediately call on the Judge for help. Instead of indulging in her pain, Dani did two things: not knowing how to reach Hesoon's family in Jejudo, she vowed to go to the South Sea one day to scatter the ashes herself. Then she applied herself with renewed energy to various projects around the house and appeared keen to forget everything that had happened. She had always been lively, but now she seemed to believe something dreadful would catch up to her if she slowed down even for a minute. She dressed as impeccably as ever, and tried new creams to hide the fact that she never slept through the night. She bought clothes and toys for Hesook and made nourishing postpartum soups for Luna. When it was warm enough Dani launched into spring cleaning, wiping down every corner of the house, putting away winter clothes, opening the drawers and airing out the linens.

"It's strange," she said, throwing her hands up in front of the paulownia-tree chest. "I can't find my favorite comforter—the one with peonies. It took my seamstress two months to hand-embroider the flowers with real gold thread."

Dani questioned the housekeeper, who swore she knew nothing. Unrelenting, Dani ordered all the wardrobes in the house to be opened and their contents laid out. At that point, Jade stepped forward.

"It was me, I'm so sorry," Jade said, staring down at her feet. "I should have told you, but my friend JungHo was sleeping out in the cold . . . I just wanted to help him." She began crying.

"What friend?" Dani asked in confusion.

"The same friend who fetched the midwife for Luna."

"And this friend sleeps outside on the streets?" Dani closed the chest and walked toward Jade.

"Yes. He doesn't have a home," Jade said. She'd barely finished answering when something exploded on her face. Dani had slapped her.

"Do you realize what you've done? You stole from me. That comforter was worth more than what Silver paid to buy you from your mother. Do you understand that?" Dani stared unblinkingly at Jade, whose face was streaming with hot tears. She nodded.

"Your value depends on how men see you. When they realize you spent time with some beggar boy, do you think they'd pay even a penny for your company?" Dani snorted. "Did you let him touch you?"

"No!" Jade said, indignant.

"You're to never, ever speak to that boy again. If you either steal anything else or talk to him, you'll be turned out of this house—and you'll find out for yourself how cold it is to sleep on the streets."

SINCE THE NIGHT LUNA GAVE BIRTH, JungHo had come by every afternoon hoping to meet Jade outside the house. He brought over the dog to cheer her up and, occasionally, pretty pebbles he'd found walking along the canal. But now she never came out of the gates.

One day he finally got up the courage to knock on the door. He heard light footsteps crossing over the courtyard and was bursting with excitement that it was Jade herself like last time. He was startled when a beautiful older woman opened the door, glaring at him sternly.

"You're the beggar boy hanging around my Jade?" she said. Without waiting for an answer, she disappeared for a moment and then returned with an envelope. She pressed it into his hand.

"That's for helping Luna last time. It's more money than a grown man makes in a week—you'd have enough food for a month at least. Take it and don't ever bother us or Jade again."

"I don't need this," JungHo managed to say, pushing the envelope back. "I just wanted to be her friend."

"You're a bold little thing, aren't you?" Dani snorted. "You can't mix with someone like Jade. She's going to be a courtesan, possibly the best one I've ever trained. And you, you're nothing but a nameless orphan."

JungHo wanted to tell her his name, but thought better of it and turned around. He could already hear Dani stepping back inside and bolting the door behind him. He still couldn't believe that Jade would not even say goodbye to him, that this was the end. He thought that if she knew how much he wanted to talk to her, she would find a way to meet him. So he came by every day and threw a pebble over the wall into the courtyard. Once, he tossed in a smooth, green sea glass that reminded him of her name. That was as clear a message as he could possibly send. But Jade never came out to meet him, and after a very long time, he stopped coming to her house for good.

PART II

1925–1937

11

JUNGHO SPEAKS

1925

MY NAME IS NAM JUNGHO. YOU CAN'T START A STORY WITHOUT SAYing your name. When I arrived in Seoul that was the first thing someone asked me. "What's your name, country bumpkin?" That was Loach by the way, who is still annoying as hell but I can't forget the fact that he is the oldest friend I've got.

I told my underlings that I was named after a legendary tiger in my village in the mountains. It's a story my older sister used to tell me and my younger sister before falling asleep. There was once a poor woodsman who lived alone with his mother. One evening as he was going back home after chopping wood in the mountains all day, a giant tiger appeared in front of him. Just as the tiger was about to pounce the woodsman started crying, saying, "Oh, my older brother! It is you! I have been waiting to meet you for years and years!"

The tiger got confused, stopped in his tracks and asked, "Um, what? What are you talking about, human?"

"Can't you remember, Older Brother?" The woodsman wept even louder. "Twenty years ago, you got up in the middle of the night and left our home. I woke up from my sleep and followed you. Then in the mountains you suddenly turned into a tiger as if from some dark curse. That same curse must have erased your human memory too. Ever since, we've been hoping to see you again. Come, let's go home—our mother has been waiting for you all these years."

In case you're wondering the woodsman was lying to get out of this alive. But the tiger started thinking and he couldn't really remember how he used to be before he was a young tiger. Then he was like, "Oh my god, I must really have been a human before!" And he started crying and hugging the woodsman with his giant paws.

"I'm so glad we finally met, Younger Brother." The tiger wept. "I can't go home looking like this. I don't want to scare our mother. But I'll always watch over you."

The woodsman hugged the tiger one last time and went back home. The next morning he found a dead rabbit in his courtyard. So he said, "That tiger really thinks we're his family!" After that there was a deer. And so the tiger kept bringing them food and the woodsman and his mother never went hungry.

Couple of years went by like that and the mother died of old age. The tiger stopped dropping by with food after that. A while later the woodsman was coming down the mountain when he ran into three tiger cubs. Each cub was wearing a white hemp ribbon around his tail. The woodsman asked, "Why are you wearing those ribbons, tigers?" Then one of them replied,

"Our grandmother was a human who lived in the village down the mountain. She passed away and our father grieved for months and couldn't eat or sleep. He died of sadness in our cave and now we're in mourning."

The woodsman cried real tears then and felt sorry for tricking the loyal tiger. So he built a monument to the tiger which was just a huge stone with some carvings in our village square. I couldn't read it but this really did exist next to the ginkgo tree by the well. So that's why I'm named JungHo—*Jung* meaning righteous, *Ho* meaning tiger—I'd say to my underlings. And even the ones who had heard similar stories at their own villages believed me.

I'm not lying about the tiger monument but the truth is that when I was born my father was overjoyed to finally have a son, so he went to the local astrologer and got my name made. My father paid a rabbit for a real name of Chinese characters when plenty of people just named their kids after the first animal or flower that grabbed their eyes, like Loach for instance who claims his mother had mad cravings for loach soup while she was pregnant with him hence his name. My sisters were also just called May and June after their birth months so that's how much my father loved me specially. The reason I don't tell this version is that every year I remember less about my father and whenever I talk about him it's like opening the lid of a boiling stew and letting the steam get out so there's less of the good stuff in the end. That's why I don't talk about him unless I have to and most of the time it's enough to look at his cigarette case and my mother's ring to remember that I'm not nobody but Nam JungHo.

EVEN LONG AFTER WE MOVED out from under the bridge, I still used to go back there from time to time. It didn't make me feel happy—the sight of the muddy water, the stony banks where we used to sleep on nothing but mushy straw mats. But I couldn't help but feel drawn to it. Do you ever go back to the place where you used to live and feel like you've been drinking soju on an empty stomach? Your head turns all of a sudden and you miss things like you don't even know what. I wouldn't call that happy but I would sometimes be in the mood for that kind of feeling.

For the longest time of course I didn't have enough things to eat let alone a drop of liquor and our goal was to keep a steady pace of eating once every two days. We were all starving every second we were awake and even in our dreams. I was often the hungriest of all of us because I'd give my portion to whoever looked like he was at the end of his rope. Sometimes when I handed my piece of dumpling to some kid cold sweat would break on my back because I'd be that hungry. I didn't do that to buy anyone's loyalty but ultimately that was how all these guys became closer to me than real brothers. Word got around that Nam JungHo under the bridge was the chief of all Jongno street children and that he feeds everyone who is loyal to him. By the time I was sixteen I had over forty kids under my command.

It was clear then that we couldn't keep on living under the bridge much longer. It was a godawful place to live even for beggars and in summer the mosquitoes attacked every inch of you and in winter you froze to death almost every night and let me tell you, that gets old after a while. Whenever there was any kind of riot our tents of sacks and straw mats would be torn apart and destroyed. We hid in crannies in the levee that no one else could find and watched as the police burned everything we had down to the last wooden bowl and spoon. This was when Loach convinced me to change ourselves from beggars to "protectors." Mind you this was not an easy thing to do to just barge into a little Chinese restaurant and demand fees for protecting the business from other gangs. Every neighborhood in every district of Seoul was claimed by one of several gangs both Japanese and Korean and those borders were strictly respected in order to avoid full-out war. I was starting from scratch having claimed no street as my own and with only a ragtag group of beggar boys who knew nothing about fighting. In fact if we weren't in such a desperate situation I wouldn't have had the courage to demand money from an elderly man who'd done nothing wrong to any of us. But it was shockingly easy at the end of the day. He took one look at me flanked by Loach and YoungGu and handed me the money with downcast eyes. I counted the money and gauged the going rate of these "protection fees" in the neighborhood and asked for twice that at the café next door. Here the owner was a lady in a floral-patterned blouse and heavy white makeup and she reminded me of a full moon with eyes drawn in charcoal. I'd seen enough women and girls around Seoul to know that she wasn't beautiful with or without makeup but the simple fact that she was female made my demand even more uncomfortable and embarrassing. But this lady listened to me and handed me the money even giving a slight bow of her head.

Once word got around that we'd been claiming our territory the inevitable happened—that is, the other gangs started attacking us. By all normal odds we should have been utterly destroyed by these bullies who were older and more experienced than us, but we surprised everyone including ourselves by winning and reclaiming our rights. This may sound like bragging but fighting comes very easily to me. I once fought six guys simultaneously on my own and they had long Japanese swords but I ended up putting my knife straight through their leader's left palm. He dropped the sword from his right hand and before it hit the ground I grabbed it and sliced off his ear with it and said next time I will strike off his head instead. No one challenged me after that and even the police stayed away from threatening my group.

Some people can't hide their surprise when they see that I, the skinny and short one, am the chief and the best fighter in the whole district. They started saying that this was because I was the son of a tiger hunter who used to kill beasts with his bare hands, which of course wasn't true but I didn't exactly deny it. What I am is just faster than anyone else and I know how to use my opponent's own power and weight against him and most importantly I am not afraid of sticking things into people if they get in my way. But I didn't have to resort to such extreme measures to get the owner of that Chinese restaurant to "rent out" his back room to us for free and I settled several small groups in similar places nearby.

Pretty much overnight, we'd gone from sleeping outside to having a floor and a ceiling over our heads. This was actually not easy at first. It was hard to fall asleep at night with the walls that seemed to close in on me. It was so hot that I actually missed sleeping under

". . . But are we giving up on Primorski? We should never have trusted the Red Army . . ."

When he'd first moved to MyungBo's guesthouse, these phrases were meaningless to him as though they were in a foreign tongue. He wasn't even interested in knowing these windy words and cloudy ideas; he liked to reserve his thinking for Jade, his friends, food and shelter, and other tangible things that made his heart warm, stomach full, and feet firm and heavy on the ground. Then MyungBo started explaining things to him one by one, using the words that he *could* understand. *Primorski* was just the Russian word for Yeonhaejoo, a frosty northern land that horse-riding Koreans conquered two thousand years ago. They were hunters, mountain people, warriors—and their capital was PyongYang, which was close to JungHo's own village. When JungHo listened to these tales, he felt a strange yearning and pain. It was a pain that originated outside of him and seeped through his skin, like the pale blue moonlight, the howling of wolves, and the sound of snow crunching under his feet.

The door opened; several men dressed in suits came out, along with a few women in *hanbok*. They barely nodded at JungHo while passing by and whispering among themselves. JungHo flushed a little, remembering how deeply MyungBo bowed to him at their first meeting. These revolutionaries all talked about abolishing class, but MyungBo was the only one who treated everyone—including JungHo—with equal respect.

"Comrade JungHo, I'm sorry the meeting ran late," MyungBo called, and JungHo walked inside.

His mentor did not get up; that was the one gesture of informality that he allowed himself as the months passed. Instead, he busied himself with spreading out a book, sheets of paper, and a pencil over a low table. JungHo sat down across from him and peered down at the book. Instantly, he lost all memory of the shapes of characters he'd learned. Instead, his mind let the black marks turn into cranes flying across the page, then strips of charcoal scattered in the snow, and he shook his head firmly to get rid of these unhelpful associations.

"Let's start from the top," MyungBo nudged gently. "You remember this syllable . . ."

JungHo searched in the innermost depths of his being for the answer. His eyes felt watery from the effort, but he came up to the surface with the correct name: "It's *dae*."

"Very well done! Excellent! And then the next one?" MyungBo said, brimming with excitement. JungHo forged on in order to not disappoint his mentor, diving into his mind and bringing back answers one by one.

After an excruciating hour, MyungBo closed the book. "That's enough reading for today I think," he said, then smiled, as if to reassure JungHo. "I know it's very difficult, Comrade JungHo. But my instinct tells me you'll play a large part in our independence, and that's what I'm preparing you for. Now let's try writing."

For the past several months, MyungBo had been asking JungHo to copy all the dozens of consonants and vowels from their workbook. Instead, MyungBo now wrote out just three syllables on the sheet of paper and asked JungHo to read them out loud.

"*Nam . . . Joong . . . Jung . . .*" JungHo looked up at his mentor, who was beaming. "It's my name."

"I haven't been teaching you the right way—that was hampering your progress. Let's first learn the most important word. Everything you write henceforth under your name has to be done in honesty and good faith. That's what it means to have a good name—not who your family is or how rich or famous you are."

JungHo copied from MyungBo's example, writing the first syllable again and again, then the second, then the third, until he filled the page. Then he turned that sheet facedown, took a blank sheet of paper, and shakily wrote out the three syllables of his name together for the first time. When he finished, he looked up eagerly like a schoolboy and saw that MyungBo had tears in his eyes.

"Well done, my friend," MyungBo said, trying to conceal the breaking of his voice. "You have a lot of strength in your penmanship—it's like your personality."

The childish letters were overlarge and uneven, but JungHo knew it was a genuine compliment and not a mockery.

That night, JungHo inwardly promised himself to live his life as to make MyungBo proud; before, he'd only wanted a way to improve himself in order to win Jade. MyungBo was connected to him through neither blood nor love—it was honor that bound them irrevocably together. Upon this realization he added MyungBo to his list of people to keep safe, no matter what.

Despite being one of the forty richest men in Korea and unfathomably influential, his mentor was living in constant mortal danger. His life was at an even greater risk since he renounced pacifism and compromise. MyungBo told JungHo that peacefully marching for independence had sacrificed too many lives for little gain, and that in order to gain their freedom they had to fight back. (JungHo had no problem understanding this portion of their lessons. He rather felt like saying, "Of course, what did you expect, you rich people?" but bit his tongue out of deference.) Unfortunately, the wings of the Korean armed forces had largely been clipped. The independence army based in Vladivostok had won victory after victory for a decade, sometimes joining forces with the Red Army against Japan. But afterward, the Bolsheviks demanded the Koreans disarm and disband, or be absorbed under the Russian command. Those who refused were killed or imprisoned.

The independence army in Manchuria had fared only a little better, severely weakened after the Japanese army massacred tens of thousands of Koreans living there, civilian or otherwise. That left Shanghai as the only viable center of armed resistance, although raising an army there in the heart of China was impossible. MyungBo therefore believed that the only effective course was to attack singly those places Japan valued the most: their police stations, banks, government offices, armories, and the like, in Korea, Japan, and China. MyungBo was trying to establish a group of exceptional snipers in Shanghai for these high-profile targets.

"We're at war, Comrade JungHo. And sometimes, despite your best intentions and efforts, war is inevitable," MyungBo had once said, almost like an apology. JungHo hadn't needed that explanation, but he nodded and grimaced to show he didn't take any of this lightly. He believed that his mentor would never lead him astray or ask him to do something shameful or unjust. He would live up to MyungBo's expectations, when the time came. Until then, he was called to a hundred different tasks MyungBo couldn't do himself: deliver forbidden manifestos to the socialists in the South, hide fugitives in safe houses and deliver them food, discreetly exchange a suitcase with a stranger at the train station under the plain gaze of the gendarmes. JungHo gave his all to these assignments, and MyungBo rewarded him—not with money or promotions, but with his unspeakable goodness.

The closer he became to MyungBo, the less intense JungHo's yearning for Jade became. The occupation of his mind and body to all that he needed to do in order to be worthy of her left him with very little time or energy to spend with her. He was going to her house once a week for a while, then once every fortnight, then just once a month. The worst part of this was that Jade no longer seemed to mind that he'd stayed away—she seemed preoccupied with rehearsals, performances, salon appointments, photo shoots, interviews, shopping, cinema, and a hundred other obligations and amusements. She always greeted him warmly, looked more and more beautiful each time they met, and talked breathlessly about some artist or a new novel of which he had zero knowledge. It seemed she always had something to do after ten, fifteen minutes. She was sometimes not home when he came by at noon.

So JungHo made a promise to himself that he'd stop calling on her until he was as important to her as she was to him. If he was being honest, he didn't know if he could ever take the place of her work, her art. Just from watching her dance once, he'd seen that this was a place in her soul that men couldn't touch. But he wouldn't even wish for that—he would only wish that he'd be the first among the *people* that she loved. That seemed possible so long as he could prove his worth as a man, although how he might do that was completely beyond his imagination. These thoughts came to him suddenly as he went about his day doing unrelated things, eating with his friends, delivering messages for MyungBo, getting up in the morning and shaving. Most often, it was when he felt the caress of the spring breeze or glimpsed the crystals of white moonlight salting the Han River. Then he would wonder how she had changed since they last saw each other, and whether he was now good enough for her.

IT WAS A WARM SPRING afternoon when the atmosphere shimmered under the quick-drying sun and everything from trees to grass to houses had a secret air of movement, of growing. HanChol narrowed his eyes against the white light, leaning against a wall and resisting the urge to put his hand on his stomach. Looking doubled over in hunger wouldn't exactly help attract customers. He had only made one won since dawn, when he broke his fast with steamed potato and barley. He'd decided not to go home for lunch until he hit the one-won fifty-cent mark, and now it was past four.

A woman in a kimono was walking toward him, and he straightened up. It was hard to know how old she was under her white makeup, but her coquettish gait and mannerisms looked young.

"Koko kara Honmachi made ikura kakarimasuka?" she said, smiling. How much to go to Honmachi?

"Ni ju-sen desu," HanChol replied—twenty cents. She nodded,

and he helped her climb inside the carriage. He almost never had Japanese customers, who were mostly concentrated in MyungDong and Honmachi and didn't venture outside, even somewhere as close as Jongno. But money was money. And the woman seemed pleased—perhaps it was the novelty of riding a Josenjing rickshaw. She broke the silence a few times to murmur about the weather, which could have been directed equally toward him or herself. The trailing sleeve of her kimono flapped rhythmically against the side of the rickshaw as they gained speed. HanChol stayed quiet until she got off at Honmachi and pressed a one-won bill into his palm, refusing change. He watched as her embroidered obi disappeared into the crowd. She didn't move him; nevertheless, he was instinctively cataloguing her in his collection of women.

HanChol was only nineteen years old. Yet he had long ceased to consider himself young or to give in to juvenile fancies. He was proud of the businesslike attitude he had toward everything, which was necessary to make any progress. What he thought of, day and night, was first success and then much later, duty. As for love, he never regarded it as something valuable to himself. Love felt to him like a distant and mysterious mountain, which was potentially real only because others spoke of it with reverence and conviction. He just had no particular impulse to see the mountain himself; it had as little bearing on his reality as the idea of heaven and hell. The only time he thought of women with longing was when he masturbated quietly in his room, not even daring to breathe freely, since his mother and two sisters slept in the next room. Then, he would close his eyes and recall a beautiful woman he'd driven that day, perhaps a flirtatious courtesan who had called him "as handsome as a prince," or a Modern Girl whose shapely legs encased in silk stockings were clearly visible if he just turned his head around.

And yet. As he turned west out of the Japanese district, his thoughts turned to the one woman whose image wasn't confined to these nightly indulgences, who surprised him with her strange relevance to his being. When he first saw Jade outside the theater, he'd also had a sensation that he'd never had with the others: the strongest urge to talk to her. At the same time, HanChol had gotten the distinct feeling that she too wished to speak to him intimately, although the presence of her friend prevented too much openness. They had exchanged a hidden, subtle, and precious mutual understanding with fleeting glances and twinkling eyes, the way young people communicate only in the first few loves of their lives. At home that night, he had touched himself and come more powerfully than ever before.

Yes, at the beginning it had only been a physical desire and a curiosity, and nothing more—he was certain of it. Nevertheless, as he became her favorite driver and saw her several times a week, his regard for her began to acquire a specificity that he'd never felt before. To HanChol, all people belonged to certain categories: family, schoolmates, close friends, other rickshaw drivers, customers, people from whom he might benefit, and so on. He behaved toward anyone according to his or her category without any partiality. But how he thought of Jade defied his normal attitudes toward courtesans, customers, or women in general. She was all those things, but she looked and acted nothing like the others and he only thought of her as Jade.

HanChol caught himself drifting into a reverie and shook his head forcefully. It was close to five; he'd stop by his house and eat a meal, which would be both his lunch and dinner. When he pulled inside the front yard of their thatched-roof cottage, his mother rushed out of the room where she was sewing with one of his younger sisters. The other one was out washing laundry at a creek; the three women together made a meager income by cleaning and mending laborers' clothes, a sum that amounted to only half of HanChol's.

"Hurry up and fix your brother's meal." His mother turned sharply to his sister, who was still seated inside the open door. The girl was used to their mother's abuses, but now she looked frightened. There was no more barley after their morning meal; as the oldest daughter, she was continuously called upon to make food out of nearly nothing, yet even she couldn't make miracles happen. Before sharper rebukes could fall upon his sister for his sake, HanChol stepped in.

"Mother, don't worry. I already had a bowl of soup at a tavern. Here, that's for dinner," he said, handing her the two won. She creased into a smile. "*Aigoo,* my son. My firstborn."

She urged him to stay and rest, but he shook his head and went back out with his rickshaw. His mother doted on him as she never did on his sisters; she respected and even feared him as the head of the household since age fourteen, when his father passed. Nonetheless, her constant fixation upon his bloodline, which was some obscure cadet branch of the mighty House of Andong-Kim, made him uneasy around her. Her common refrain was "If your father were still alive, his cousins would have taken us in . . ." and "You must restore our family's name, you must live up to our honor . . ." The clan still lived in prosperity in the wealthy enclave of Andong, but their family had been living apart since HanChol's grandfather's time. They were now no better than peasants, except in their strict observance of formalities and the expectation that HanChol would go to university and enter into a respectable career, lifting them all out of their misery.

The sun was still shining above the buildings, but its warmth was being replaced by an earthy coolness, as happens on fine spring evenings.

HanChol's next customer was a well-dressed gentleman with round eyeglasses, who sedately read his newspaper the entire time to the new baseball stadium in EuljiRo. When HanChol stopped in front of his destination, he dreamily peeked out from behind the newspaper, hopped off the rickshaw, rummaged through his pockets, and said, "Oh, I didn't realize I only have ten cents on me. I'm sorry, my fellow." Before HanChol could say anything, the gentleman gave him a ten-cent bill and disappeared into the crowd. HanChol crumpled up the money in his hand and shoved it into his pocket, disgusted. People!

Hours passed more or less in the same vein. At half past ten, Jade came out of the side entrance, where HanChol was waiting for her as usual. When his eyes found her, his mood brightened immediately. It was the opening week of Jade's new play, about a girl from a once-genteel family who becomes a courtesan in order to pay for the treatment of her invalid father and gravely ill brother. Tonight she was wearing a pale blue skirt suit with high-heeled pumps. A medium-brimmed navy hat, with a silk satin band in the same shade as the suit, was pressed above her head. She held the strap of her purse with both hands and looked around searchingly, almost exactly like her character when she arrived at the harbor. The effulgence of streetlamps gathered into golden pools of light at her feet. HanChol felt in awe of her loveliness. He pulled the rickshaw toward her slowly so as to resist her effect on him.

Jade was silent as he helped her onto the rickshaw and started heading automatically toward her home. She seemed to be lost in thoughts that had nothing to do with HanChol, and that secretly bothered him. On the rare nights when Jade sat silently with a sad and pensive air, he found himself wanting to know what was wrong and to make her feel better. In the past, Jade had often gossiped cheerfully with Lotus, knowing that the driver could hear them and yet not sparing any details of rich lovers who were paying them court. But since Lotus had moved to a different theater, Jade rode quietly and often in a more subdued state of mind, gazing at the jazz-soaked storefronts and the people walking under the cool white moonlight.

As they got on the boulevard, she broke the silence.

"Mr. HanChol, I've known you for a long time now, but you never talk about yourself."

He had the impulse to stop pulling, resisted it, and kept trotting. The quickening of his beating heart didn't have anything to do with running, however.

"I don't know what about my life could interest you," HanChol said in his deep bronze voice, without glancing back.

"Anything. Everything." Jade's eyes were full of smiles, he imagined. "For example, how old you are."

HanChol told her that he was nineteen, and she sighed.

"Younger than me, then. I'm twenty already. And you're still studying at the night school?"

"Yes, miss."

"I am sure you're brilliant. I can tell how smart a fellow is just by looking at his eyes."

HanChol was trying to process both that she thought he was intelligent, and that she'd studied his eyes. When had she even looked straight at his face?

"I can follow the others. I try my best," HanChol said modestly, though in fact, his teacher—a Christian who had studied in Hiroshima—had complimented him more than once on his uncanny brightness and exhaustive memory.

"You're being humble. I'm sure if you could've gone to school full-time, you would have passed university entrance exams already," she persisted.

HanChol had himself thought this hundreds of times. After paying for the living expenses of the household, he hardly had any tuition left even for the night school. It was impossible to tell when he'd be able to take the entrance exams, let alone how he'd be able to pay for university. Would he be able to matriculate by twenty-five or twenty-six? He had no way of knowing. Instead of talking about his abject circumstances, he turned the subject around.

"You're intelligent as well," he said. He didn't know what he was saying until after the words were spoken, and realized he'd always thought that.

"Me?" Jade sounded full of surprise. "Why would you think that?"

"I can always tell when I look at someone's eyes," HanChol said jokingly, and feeling emboldened, turned his head over his right shoulder to steal a glance. She was staring at him with such wide eyes under her navy hat, her rosy lips in a half-moon smile.

"No one's ever told me I'm intelligent before," Jade muttered sheepishly as he turned back around to face the road.

"You just always say the right things. When you and Miss Lotus talk, for instance."

"Oh, so you were eavesdropping on us?" She pretended to be scandalized. They continued talking in a careful, but excited manner until they reached her home. He helped her down as usual; but this time, instead of keeping his head lowered as he held her hand steady, he met her eyes and smiled. Neither could say which one was holding on to the other, but for an imperceptible second, they didn't let go. It was unconscionably, irrationally sweet—that brief moment when they both knew how reluctant they were to separate. And when their hands finally parted, each one was already missing the touch of the other. Jade hid her confusion by busying herself over the fare.

"This will give you some change to buy books," she said, pressing folded bills into his hand.

"I don't want to take money from you." He shook his head, still boldly looking at her. But she gazed out above his right ear, like someone suddenly confronted by the blinding white sun. From such a lovely girl, who usually acted as though she could get any man she wanted, this was an unexpected symptom of shyness. He found it irresistible.

"If you give this ride for free, I will never hire you again for fear you might never let me pay. So just take it." Jade pressed the money into his palm more firmly, and this time he relented. He stood there watching her lithe form slip inside the gates, and on walking back, felt that everything—cars, bicycles, singing of drunkards, freshness of night air, liquid light spilling onto the dark road—was more vivid than ever before. As he neared his house, the singing died away and the stillness was only felt more purely by the innocent, rhythmic call of the *sochuck* owl. That spring bird call had never moved him so achingly. It seemed to say all that there is to life.

AFTER THE PERFORMANCE on the following night, Jade sat primly in the rickshaw without initiating a conversation. She seemed determined to pretend that nothing had happened between them. Han-Chol was disappointed, but not hurt. If anything, her reticence only confirmed to him that something significant had taken place. He was wondering how he could break the silence when the sound of a *sochuck* bird was heard in the distance.

"Did you hear that, miss?" he asked, slowing down to a walk.

"Hear what? That bird?" Jade leaned a little forward, closer to him.

"Yes, miss. It's a *sochuck* bird."

"I always heard that song and never knew which bird it came from," Jade confessed.

"It's a brownish owl with big round eyes. When I was little, my father and I went to the South Mountain one day and found a baby owl that had fallen out of its nest. It was just a tiny thing that fit into my palm—like a small, fluffy potato."

"Oh my!" Jade couldn't feign indifference any longer. "So what happened?"

"It had a broken leg, so we brought it home. My father wrapped its leg in a bit of cloth to help it heal. My sisters and I took turns feeding it cicadas. We named it Potato."

"How precious!" she exclaimed. "Did his leg heal?"

"It did. He walked around, following me everywhere. When he got tired he would cry, asking to be put on my shoulder. And when I'd be out of the house, he'd cry then too, waiting for me by the gates for hours. But then, he got bigger, and fall came . . . And we couldn't always keep looking for insects to feed our pet owl, even if we were still children. Our parents told us to get rid of Potato.

"So I brought him to the woods where I found him. At first, he kept crying and running after me. So I finally picked him up, put him on a tree, and said goodbye."

"That's awful. What if he just stayed there on the tree and starved to death?" Jade sounded close to tears.

"He'd been flapping his wings for a long time. I think he made it," HanChol said. Only later had he learned that *sochuck* owls have to migrate across the South Sea in the fall. He didn't tell her this because it would have caused her pain.

Jade was trying to contain the mysterious stirring within her, which started in her chest and radiated outward throughout her whole body, similar to intoxication. Love happens all at once, and also in stages. Having already fallen in love with him by sight, she was now experiencing that revelatory moment when a woman realizes what kind of soul her lover has. She felt that he had a special, tender soul—and that he could share this hidden self only with her, perhaps even that she brought it out of him. Seeing his broad-shouldered and lanky frame with its strong back, narrow waist and hips, she felt pity for the young man that he'd become—handsome and intelligent and capable, but also weighed down by his family and his circumstances. Already she wished she could lessen that premature sense of responsibility and see his face relax and light up, as it had while they were talking the night before. As naturally as some people take to books or sums or the making of money, Jade's heart was predisposed to give love. It had already reached forward in order to make this person happy.

"You must be exhausted, Mr. HanChol," she told him. "I want to get off here."

"Here, miss?" They were still several blocks away from her house.

"Yes. I'll get off here," she said firmly. "You can walk beside me if you like."

He helped her off, and she was thrilled to notice the tiniest squeeze of the hand he gave her before letting go. They walked side by side without further conversation, and that was sweet too in its own way, being able to focus on each other's presence. Had walking ever been more pleasant? Jade wondered. She could not stop smiling. They didn't tell each other much, and yet understood each other so well. So many words could be exchanged between people without any real desire to know one another. But with the right person, one could speak much or not at all, and feel completely connected. This was what Jade realized as they walked together to her gates.

When Jade tried to pay him, he preemptively pressed something into her palm—a letter. While she blushed and gathered her composure, he gave her a handsome smile (not quite as relaxed as before) and left. She came inside the house and, in the safety of her own room, lit a candle and began reading with a pounding heart. He had admired her for years, ever since he first saw her. He had no reason to hope that she would return his feelings, but he was happy now that the burden of secrecy was lifted. He would understand if she refused to ever see him again, since he had nothing to offer her. But he only wished that she would be very, very happy, because that was what she deserved.

"But that's exactly how I feel about him! I only wish for his happiness," she said to herself, curling into her bedspread, exhilarated and pained at the same time.

The next night, HanChol waited anxiously outside the theater, not knowing if she'd be there. Months before, Jade had once alluded to Lotus's lover, who either had his chauffeur pick her up or himself drove her home in a black car. There was no reason to think Jade wouldn't also be able to secure a lover like that. Some rich man had to want her as a mistress or as a second wife—perhaps even as a legal first wife. All Seoul had admired her in *The Story of ChunHyang*, and her photographs had been in the newspapers and the magazines. And even if he had flattered and intrigued her, he was hardly in a position to start anything with a woman—not even a suitably innocent and hardworking girl, let alone an actress.

As he reflected, the side exit opened and Jade came out, her whole body seemingly looking for him only. The streetlamp cast its light from her left, shimmering on her small but shapely forehead, the tops of her glossy eyelids, the bridge of her nose, and her left cheekbone, leaving the right side of her face under a shadow. When she found him, she lit up with a smile, and it was like when the sky turned pink before the sun rose. She looked not just beautiful, but vitally significant—full of mysterious meaning like the songs of nocturnal birds. He forgot all his inner arguments; instead he could only think about embracing her.

16

BECAUSE YOU WERE YOU, STANDING THERE

1928

OVER THE MONTHS, LOTUS HAD LEARNED THAT PRESIDENT MA DIDN'T act the same way normal people did. He let his feelings be known: once at a restaurant, he'd forced the chef to remake the entire spread of twelve dishes because in one of them he'd tasted onions, to which he was allergic. For this reason, Lotus had been anxious about telling him her news. She waited until he was in a particularly good mood one night following the signing of a deal—a purchase of a lucrative factory in KaeSong.

"It's a huge win. One of only a few chemical manufacturers in the country. I'm going to go up there on Friday," he said, his hands on the steering wheel. He'd picked her up after her performance and they were parked near her house. "You should come with me. It would be a nice drive out in the country." He paused, noticing her silence. "Why, what's the matter?"

"I'm pregnant," Lotus blurted out, hiding her face in her hands. For a while, neither of them said anything. Then she felt him take her left wrist and slowly lower it down.

"Look at me," he said matter-of-factly. "Are you sure?"

Lotus nodded through the hot tears streaming down her face, clutching her still-flat abdomen.

"You can't keep living at your aunt's. I'll have to find you your own house. And a maid and a housekeeper. You'll be comfortable. But why are you crying?" he said.

"I thought you'd be angry with me." She sobbed, nostrils flaring. At that, President Ma laughed out loud.

"Angry? I've never been less angry in my life," he said, kissing the top of her head. "I might finally get a son."

The next morning, Lotus told the family at breakfast that she would soon be moving out. But she didn't tell them her news, basking in the power of withholding a secret. If she was being honest with herself, she could admit that she was primarily hiding it from Jade. Some irreconcilable awkwardness had entered into their relationship ever since Lotus joined the Grand Oriental Cinema, and while they still smiled at each other and exchanged pleasantries, they both acutely felt the impossibility of being frank with one another. Lotus believed that their present iciness was caused by Jade's jealousy. Now that Lotus was the star of the most prestigious theater in Seoul, and mistress to one of its wealthiest businessmen, Jade was insincere and cold, and not genuinely happy as she ought to be. On the other hand, Jade believed that their relationship was strained because Lotus had hidden her decision to move to a different theater, not even telling her almost until the last day. How could Lotus believe that Jade, her own best friend, would stand in the way of her success and happiness?

On the day of the move, Dani, Luna, and Jade helped Lotus carry the trunks of clothes to the car.

"This is a lot more than what you brought here, ten years ago," Dani joked, pretending to grimace under the weight of the package. "My arms feel like they're going to fall off." Still, it was she who had insisted on helping instead of leaving it to the maids. When everything had been stuffed inside the trunk and the backseat, Dani took Lotus's face in her hands as if she were still a child.

"You're my cousin's daughter, so we are five degrees apart. But I've always treated you as if you were my own daughter. We were a family, together in this house for ten years, eh?" She had no trace of tears in her eyes, but her voice quaked.

"We'll always be a family, Aunt Dani," Lotus said softly as she embraced her. She went to Luna, Jade, and Hesook and hugged each one. The car was already started, rumbling and emitting a stream of warm sooty smoke. The chauffeur opened the passenger-seat door for her, and they were off.

• • •

LOTUS'S DEPARTURE CAST a subtle gloom over Dani's house. Breakfast was the time when her absence was most conspicuously felt, since that had been the meal that they all shared together. As usual, Dani vacillated between experiencing emotions passionately and restraining herself from sentimentality; the former was her nature and the latter was her principle. She never admitted to feeling sad or empty, and only the keenest observer could perceive a change in her confident self-possession. But Luna, who was familiar with Dani's inner workings, knew that she missed the girl dearly.

Luna herself felt the loss but was not devastated by it. She had grown to love her younger sister as they both got older. But that had also coincided with the shaping of their individuality, and they had needed each other less with every passing year. She was simply glad that Lotus had blossomed and found what she wanted. Luna knew that her younger sister needed only two things to be happy: a man's love and music.

As for what she herself needed to be happy, Luna was less certain. Rather, she never stopped to think about this, since for her even the very idea of happiness seemed alien and out of reach. It was no more sensible than being asked, "Would you like to live on the moon? How does that sound?" The closest thing to happiness was how she felt when her daughter curled up to her at night, begging to use her arm as a pillow. "What about your pillow?" Luna would ask, pointing at the soft silk cylinder filled with dried chrysanthemum petals and mung beans. "No, no. I want to sleep on Mama's arm," Hesook would protest, snuggling her head toward Luna. Luna would sigh, as though exasperated, making the child giggle. They would play silly games that only they understood; Hesook would call out, "Nose, forehead, chin, cheek, eyebrow" and so on, and Luna would kiss rapidly each part that was named. Messing up and kissing the wrong place caused both of them to break into utterly senseless and joyful laughter. Looking at the pure adoration in her daughter's sweet little face, Luna welled up with the conviction that nothing and no one else mattered.

That, perhaps, was Luna's happiness, although calling it so made her feel selfish and undeserving. Luna did not particularly wish for it, and only looked forward to saving enough money to secure her and her daughter's future. She had the idea to raise Hesook as a normal, modern kind of girl. This was the reason Luna had been careful not to get into any affairs, so that Hesook might have the liberty to get educated and marry a proper man. Girls from upper-class families would often study abroad in Japan or even Europe, and Hesook would also get the best education money could buy. Luna carefully saved up almost everything she made from parties and modeling—less than either Jade or Lotus, but still substantial—so that Hesook would lack for nothing in terms of schooling or clothes. She was proud that Hesook was a good student, getting high marks in most subjects and praised by her teachers.

This was why Luna was all the more devastated when Hesook came home one afternoon and gave Luna a letter from the principal, asking her to visit the school the next day. She questioned her daughter and threatened to use the switch. Hesook, who had never been beaten in her life, broke into rivers of tears and ran away to her room. Luna immediately regretted her harshness, stroked her daughter's hair, and promised her that she wouldn't get angry again. Between sobs and hiccups, Hesook explained that she'd gotten into a fight at the school but wouldn't say anything more.

The next morning, Luna got dressed especially carefully. She picked out her most elegant summer outfit: a cropped white silk blouse and a floor-length lavender skirt. Unlike Jade and Lotus, who increasingly preferred to wear Western dress, Luna almost always wore traditional clothes. She was the only one in the house who still dressed her hair in a braided chignon. On this day she chose a green jade *binyuh* to hold it in place.

Around noon, Luna got out of the cab in front of the Christian girls' school that Dani had also attended. The relentless July sun was reflecting on the light pink sand of the courtyard. At the moment, it was filled with an eerie silence peculiar to an empty playground in the middle of classes, lying in wait for the cheerful children. A gray-haired porter stopped her at the gates and waved her in when she said she was Hesook's mother, not knowing or caring that she was a famous courtesan. "Oh yes, you got a letter from the principal? You'll want to go to her office on the second floor," the porter said good-naturedly. She thanked him and started crossing the sun-drenched courtyard, trying to hide how she herself felt like a little girl in trouble.

• • •

UPSTAIRS IN HER OFFICE, the principal was having coffee with a visitor, Deputy Consul Curtice. She originally hailed from Rochester, and he grew up in Ithaca; and by virtue of their neighboring hometowns, they'd relied on each other more than on anyone else among the Americans in Seoul.

"I believe you will find our students are very well-educated, polite, and devout. I have a few in mind whom I will recommend," she said, putting her cup down on the saucer with a crisp and cheerful clink. "Some very smart girls from poorer families, who would surely be forced to marry as soon as possible. This would give them a chance to use their education and earn their independence, perhaps."

Deputy Consul Curtice nodded thoughtfully. He had come to ask her help in finding a new translator and secretary at the consulate. The old translator had passed away from tuberculosis the previous winter and it was imperative to find a replacement soon. There were young men who graduated from missionaries' schools as well, but the new consul-general had the notion that women translators and typists were cheaper and more obedient than their male counterparts. The men were more likely to get involved in political activism, whether that meant communism, the independence movement, or both. His predecessor, the former consul-general, had been more sympathetic; he'd sent the AP reporter's photographs to the secretary of state and urged the Wilson administration to take a stance against such atrocities. That integrity had a cost, and he was quickly removed from his post and reassigned to Canton.

The new consul-general stuck with the official program that the regime here was an American ally. Curtice found it difficult to agree with his supervisor on many issues; but insofar as the translator was concerned, he saw no harm in bringing a modern-educated Korean woman into the fold.

"Yes, that would be tremendously helpful, thank you," he said with a smile in his bright blue eyes, which had stayed young even as his red hair climbed higher on his forehead and his body took on the pendulous hints of middle age. As he was searching for a way to bring their meeting to a close, someone knocked quietly on the door.

"Come in," the principal said in English. But her face showed surprise when a beautiful young Korean woman walked in, blushing brightly from nerves.

"May I ask what this is regarding?" The principal switched to an unexpectedly firm and flexible Korean that she'd acquired in the past two decades. The young woman looked shocked at hearing her language come out of a white person's mouth.

"I'm Hesook's mother," the woman said in Korean, then added in English, "I am here to talk about her."

"Oh, yes, of course! I am sorry, now I remember," the principal said in a mixture of Korean and English. She rose from her chair in greeting and Curtice followed, giving a slight nod of the head in the woman's direction. "I should get going," he indicated with his eyes to his host. But she signaled that he should sit and wait for this short, unimportant meeting to finish, and he obeyed.

"Please sit down," the principal told the new guest, who shyly slid between a chair and the coffee table and settled down, resting her white hands on her lavender skirt. As sometimes happens when meeting a stranger who is either unquestionably good-looking or ugly, the principal and Curtice were startled by the woman, who was remarkably pretty. Out of their good breeding, however, they both behaved as if they hadn't noticed. Curtice looked out the window to show that he didn't wish to intrude on their meeting. A warm breeze was coming in from the courtyard, causing the white linen curtains to flap around.

"I teach only the senior girls myself, so I don't know Hesook well," the principal said in English. "But from what her teacher tells me, Hesook is a very bright girl."

"Thank you," the woman said quietly with a bow.

"She's never caused any trouble before, so we were surprised when she got into a fight with a few of the other girls. It appears that those girls were taunting Hesook, but she was the one who started kicking and punching. Do you understand?" the principal said in a stern voice that she used indiscriminately on troublesome students, faculty, and visitors alike.

"Yes, I do," the woman said meekly, studying her lap.

"Those girls were making fun of Hesook for not having a father, which is a terrible thing, but I can't have anyone who acts violently at the school."

"You mean, you're expelling Hesook?" The woman became agitated and looked straight into the principal's eyes. "No, she is just a young girl. She made a mistake . . ." She switched to Korean and appeared to beg for forgiveness. Still seated awkwardly at the table, Curtice resisted the urge to intervene and say to the principal, Why not just let this one go?

"I know that Hesook is young, which is why this time it's only a warning," the principal said. "But please, have a talk with her about not fighting. I won't be so lenient next time."

"Thank you, thank you so much," the woman said in English, bowing deeply at the waist.

Having overheard snatches of the conversation, Curtice wondered to himself who this stranger could possibly be. She looked young enough to be a student at the school, and it was also curious that she spoke English. Soon, his curiosity was partially satisfied: when the principal asked her where she had learned the language, the woman explained that she'd been taught by her aunt, who had been a student at this school.

After the visitor left, the principal turned to Curtice and said, "I'm sorry about that. She could have waited for us to finish, but . . ."

"No, it was no trouble, I didn't mind at all," Curtice said. "Who is she?"

"Just the mother of one of our students," the principal replied.

"She looks much too young to be a mother." The deputy consul raised his eyebrows, not bothering to conceal his thoughts. "She speaks English. You don't think a married woman could possibly want to work at the consulate—?"

"She is not married, Mr. Curtice, although I highly doubt she'd want to be a translator or a secretary," the principal said tartly. Curtice blushed, wondering how he'd offended her. The principal was at least ten years older than he was, and they had always had a mutually respectful, sexless dynamic. Nevertheless, it was clear that his interest in this stranger made her feel indignant and insulted.

"She's—what's known as a *giseng*. A very successful one, I hear. Her daughter doesn't have a father," the principal pronounced, clasping her hands together on her lap, as though that would be the end of that discussion.

Curtice looked out the window again so as not to betray his astonishment. A sudden thought came to his mind that if he could see the stranger crossing the courtyard, he would take it as a sign. A sign of what? He didn't know yet. A light breeze lifted a veil of dust and carried it up to the blue sky. When Curtice was beginning to feel afraid that he'd been looking away too long, that the principal would be offended by his inattention, the woman in the lavender skirt appeared in the frame of the window. Amid the pink sand that was blowing up, she looked a little like a traveler crossing the desert.

• • •

HANCHOL NO LONGER BROUGHT the rickshaw to the theater after Jade's performances. Instead, they strolled home side by side slowly every night. The walk lasted nearly an hour, but neither of them felt any fatigue, even after a long day of running around town, rehearsing, and going onstage. They both felt so keenly alive simply by wandering and holding hands. They pointed out to each other the things that they saw: "Oh look at those arched windows of that department store . . ." "Did you ever notice that statue there?" Though none of those things were particularly profound, everything seemed significant and delightful and memorable. When they reached her house, he gently, almost reverentially, wrapped her in his arms and they kissed.

One night when the weather was particularly beautiful and the moon was bright, Jade pulled away from kissing him and said,

"Wouldn't you like to come in?" She knew he'd been thinking of this for a long time, but that he'd never have the courage to ask her first. She led him by the hand to her pavilion, proud to be showing him where she lived.

She knew this was his first time, and that he had to be nervous. But despite being inexperienced and younger than she was, he took her as if he knew what to do. His touch was urgent, but gentle. Even when they were both undressed, he kissed her from the crown of her head to her fingertips, then all the way down to her toes. His lips traveled along her body like a cartographer, making a map of her sensations. Little sighs escaped her mouth—not like with others, to show that what they were doing was suitably pleasing, but because she couldn't help it. She looked up mesmerized at his lean but well-muscled body above her own, so patiently caressing her while delaying his own gratification. She said, "I don't want to wait any longer," and reached for him, but he kept touching her all over. "I could kiss you forever," he whispered. When he finally pressed into her body, they looked into each other's eyes in awe. The sensation of being so close was painfully exquisite. They held each other motionlessly for a while, before moving and dissolving into each other. He came first, and she expected him to roll off of her and fall asleep as others had done. But he stayed inside her and became hard again until she also climaxed.

He lay on top of her, panting and resting his tired head on her chest as she stroked his damp hair. He caught her hand and brought it to his lips, and she glimpsed him smiling unconsciously, as though he couldn't believe his good luck.

"Your skin . . ." he said, melting into softer, fluttery kisses over her chest. And she knew exactly what he meant; the feeling of his bare skin against hers was so comfortable yet intense that she felt hungry for it even in the moment. Without speaking, they shifted positions to touch each other as much as possible, and then laughed at their silliness.

"I can hear your heart beating," he muttered. She could also feel his heart pulsing hard above her stomach. No one else had said this to her, but then no one else had made it worth noticing. Feeling his heartbeat was something she knew she would treasure for the rest of her life.

"Do you love me?" she asked.

"Yes, I love you," HanChol said simply. "I really do."

"Why? Since when?"

"Since I first saw you outside the theater. Why? Because you were you, standing there, and I was also standing there . . . It's that simple and that complicated. But it couldn't have been otherwise." He sighed and turned his face so that his right cheek pressed into her chest.

Ever since then, nothing else mattered to Jade more than loving and being loved by HanChol. She rarely spent time dwelling on her estrangement with Lotus or her success in theater. She knew she had the most important thing, something so pure and rare. When she came to Silver's house, all she'd imagined for herself was becoming a maid. Then later, she wondered whether her fate was to lie with men toward whom she had no feelings except revulsion, until cast aside for younger women and newer amusements. But by some miracle her reality was now better than anything she'd ever dreamed. In a relatively short amount of time, it turned her into a different person. The change was mostly internal, although as happens when there is a seismic inner shift, her physicality changed as well. She would sit in front of her mirror and be startled that her eyes or her nose looked strangely different than just half a year before. She now felt so well adored that her soul itself had transformed, and her features had shaped themselves to reflect that. Jade had always been charming yet imperfect, with a narrow forehead and regular, unremarkable eyes laced with thin lashes, but now those flaws were unnoticeable. She was used to attracting attention, but never so much as now—she felt people's eyes following her as she walked down the street or went onstage. None of that mattered to her, however. She only cared about being beautiful in his eyes.

Women, more so than men, are apt to polarize love as either giving or receiving. A wider expanse exists between those women who understand love as selfless caring, and others who cannot abide by a relationship through which they don't somehow benefit. To Jade, even the idea of gaining something through HanChol would have tainted their love. None of the gifts and money Jade had received from her patrons had made her as happy as when she was thinking of ways to help HanChol. She had more than enough money to support him while he finished school. After losing his biggest customer, Jade, HanChol was having trouble making enough money. But Jade knew that he would have a hard time accepting her help. When she brought it up, HanChol looked offended for the first time in her presence.

"I could never take your money," he said tautly. "I'm a man who knows how to make his own money—not take it from a woman."

"Don't think of it that way," she pleaded. "I am older than you. Think of it like this: in life, there are times when you should accept help from people who are perhaps older and in a better position. And then when you're successful, you return the favor and help out those who need it. You can't keep going like this, spinning wheels! There has to be something that lifts you up out of the muck, and now I'm saying I want to be that something."

She was looking at him with such loving and innocent eyes. She was completely selfless in her offer, and wasn't seeking anything in return. He kissed her hands and said, "I don't deserve you."

He had been considering dropping out of night school altogether rather than struggling for another six or seven years, just to get a shot at university. He had been looking at a lifetime of driving rickshaws or, when those became obsolete, becoming a hard laborer carrying bricks on his back seven days a week until his death.

Jade not only paid for his school fees, but also covered the living cost for him and his family. Unable to explain that a courtesan-actress was his benefactress, he told his mother that he'd won a scholarship. She replied, "At last you are starting to live up to your potential. But don't become arrogant and slack off. You mustn't rest until you're admitted—our family depends on your success."

HanChol went to school nine hours a day and studied at home even longer, often until after the night birds fell silent. Sometimes he found himself reading until sunrise. But after running around the city every day for years, simply learning in his seat was something he could do gladly. He caught up on several years' worth of education in just a year and finally took the university entrance exam.

The results were announced in the newspapers, and when he saw his name near the top out of all the students in the country, he was exhilarated to the point of tears by two things: first, that his life could have gone the path of abyss or that of success, and that it had taken a decisive and irrevocable turn toward the latter; second, that he had done this all on his own.

17

CAFÉ SEAHORN

1933

WHEN YOUNGGU HAD FINALLY GOTTEN THE COURAGE TO ASK THE RES-taurant owner for his daughter's hand in marriage, JungHo had offered to make the match. But YoungGu had refused.

"JungHo, you know I'd trust you with my very life," he'd said. "But I'm worried you're going to speak with your fist again. That won't do for the father of my future bride."

He'd also ruled out eloping, although stealing a bride was a rather time-honored practice among men who couldn't pay the dowry. Instead he went to the father, knelt on his floor, and asked for his blessing. He begged for forgiveness for coming into his home and taking advantage of his restaurant, and promised to work to repay the debt.

"You hooligans have ruined my life for years and now you rob me of my daughter too? Is this some kind of a sick joke?" the father shouted. "Fine, if you really can't live without her, as you say, go out there and kneel in the courtyard. If you get up before I say you can, you won't lay a finger on my daughter. And trust me, I'll know if you get up for even a second!"

YoungGu obediently left the room and knelt in the dead center of the busy courtyard, while restaurant workers looked on and gossiped, neighbors peeked over the walls to laugh, the girl cried miserably in her own room, and his loyal dog tied to the chestnut tree barked his heart out, sensing something grave had fallen on his master. The commotion was extraordinary. But YoungGu stayed in his spot, shins digging into the dirt, head bowed in penitence, and did not get up the entire night. The next morning, a servant was trying to convince him to just give up when he collapsed and sprawled out on the spot.

Finally, the father came out of his room, shook him by the shoulders, and said, "If you swear to sever all ties with your gang of hooligans, especially that red commie JungHo, and to work hard like an honest man from this point forward . . ." He couldn't finish his words, because the idea of giving his most adored daughter to this wretch was still so appalling. Then he remembered the old saying that there is no parent who can win against his own child.

"Thank you, Father," YoungGu whispered faintly. "I will take good care of her."

From that point on, YoungGu had ostensibly dropped out of the group. He stopped going to the meetings and doing JungHo's work and started helping out at the restaurant. Soon, he was managing the place instead of his old father-in-law, who had softened with time and the birth of his beloved granddaughter.

JungHo had every right to be angry at YoungGu's defection, but he felt it was okay to let his friend go. Loach had also left the organization, saying he couldn't swear the oath that was required. In reality, the oath was hard for even JungHo. Renouncing his worldly possessions was not insurmountable, since he owned so little to begin with. (MyungBo himself had given up half of his estate to be distributed among the poor and to be used for missions—and that took true fortitude, JungHo believed.) The second part of the oath, being ready to give up his life for independence, was another matter. From observation, JungHo knew that there were two kinds of activists: those who were destined to die young in action, and others who would live on to govern, to negotiate, to write manifestos, and so on. It was obvious that MyungBo was the latter—he was much too essential, and his scholar's hand was more useful for writing letters and declarations than firing guns. On the other hand, it had already been several years since JungHo (and MyungBo) quietly realized that he would never read or write well. This was a disqualifying weakness, he knew. JungHo let these thoughts roll through his mind in waves—they sometimes roared and clashed, and sometimes quieted down into a narrative that made sense. When he felt most calm, he believed that MyungBo would ask him to do something only he could do, at precisely the right moment.

One evening after YoungGu and Loach left, JungHo saw them for dinner at the Chinese restaurant. They were in a fine, drunken mood familiar to old friends gathered in a place of fond memories—a feeling like sitting on the grass in summer twilight. It was blissful at first, and as the night went on, took on a shape of indistinct sadness. Even though they were all still young, JungHo felt strongly that something was completely behind them already. YoungGu was a father of a daughter with another one on the way. Loach had himself saved enough money to open a general store near YoungGu's restaurant. JungHo hadn't sought to do any of those things. But if he'd been able to build something small and real with Jade by his side, that would have been everything to him. He was startled to realize he hadn't seen her in almost three months. Last time he went, he'd gotten the feeling that she had a new man, and had left feeling worse than before seeing her at all. It was a unique form of self-torture that he'd no longer administer on himself.

After saying goodbye to his friends, JungHo went alone to the stone bridge over the canal to smoke and think. Resting his elbows on the railing, he took out the silver cigarette case from his inner pocket. It was tarnished in places, and the engraving was hard to make out. But—he ran his finger over the light grooves—of course it was still there. Time had the effect of muting everything, but it could never erase something real.

From time to time, JungHo went to certain low-end restaurants where there were women who took care of his needs in the back room. They were not courtesans, just whores who lay with anyone for a price, but he liked them and hungered for them. With one very young girl, who couldn't have been more than eighteen at most, he'd felt a sort of brotherly affection along with physical desire. This didn't strike him as an infidelity to Jade because it helped him keep the better parts of him for her over such a long time, and so was maybe an act of faith. He considered going to see this girl. It would be nice to lie in someone's arms for a while. Then, shaking his head, he decided against it.

It occurred to him now that he had never just told Jade his true feelings. Perhaps she knew and was refusing to acknowledge it. Perhaps she hadn't seen him that way but would now realize what's always been in front of her. When he arrived at her house, the maid told him she was out and asked if he'd wait inside. He opted to stay outside to breathe a little better in the fresh air.

He was wearing his only winter suit, one of two shirts, and an old overcoat, but everything was clean, pressed, and starched by MyungBo's housekeeper. No one could say he looked like a dirty street urchin or an outcast. Some women passed by and glanced at him with friendly curiosity, which bolstered his confidence. He was finally ready to tell her.

• • •

JADE HAD GONE OUT that morning to the set of her new film near the Han River. It was chilly and windy by the water, and she wasn't feeling well. Between takes, her costar asked her if she was all right.

"I'm just a little tired, but I'll be okay," she replied.

"It's too cold today. I feel sorry you have to be in that thin little blouse," he said with a smile. It was the kind of smile that men give to show, Yes, I care about you. Jade knew her costar liked her, and though she never planned on returning his feelings, his consistent availability made her feel immediately better.

She was suffering because HanChol had graduated from university, and instead of allowing them to begin their new life together, it had only brought on fresh anxieties. At first, it shocked both of them that he couldn't find a job immediately. Many companies had laid off workers since the market crash, and only a few were hiring new employees. There were thousands of applicants for perhaps five or ten openings at a firm, which were first given to the Japanese and then the pro-Japanese elites. Without family connections or wealth, a degree was utterly worthless. Out of pride, HanChol refused to write letters to his estranged Andong relatives or hobnob with young bourgeois men from college—although avoiding the latter, strictly speaking, was less from his integrity than from an instinctive understanding that they would not welcome him. The more Jade tried to soothe him, the more HanChol acted aloof and cold, because he found himself becoming isolated in a woman's love when he should be liberated in the company of other men. Jade knew that he felt this way. So she tried to demand as little as possible from him, even if that ground her down with unhappiness.

Jade had believed that all he required was some distance and a job, and rejoiced when HanChol finally found a position as a mechanic at a bicycle shop. It didn't even require a college degree, but he had already spent months sending résumés to dozens of different companies and banks to no avail. If HanChol was disappointed, he hid it well. Years of fixing his own rickshaw soon gave him the ability to figure out any problems that a bicycle might have just by looking and tinkering for a few minutes. The night before, HanChol had come over and told her how he had even fixed his boss's own bicycle.

"This job wasn't what I had in mind exactly, but it's at least consistent. And my boss pays better than most. He said he was very impressed by how quickly I fixed his brakes, and we talked a little about what I had studied in university," HanChol said in bed. His right arm was wrapped around Jade, whose head with its cropped, wavy hair was resting snugly on his shoulder.

"See? He recognizes your talent. Before long, he will give you more important tasks and promote you. And then you'll be set." Jade beamed at him. Although she refrained from even thinking this directly in her head, she had a growing anticipation regarding their future, and she thought that HanChol would bring it up once he felt stabilized. While he was studying, he used to say from time to time that he wouldn't let her down and that he would make her happy. More than a few times, he had said he wished that they could be together forever. Hearing these words in his arms had given her a feeling of pure luminescence, like a firefly that stores up the sun's rays by day and fluoresces by night—humble yet miraculously alive. It was that awareness of having tasted life, of being *kissed* by life. But her happiness was dependent on him and thus easily broken.

HanChol had stopped saying that he wished they could be together forever. Since when exactly, Jade could not know.

Instead of those tender words, he mindlessly squeezed her shoulder and said, "Yes, I hope I'll move up in this job. I mean to show him what I can do. He is rather absent-minded, and the business is run very badly by an associate . . ."

What she had wanted to hear was that once he was established, he would tell his mother about her and that arrangements would be made. With disappointment Jade sensed that he spoke rather more about himself than about her or them together. So she clung to him all the more affectionately. "Kiss me," she whispered, guiding his narrow hips over her. She fell into the familiar pleasure as he kissed her breasts and plunged himself into her with the same longing and urgency. Her face lit up when she became certain that he still desired her just as much as at the beginning. A man's eyes revealed everything while making love. But after finishing, he no longer kissed her or broke into that unconscious smile.

All afternoon, Jade mindlessly went through her scenes, preoccupied by HanChol. When the filming wrapped in the early evening, her costar asked, "Aren't you in the mood for something hot after all this? Would you like to come with me to get some udon?"

He had a wonderful, anxious twinkle in his attractive eyes. His elegant wool suit was impeccably cut and pressed, and she had once laughed to herself imagining that it could stand up on its own without a wearer. But he really was a very nice man.

"Oh, thank you but I can't today," Jade replied, blushing. "I have plans already. Some other day, perhaps." She pulled on her pale blue coat with a rabbit fur collar, noticing how her costar was trying to hide his disappointment and feeling both pity and elation. She bowed to him and got into a cab, which took her to Lotus's villa.

"It's been such a long time. Oh, you look cold! Hurry up and come inside." Lotus greeted her at the front gates herself, placing a hand on her friend's back. They rarely spent time together, and several months had passed since Lotus had last come to Dani's house. But Lotus had called her, asking her to visit, and she'd accepted. They both felt a little disingenuous in each other's presence but tried sincerely, as old friends do, to conceal that artificiality.

"Where's Sunmi? How is the little darling?" Jade asked, looking around for Lotus's daughter, who had turned three. Sunmi had gone for a walk with her maid, and her mother had the happy look of a parent relieved of a toddler.

"You are so lucky you don't have a child, Jade," Lotus said in her old familiar tone, once they were settled in her room. "Not that I don't love her, because of course I would do anything for my daughter, but . . . I miss my old life. The stage, the performances . . ."

"You can surely go back? They still play your record at all the cafés, you know." Before Sunmi was born, Lotus had recorded some songs that had turned her into a household name. It had given her a small fortune, and President Ma a larger one.

"Do they really? I'm hardly the one to know—I haven't gone out at night in ages." Lotus sighed. "Sometimes I just really miss the old days, don't you, Jade? When everything wonderful seemed possible? Now I'm not so sure. I just try to—" She faltered. "I just try to keep my head up."

"I do miss the old days. We were all so innocent." Jade fought the tears in her eyes. She was thinking of Lotus and HanChol and every other person she had once loved with absolute certainty and purity, without fear of getting hurt. Even JungHo had quietly slipped away from her side, and she regretted not being a better friend to him. Lotus reached over and patted her arm, and she laughed. The hotness of tears was somehow very healing.

"I have an idea," Jade said between sniffles. "Why don't we go out this evening? To be honest, I could really use a drink."

Lotus resisted the suggestion for only a moment; she was actually thrilled to have an outing. Humming softly, she sat down in front of her vanity with its powders and rouges. Although she was never beautiful, she still looked young. Her new hairstyle was similar to Jade's, cut to shoulder length and curled with tongs, and it suited her features.

The maid and Sunmi returned as she was choosing her outfit. Jade noticed that Lotus's daughter was not a pretty child, felt guilty for having this thought, and thus acted overly awed by her. The nanny prompted Sunmi to say hello. She only put a tiny finger on her lips, staring around the room with a slow watchfulness that struck Jade as unendearing.

Lotus said distractedly, "She's so quiet, so polite. She never cries in front of me. Once she fell down while the nanny was away, and she screwed up her whole face trying to keep herself from crying." Hearing this, Jade resolved to show Sunmi genuine warmth and kissed her on top of her head. Lotus lightly raked the child's new hair, uncut and translucent like dewy spider silk. "There, there . . . And now it's time for bed," she said, sending the girl and her nanny away in a hurry.

The evening was blustery and overcast. Lotus selected a maroon silk dress, a cloche, and a dark green overcoat—autumnal and rich against the grayness awaiting them outside. She was buoyed by the voluptuous pleasure of being perfectly dressed for a certain kind of weather. Jade was already putting on her shoes when Lotus stopped at her vanity to roll a cigarette. She smoked it halfway before she noticed Jade's impatience.

"It's mostly tobacco and a bit of opium. Just to take the edge off," she said. "You want to try it?"

"No, I'm fine. At this rate we'll still be here at midnight," Jade said, and Lotus put out the cigarette carefully and left it on her ashtray.

When they finally set off, a hoarse wind was blowing away empty pails by the well and maids were skidding about, tearing off the washings from clothing lines.

There were countless cafés in Seoul, and each had its own following. The businessmen and pro-Japanese wealthy went to Café Vienna; the Nationalists went to Café Terrace; the Communists went to the Yellow Horse; the students and the artists went to Café Gitane; and the Japanese went to their own cafés, run by the Japanese. But everyone who was known in society went to Café Seahorn, which was owned by a young bourgeois poet. Somehow the fact that he was a pro-Japanese landowner's son with the best education, but also a Leftist and an artist who believed in free love, made it possible for him to attract the most interesting people from every corner of society. Jade was acquainted with him, and this was where she was taking her friend.

"Isn't this lovely? You can see everyone from this spot," Jade said to Lotus as they slid into the crimson leather booth. She turned toward the pretty waitress and ordered two cups of mocha.

"Why is this so much more delicious than normal coffee?" Lotus whispered.

"It has chocolate in it—isn't it amazing?" Jade giggled. "We start with this, then we'll have some alcohol. You see how people are just talking now. Later on, everyone will be dancing. Oh, they're playing 'La Paloma'!" Jade flitted from one thought to the next. She pointed out a well-known woman painter who'd married a diplomat and traveled the world with him; but while abroad, she had an affair with her husband's best friend, and he divorced her as soon as they returned. Now she struggled to make a living by selling paintings and doing illustrations for magazines. There was also a novelist who was sitting alone, ostensibly reading an American magazine that was stocked at the café, but was really there for one of the waitresses, who was his mistress.

"They all go for the café girls these days. More modern than the courtesans, I've been told," Jade said, glancing at their waitress, whose apron emphasized her tiny waist. She looked no older than twenty. "And not as demanding as high-born Modern Girls."

"Sometimes it feels strange to think that we started out learning classical poetry and traditional songs at that pavilion under the weeping willow. And my mother in her regal silks and jewels, and her lifelong devotion to the one man who gave her that silver ring . . . That feels like a hundred years ago."

"Don't you miss her? Why don't you take Sunmi to visit her in PyongYang?"

"President Ma wouldn't allow it," Lotus said quietly to her cup of mocha. The music changed. A young gentleman was headed their way, and they both smiled in preparation for his arrival.

"Miss Jade, what a pleasure. Why have you been away for so long? We've missed you here," said the gentleman, who was the poet-owner of the café. He was somewhere between twenty-five and thirty, of an average height and build. His shirtwaist sans jacket, the horn-rimmed glasses, and amiable mannerisms were proof of his bohemian status. He took hold of Jade's left hand and kissed it passionately, as if to say, "this is only half in jest." When Jade introduced her friend, he was equally overjoyed to meet the famous singer and ordered a round of American whiskey to be brought out. He had the gift of talking to two women with equal attention and flirting without implication.

"So what does the name mean? Seahorn," Lotus asked him, awash in her first taste of whiskey.

"Oh, it's something I made up. You know, we all have those things that we just love without rationality. Actually, if it's rational, then it's not really love. So the thing I love the most in the world . . ." The gentleman lingered over his words, licking the whiskey off his lips.

"It's the sound of ships. When I was a student, I once traveled to Busan on my own. I lived in a boardinghouse near the harbor for a month, just reading and writing from morning until nightfall. After dark, I would light a candle to keep going, and it was possible to believe that there was nothing in the world except myself and my books. It felt like my room was the cabin of a ship, somewhere out in the middle of the ocean. And every afternoon between three and four P.M., there would be the sound of the ships at the dock. The big ships would go, *BOO—BOOOO* . . . and the smaller ones would answer, *Doo—doooo* . . . Those ship horns made me happier than I'd ever felt in my life. If I could bottle that sound, I would pour it little by little when I'm sad and drink it like whiskey." He smiled. "Have you ever been to the sea, Miss Lotus?"

Neither Lotus nor Jade had ever been to the sea. Not even to InCheon, which was so close.

"That's right, you are both Northerners . . . Of course, that's why you two are so pretty. Not for nothing that PyongYang courtesans are the most celebrated of all. Oh, the song has just ended. If you'll excuse me, I'm going to put on another record." He bowed and turned away.

"How charming he is," Lotus said, once he was out of earshot.

"Yes, but don't you also find that he's not all there with you?" Jade took another sip of her whiskey. "His story for instance. It's like he wasn't telling it *for us*, not really. He's told that story to anyone who asks. He doesn't really care about us knowing, ultimately. Why are you smiling? Am I too cynical?"

"I'm smiling because I love you so dearly. My oldest friend." Lotus embraced Jade with one arm.

"But do you agree? Don't you think I'm right?" Jade was thinking of the story of the owl HanChol had told. He'd always made her feel that he was telling that story only for her. He'd wanted to be understood by *her*. She missed him terribly.

"Yes, you are right. But you were always pickier with men. Oh, listen, Jade!" They both stopped speaking; it was Lotus's record that was put on the gramophone. The poet-owner waved at them from across the room. Couples were starting to get up and dance, as if the music had awakened them from sleep like enchanted people in a fairy tale. The liquid light of the lamps spilled over them and their shadows whirled around the walls.

"I'm so glad you brought me here." Lotus put her head on Jade's shoulder. "You know, President Ma doesn't love me and hasn't for a long time. He doesn't even pretend to love Sunmi—a fourth daughter and a bastard at that, when he'd really wanted a son. I'm pretty sure too that he's been sleeping with that whore of a secretary." Lotus actually hadn't thought about the last part, but once she'd spoken it out loud she knew it had to be true.

"I'm afraid he will leave me. Or I think about leaving him. It sounds like two completely different things but the end result is the same—he'd be fine, better than fine, and I'd be destroyed. So I dread both options . . . but I'm so unhappy now. What should I do?"

"You don't have to stay with him forever," Jade said, taking her friend's hand.

"But no one else will ever love me again. I will be an old and abandoned woman, a cast-off mistress."

"You see that painter, the one who was married to the diplomat." Jade indicated with her glance at the woman in a crimson velvet dress, who was now dancing with the poet-owner. "She was thirty with four children by the time she was having affairs in Paris and Berlin. You're only twenty-five and with one child." The painter whispered something in her partner's ear and then they threw their heads back in laughter. It was possible to believe that she didn't care about her ex-husband, or his best friend—her lover—who had also abandoned her.

"And now no one in her family acknowledges her and people jeer at her behind her back. No, that's not for me." Lotus sighed. "The luckiest one among us is my sister, right?"

"Right."

Luna was thirty years old and still as lovely as ever. She had bought herself out of the courtesan guild registry and worked as a secretary at the American consulate. It paid her decently and allowed her to be independent. Her supervisor was besotted with her, but she pretended not to notice. Unlike the two younger women, Luna seemed content to be left alone. Solitude became her like a beautiful coat.

The pretty waitress returned with two glasses of golden-brown liquor. "Cognac, compliments of the gentleman in the corner booth," she said, pointing with her glance. "Not the officer. The one with the bow tie," she added. Jade froze when she recognized his face. He was no longer in uniform but still wore the same arrogant smile while studying her from across the room. He said something to his friend, picked up his own glass, and started heading to their table in his confident, quick strides.

18

RAINY NIGHT

1933

"WHY DON'T YOU COME WITH ME? DON'T BE BORING," COUNT ITO said to Colonel Yamada, putting out his cigarette on the crystal ashtray.

"What is this about? I can't keep up with your whims."

"Don't you have eyes? You can see that there are two women at that table. One of them is quite beautiful, maybe even extraordinary. I actually met her years ago."

"I don't understand your fascination with these café girls and prostitutes." Colonel Yamada smiled coldly, shaking his head. He was on leave from the war in Manchuria and was meeting his brother-in-law for the first time in three years. After the harshness at the front fighting both the Chinese and the Korean armies, the carefree and ignorant ways of Ito and society in general rankled him.

"She's not a café girl. She's a movie actress," Ito countered, already slipping out of the booth.

Ito was one of those men who obsess over a woman and then forget about her quite completely and suddenly. Since walking out of Jade's dressing room eight years ago, Ito had not thought once about her. That encounter had satisfied his appetite, and he'd found other cravings. Some of that was for other women, but he never was truly interested in women or even people in general. There was always an element of lowering himself when he got too near another person—this, indeed, was why he preferred Yamada, in whose company he felt the debasement the least. Instead of people, Ito liked beautiful objects, ideas, and the empty space between things and ideas. He would have been perfectly happy to slip inside that white void and breathe in the cool, fresh air for the rest of his life.

Occasionally, however, Ito became interested in others almost in spite of himself. Jade had completely changed since the last time he'd seen her. It wasn't just that she was wearing a Western dress or that she'd cut her hair and curled it with tongs. Even her features looked quite different and somehow more captivating. Yet he'd recognized her by her immutable essence, a certain halo around her physique. He wanted to study her up close.

"It's been a very long time since we last saw each other," he said as he sat down next to her in the booth. She glared at him with eyes that seemed even brighter than before. Her friend, fashionably dressed but unquestionably homely, also looked insulted by his overture. He paid her no more attention than to a piece of counterfeit antique.

"How have you been? I've noticed your films," Ito said, his gaze fixed on Jade.

"Colonel," Jade said in slow and measured Japanese. "I've no doubt there are plenty of women here who would be happy to talk to you. I'm not one of them."

"But they don't interest me. Look, do you know what it's like when one has everything?"

"Can't imagine," Jade said sarcastically; nevertheless, Ito knew she was being pulled in.

"I have wealth, youth, intelligence, power, women . . . There's nothing I lack. I never have to try very hard. It starts to become very dull—even the company of pretty women. It's so rare to see something that genuinely piques my interest, as you do."

"Why?"

Ito rested his chin on one hand and looked into Jade's lovely black eyes. Her skin was lucent and velvety, from her cheeks all the way to the marble-like décolletage above her V-shaped neckline. She was at her peak radiance as a woman and was not even aware of it. It almost gave him pain.

"I will tell you if you dance with me," he said at last. "Don't refuse. You're a dancer and this is a terrific waltz."

He stood up and extended his hand. People were watching them out of the corners of their eyes: the handsome Japanese millionaire, newly made a count, who had just bought gold and iron mines from a French businessman; and the famous actress in all the movies. She took his hand.

Everyone watched them dance. The normally well-trained café girls stopped serving the guests and stood off to the side to whisper to one another. The count and the actress made a brilliant pair.

Yamada observed the change in his friend with quiet fascination. Ito moved with easy confidence, drawing the woman's waist close to his body with one arm. Yamada had never danced before in his life. For a moment he imagined it was himself whose arm encircled the beautiful woman in the middle of the dance floor. Ito had been right about her—she was exceptional. It was not just her face and body, which were both imperfect, but the quality of her presence and movement that drew one's eyes.

The couple parted when the song ended, and Ito walked over to Yamada's table.

"She wants to leave, and I said I'll give her a ride back. Will you be okay taking a cab?"

"Of course."

"I'll see you soon. Tell Mineko I said hello."

LOTUS AND JADE WALKED OUT together and Ito followed, putting on his coat one sleeve after the other; he opened the car door himself

20

THE DREAMERS

1937

EVERYONE DREAMS, BUT ONLY SOME PEOPLE ARE DREAMERS. THE NON-dreamers, by far more numerous, are those who see the world as it is. Then there are the few dreamers, who see the world as *they* are. The moon, the river, the train station, the sound of rain, and even something as mundane as porridge become something else with many layers. The world feels like an oil painting rather than a photograph, and the dreamers are forever seeing hidden colors where others just see the top shade. The nondreamers look through glasses, and the dreamers through a prism.

This is not a quality determined by intelligence or passion, two things most often conflated with dreaming. Dani, the most intelligent and passionate person Jade had ever known, had a vision that was as crisp and sharply outlined as her mannerisms and principles. Dani was not interested in the unfathomable when there were wrongs to be righted, preferably with utmost grace and aplomb. When Jade stopped dancing and acting, she felt as if all the colors had gone out of her life. She was now in the world of the nondreamers, a strange and suffocating place, and felt lonelier than she'd ever been; but Dani acted as though she just had to accept reality and move on.

"It's the depression," Dani said one morning, poring over her newspaper through her magnifying glass. "People don't have money to spend at movie theaters. Many restaurants are closing now, too. You can't be too hard on yourself."

"But, Auntie, you know *Hong GilDong* just came out and it's a hit. And last fall, the remake of *One Lucky Day*. It's been only six years since the original, did they have to make a new one already?" Jade said, picking at her breakfast of pine nut porridge. "It sold out every night for almost six months."

"That's because it's a talkie. People are mad for anything new. Your studio should have foreseen that. Can't you talk to them?"

Dani folded her newspaper in half and looked up at Jade as though nothing could be simpler. Despite the trauma of her arrest and her heartbreaks, Dani didn't understand defeat. To her, failure was like stockings with holes: it could happen to anyone, but if you allowed it to show in public then you were to blame. Taking care to contain and discard your failures was as much a matter of good manners as high principles. It was a kind of cool, aristocratic sensibility that made Dani a better role model than a friend. So Jade hadn't been able to talk about her studio's bankruptcy or her dwindling savings at thirty, the precise age at which she was supposed to be wealthy and independent, because her value as a woman had reached its logical expiration.

The only person who would understand her predicament was Lotus. Even though they hadn't seen each other in months, Jade was certain that her friend would make her feel better. They would laugh about the old days, their girlhood dreams of becoming celebrated courtesans, the many handsome and rich lovers they were each supposed to have by this age. She even felt that they could take this moment of vulnerability to renew their friendship and plot out the future, whatever that may be. For all her faults, Lotus had always had an inspiring appetite for life. Whereas others thought of the world as a vast insidious sea or some such field of battle, Lotus took the approach that it was all just a game or a basket of fruits—to be played and to be tasted. That was her virtue—and she often had the effect of transferring her attitude to whoever was around her. Her thoughts thus gathered, Jade put on her hat and started walking toward Lotus's house.

It was a lovely day, hot in the sun and cool in the shade, and she strolled on the road half dappled with shadows of the storefronts. People were ambling along, students were just getting out of school and flocking to the sweets shop. Delivery men whipped past on their bicycles. Light danced off the glass windows of the department store, and pasted on its walls were posters for new talkie films and singers. There were tables displayed outside the bookstore and she stopped here to leaf through the titles. These were mostly novels and periodicals, and in one literary magazine she found some names she knew from Café Seahorn. She flipped to a random page and found an illustration by the painter in the crimson velvet dress. It was not a drawing of women's liberation and free love, which she was known for, but a painting of a little girl wearing a yellow headband, entitled *Daughter.* Jade closed the magazine and kept walking.

When she reached Lotus's house, an unfamiliar housekeeper answered the door.

"Is your mistress home?" Jade asked.

"She hasn't been home for the past three days," the old woman replied grudgingly, as though Jade had asked the most inconvenient question.

"What do you mean, she hasn't been home?" Jade frowned, walking in without being told. Looking around her and calling for her friend, she opened Lotus's bedroom door. A faint ambiguous smell that she'd first detected in the hallway rushed over her like a wave. The room was empty, but that odor—floral and musky like young girls' clothes just taken off, still warm with body heat—reminded

Jade of the last time she'd visited Lotus. It had been a warm spring day, but Lotus had insisted on staying under a thick winter comforter as they talked.

"I want to go out somewhere fun, like we used to in the old days," Lotus had said then. "But not today. Today I feel tired."

"Okay, we'll go out as soon as you feel better, I promise," Jade had said, and Lotus smiled and grasped her hand. More than anything else, it was that lopsided smile that broke Jade's heart. Lotus had grinned so much as a child, even while her mother and older sister treated her with disdain. There had been beauty in her innocence—Jade could only recognize that now, as a woman.

The housekeeper was waiting for her in the hallway with a look of annoyance. Jade suppressed the urge to yell and said as calmly as possible, "Did she say where she was going?"

"Not a clue, miss." The old woman shrugged. "She wasn't in her right mind for a while, as you know."

Jade blushed and choked down the anger that was directed toward the housekeeper, but was really meant for herself. Had she really been so blind to how badly her friend had become addicted to opium? It was a common vice, almost as common as drink and tobacco. The most fashionable men and women and the most admired artists made a ritual of visiting the dream world once or twice a week. But the majority of them also didn't spend their days lying on their cots, wasting away until they were old and weak before their time. It sickened Jade that she had made excuses for Lotus instead of confronting her—simply because she'd had enough problems of her own.

Jade returned to Lotus's room, hoping to find any hints of her whereabouts. Some of the furniture Jade remembered seeing had been removed, but in the corner above the sideboard, there was a telephone. She picked it up, hesitated for a second, and said, "Operator, President Ma of the Grand Oriental Cinema, please."

There was a pause as the operator put her through, and Jade felt her heart beat fast. She had never spoken directly to this man, whom Lotus had described with so much infatuation, then possessiveness, and finally, hatred. There was a clicking sound and a male voice answered, "Hello?"

"President Ma. This is Jade Anh—Lotus's friend," she said. The silence that followed lasted only a few seconds, but felt much longer and colder.

"Yes, of course," he said at last. "How can I help you?"

"I've just come by Lotus's house, and she's not here . . . The housekeeper tells me she hasn't been home in the past three days."

President Ma cleared his throat. "Yes, I heard," he said, and his indifference snapped Jade's self-restraint.

"Aren't you worried about her? Are you even looking for her—and what about Sunmi?" she said, noticing as she spoke the child's absence in the silent house.

"Sunmi is with me. She'll be going to school in Japan in a couple of weeks." His voice was not angry, just contemptuous. "If you're as close a friend as you pretend to be, you'd know that Lotus has always been a terrible mother. Even in the best of times she was not fit to be raising my daughter. Now she's half out of her mind."

A nauseating thought came into Jade's head. "Did you make Lotus leave?"

President Ma laughed mirthlessly. "Can anyone really force another person to leave or stay? But she certainly can't come back."

Jade hung up, shivering. The housekeeper was standing by the door, not even hiding the fact that she was eavesdropping. Her face was lit up in the smug smile of servants who discover their employers' vulgarity.

"Just yesterday, he told me to get the house ready for a new mistress. He's ordered new furniture for her too. She's young, and he thinks she'll give him a son. It is shameful, even for a man like that." The housekeeper clucked her tongue.

"Never mind about the new woman. She doesn't concern me,"

Jade snapped. The old woman glared at her and then shook her head, swinging her loose jowl side to side.

"It serves you courtesans right to be abandoned—stealing other women's husbands for a living," she sneered darkly as Jade walked out the gates.

JADE BEGAN HER SEARCH in the very first place she and Lotus had been in Seoul—the train station—and made her way through all the landmarks of their shared lives, from MyungWol to the Joseon Theatre. She inquired with the staff at each place, but no one could remember seeing Lotus recently. Standing awkwardly outside the theater, she watched the matinee goers leave in groups of three and four, and recalled how Lotus had pleaded to go out and have fun when they last saw each other. She ran as fast as she could to Café Seahorn.

It was already past six thirty when she arrived at the café. Even under the circumstances, she was enveloped by the comfort of its familiar decadence, the intimate air of everyone knowing everyone. But the café had changed since Japan began clamping down harder in the peninsula, spurred by its conquest of vast Manchuria. The guests were whispering in subdued voices, and even the music sounded softer. Jade remembered her first visit to the café, when she'd marveled at the crystal ashtrays on every table. "Aren't these a little too fine to be left around like this?" she had asked the poet-owner. He had answered cheerfully, tapping his cigarette smartly on the side of an ashtray: "Why, Miss Jade, that's what true luxury is—using fine things in a casual way." Those ashtrays were now gone. But more changed than all those things was Jade herself, with her tired skin and unfashionable clothes.

There were only a few women in the café, and it didn't take long for her to realize that Lotus was not among them. She felt the energy give out from the back of her knees; she'd walked everywhere in

Seoul for a good seven hours. She collapsed onto the nearest booth and folded her head over her arms. Warm tears were prickling her eyes, as much from missing her friend as from the fatigue. *I'm not going to break down. Not here,* she thought, taking a deep breath. Raising her head, she spotted the poet-owner across the room, weaving through the blur of the blinking candles. She waved at him, but he didn't see her. He slid into a booth, which was curious, Jade thought. Although he often chatted and danced with his guests, he never sat with them. His face was turned toward Jade, and the one guest at the booth—a man—was facing the opposite way. The poet-owner was sinking deep into his seat with his hands down, and she realized that he was passing something to the man under the table. They appeared to chat for a few more minutes, then the guest rose. As he turned around to head for the exit, his eyes met Jade's and she inwardly staggered in recognition. It was JungHo.

"I didn't expect to see you here," Jade said as he sat down next to her and she clasped her hands around his.

"The owner is a friend of mine . . . Are you okay?" JungHo replied, deliberately changing the subject.

"As a matter of fact, I'm not," Jade said, her panic finally rushing out in his presence. "Lotus is gone. She's been missing for three days. I went everywhere looking for her."

"Hey, slow down. Everything is going to be okay," JungHo said, rising. "Let's get out of here. We can talk while looking for her."

Jade explained from the beginning: how cruel and indifferent the housekeeper had been, how President Ma was already preparing the house for his new mistress (JungHo blushed a little upon hearing Ma's name, but listened without interjecting). Most terrifying of all was the fact that Lotus was out wandering Seoul with little money and even less presence of mind, without having told any of her friends.

"She's really gotten herself in a bad way," JungHo said when they'd been walking in silence for a while.

"I knew for a long time, but a lot of people do it," Jade replied, feeling calmer in JungHo's presence. The sun was sending its last rays through the breaks in the buildings. There was a sense that all visible things in the world were the shadows of a truth, which radiated out only through the chinks. "Without alcohol or opium, how would they cope? There'd be even more suicides than now," she said, thinking of the deaths that had become as common as a cold. "Sometimes people just seem to get up one morning, have breakfast, and decide to hang themselves."

JungHo stopped walking and turned to her. "Hey, don't talk like that," he said, a bit roughly. She felt offended until he resumed walking and added:

"I've been within an inch of death countless times in my life. Do you know what happens then? You can actually feel it physically. Sometimes it's like a heavy blanket, when you've been starving and there's not an ounce of strength left in you. Sometimes it's like a dog, lurking in the corner and ready to attack." He squinted his eyes at the sun's last outburst.

"Each time, I knew it would be easier and less painful if I just let it take me. No one is holding their breath wishing me a long life, you know? And each time, at the last moment, do you know what happens?" he asked. Jade shook her head, frightened.

"You get one, clear chance at giving into it, or refusing. And I've said No every time. I don't know why—but the more reasons I have to die, the less I want to give in," he said. "Even when the sky is falling down, even when no one will miss you, life is still better than death."

It was Jade's turn to stop and stare at him. "I wish you'd stop saying that no one cares if you die. What am I, then?"

"If you care, that matters more than everyone else in the world combined. I just might never die!" He chuckled, and she laughed with him, feeling at ease for the first time in a long while.

"Hey, I almost forgot," Jade said, nudging his ribs. "What were you doing in there?"

"What do you mean?" He shrugged. "Now and then, I like to have coffee."

"Don't even *try*, JungHo." She snorted. "You think you can lie to me? To *me*?" She poked playfully at his side again—then stopped walking, seeing his changing expression. JungHo looked around; once he was sure they weren't being watched, he opened his jacket just an inch to reveal the muzzle of a revolver. She blushed, realizing with a start that she had been elbowing the gun.

"Was that what he gave you under the table?" Jade whispered as they started walking again. He nodded.

"A Japanese officer got too drunk one night and left it behind. It's been harder and harder to source weapons within the country—every single gun counts," JungHo said softly. It had never been very clear to Jade what he did; she knew this was to protect both of them. But just then, under the fresh darkness of the sundown, she felt his urgency to share a little of his secrets before it became too late.

"With the crackdown getting worse, we don't know how much longer we can keep up the resistance, at least in the peninsula itself. It's frustrating. I wish I could be of greater service than being the delivery man . . . But for that I would have to read and write better, and speak some Chinese besides. No matter how hard I try, my mentor doesn't think I'm ready." He bit his lips in bitter disappointment. Jade didn't know how to comfort him, so she reached out and patted his arm. That seemed to soothe him, as always.

"I thought the owner was just a dandy," she said after a long pause. "Soft hands, pretty hair."

"People are brave in different ways, Jade."

Because it had been such a nice, sunny day, it stayed balmy even as the darkness ripened. Many young lovers were promenading on the boulevard, and the shops played their SP records outside so that passersby could join in. Soft, hazy, nocturnal noises—laughter, a car engine, a dog barking—broke through the calm surface of silence, like muffled voices behind a drawn curtain onstage. Jade breathed in deeply the mixture of sounds and the smell of lilac. Everywhere around them, life was happening without their knowing, and their lives were also happening in the presence of all else. All existences were touching lightly as air and leaving invisible fingerprints.

"It's too dark now," she said softly.

"Let's get you home. But we'll find her soon, Jade. I go everywhere in the city, and know many people besides. I'll find her for you."

They turned a corner and headed in the direction of Jade's house. Somewhere nearby a record was playing and grew louder as they approached. A crowd of a few dozen people were standing in front of the record store, singing along to the latest hit. The SP had a vellum quality that caressed the atmosphere. The rounded plucking of the double bass was like rain pattering on water.

"It's 'Manchu Tango,'" Jade told him. "It wasn't going to pass censorship with that title though, so they changed it to 'Mandu Tango.' But everyone knows it's really about moving to Manchuria and missing home. Apparently the activists in the north took it up as their anthem." The crowd was changing mandu to Manchu in the refrain, and young couples were discreetly swaying side by side with their hands intertwined.

JungHo turned to her and held out his hand. "Would you like to dance?" He had a nervous twinkle in his eyes. The crisp crease of his pants, the carefully combed hair—all the effort he made, principally, for her—made her wish she liked him that way.

"We can't, we'll get arrested." She smiled in apology. Ballroom dancing was officially illegal, and although everyone knew that people danced in cafés and secret clubs, doing so on the streets was out of the question.

"It's so dark and no one will notice," JungHo said, hand still outstretched. He appeared determined but just under the surface she knew he was terrified of embarrassing himself. Even the darkness of the night and his own permanent tan couldn't hide the redness rising to his cheeks. She took his right hand with her left, then they stood both facing the gramophone and rocked side to side.

Jade closed her eyes. JungHo's hand locked around her own was hot and clammy. She tried to imagine that it was HanChol's hand that she was holding, but nothing about their hands was alike. HanChol's had been well shaped with long and sturdy fingers and she'd loved even the greenish veins that stood up under the skin. But more than their appearance it was the touch that revealed all their differences. The older courtesans used to joke that men were indistinguishable once you blew out the candle. In reality, when you stopped looking at their expressions and hearing their words and focused simply on how they felt, you perceived their disparity more keenly. If love was just the deepest shade of friendship, so deep as to look like a distinct color but actually on the same spectrum of loyalty, then she loved JungHo. So much. But if it was something else altogether, then she did not.

The calm fabric of the night was torn by a sound like an approaching thunderstorm. But the moon was still visible in the blue-black sky—it was the roar of engines that buried the music. People stopped singing and watched as army trucks rolled by, flying the Japanese flag on their hoods and carrying soldiers in the back. Suddenly, people were murmuring among themselves: "Japan is attacking Beijing. It's finally happening."

"China gave up Manchuria, but it will rouse itself for its mainland."

"They've woken up the sleeping giant."

"Shh, the birds and the mice have ears. Watch what you say."

"It was bad enough as it is . . . A full-out war and we'll likely all get killed."

"What's going on?" Jade asked, rapidly being pulled out of her dream world by the noises rushing around her. JungHo was saying something but his words were being drowned by the sirens. The yellow headlights of the trucks glared into her face and she closed her eyes once more. The only thing she felt sure of was the firm grip of JungHo's hand, not letting go.

PART III

1941–1948

21

PURPLE SHADOWS

1941

WHEN JUNGHO ARRIVED AT THE BACK GATE OF THE OLD CHINESE RES-taurant, an unfamiliar guard with a shaved head was posted outside.

"Password," the guard said, crossing his arms over his vast chest. JungHo paused; he hadn't heard that there was a new door policy.

"Nam JungHo," he said at last.

"Ah, *oyabun*!" The numbskull—as JungHo called him in his mind—snapped to attention and bowed deeply from the waist. "Please forgive my ignorance!" He opened the door as wide as the hinges would allow, and the shorter man passed through.

The courtyard was unrecognizable from his boyhood years. The chestnut tree in the center had been cut down and YoungGu's dog that had been tied to it had also died long ago. The disappearance of its howls and yelps left a strangely lasting void in the air, like a place on the wall where an old frame has been removed.

JungHo felt a sharp pang at this, more than he felt at the death of many humans—both the ones that had nothing to do with him, and others for whom he'd played a crucial role in speeding up the mortal process. He would not, would never, become a habitual killer; but he'd long believed that with the exception of very few individuals there was no one who was truly good and honorable. They lied, cheated, betrayed their friends, family, and country—then doubled back, then doubled back again, just to save their skins. When the government-general decreed that all Koreans had to change their names to Japanese ones, half the country had immediately lined up to cast aside what their parents and their forebears had passed down. They believed in nothing, he thought, if they could give up their own names so easily. His contempt for humanity was becoming more pronounced as the years went on, and even made him value his own life less. He took a deep breath to clear this thought; there was a side of him still that wanted to hold on to his little remaining innocence.

The courtyard was filled with people waiting in silence to barter their gold and jewels. At the top of the queue, YoungGu was seated in a booth, flanked by a guard on each side and receiving the supplicants one at a time. He had stopped running the restaurant when the war broke out and started buying goods from the provinces and selling them for an unspeakable price in Seoul. The army had long ago confiscated all the valuables they could, but somehow the heirlooms kept surfacing from inside silk-filled comforters and jars hidden under wooden floors. Once those ran out, desperate people brought land deeds and promises of repayment with staggering interest—JungHo knew this part without being told.

With a hand over his heart, YoungGu insisted to JungHo that he didn't do any of this for money. It was something that had to be done, and it was better done by him, a man of the people, was it not? Nonetheless, he took to the black market business wholeheartedly, the way some people enjoy themselves and become more sharply alive during crises—those ambiguous spaces between clear life and death. To chaos, they reacted with a kind of meaningless sanguinity, unlike those limp-wristed intellectuals who lost their desire to keep on living. What other alternatives there were to these two modes, JungHo did not know. He noticed that YoungGu looked happier than in the early years of his marriage when the children were small and the restaurant was thriving.

Upon catching sight of JungHo, YoungGu waved away his subordinates, rose, and walked briskly toward him with open arms. He had lost some weight around his middle since the start of the war, but in a way that made him look younger and healthier. He was wearing a brown corduroy waistcoat over a clean cotton shirt and trousers, like a well-to-do pharmacist receiving helpless patients.

"Why did that numbskull at the gate call me *oyabun*?" JungHo said, once they'd finished trading their usual greetings. "This isn't the yakuza." He frowned.

"Sorry, Chief, he really is stupid," YoungGu said, leading the way to a back storage where he kept the most precious goods for his friends.

"But you'll be happy to see what I set aside for you. One sack each of barley and potatoes, two heads of cabbage, and a bag of little, dried anchovies. You couldn't buy these nowadays even with money stacked from floor to ceiling . . . No, stop, put that away," he said, shaking his head firmly and deflecting JungHo's hand.

JungHo frowned, although not out of displeasure this time. "I can't just take this—even if we're old friends. When I went to see Loach for rice a fortnight ago, he did end up accepting some silver from me."

The fact was that when JungHo offered some of MyungBo's silver to his closest friend, he had expected it would be refused. Instead, Loach took it, recorded the transaction in his book, and then turned to talking about some other unrelated subject without any embarrassment. They both knew that Loach was hardly struggling—he was getting as many valuables and deeds as he could ever want in a lifetime. JungHo had acted as if nothing was wrong and left with a friendly handshake, but inside he'd made up his mind to never see Loach again.

YoungGu snorted. "Of course Loach took it, that selfish bastard. But remember how many times when we each had nothing but a pair of balls, you gave us your food? Remember how many times you gave me a little bit more from your bowl so I could share with my dog?" YoungGu kept smiling widely but his eyes were rather moist. "I will never forget that."

JungHo was relieved to see that his friend's generosity was real. He wrapped his arm around YoungGu's shoulder and slapped it heartily a few times. "Yes, thank you. Of course I remember, I remember," he said, regretting his earlier thought about the worthlessness of most people. It was not in his nature to stay coldhearted for a long time, even in a war.

"I'll walk you out, Chief," YoungGu said as they went back through the bustling courtyard. "It's so hot already, and summer has only just begun . . . Why, what's the matter?"

JungHo had stopped walking. In the middle of the queue, his eyes had found a man he knew better than he would care to admit. With his factory worker's shirt and pants, and somewhat more filled-out shape, HanChol had no trace left of the raw intensity of a penniless graduate. Even in the midst of war, he had the strapping look of a man ideally poised between youth and maturity, past accomplishments and future ambition. JungHo had heard that he had opened up an auto repair shop and was skillfully expanding the business even as the whole country fared like a paper boat in a hurricane. Nonetheless, he wasn't so successful that he could avoid coming to beg for food from YoungGu—JungHo thought with some satisfaction. He realized that this was his moment of revenge, a chance vindication that happens only once in people's lives. It was about three o'clock in the afternoon, an in-between time of day, and dead leaves were rustling on the sand where the dog used to lie in the sun. JungHo unconsciously took in these details so that he could recollect later the precise moment at which he felt the happiness of humiliating someone who had deeply humiliated him in the past. His ears drummed with blood and all of his veins were humming, from fingertips to toes. It was one of the most pleasant sensations he'd ever experienced.

"Do you know that guy?" YoungGu asked.

"It's a long story but he's a real"—JungHo searched for the right word—"coward. Yes, that's what he is," he said, satisfied that even MyungBo couldn't say he wasn't being fair.

"I'll make him leave right now. Or beat him to death, whatever you prefer." As the words left YoungGu's lips, five or six of his underlings filed behind them automatically, clenching their knuckles and cracking their necks.

"No, I'll take care of him myself," JungHo said, walking up to the queue with balled-up fists. The crowd instinctively quieted down and lassoed their attention on the two men. JungHo's recognition wasn't returned; in a gesture of mild suspicion, HanChol narrowed his dumb eyes that women inexplicably liked so much.

"You're Mr. Kim HanChol?" JungHo asked, without bowing or offering his hand. "I'm Nam JungHo. You may not know me, but we both know Jade Ahn."

HanChol's face was transformed at the mention of her name, as if it were an antidote that turned arrogance to sorrow. "I have heard of you. Jade used to tell me you were one of her closest friends," he said, casting his eyes low.

"Did she?" JungHo wondered, more to himself. He flushed a little imagining what they'd said about him, but he brushed this aside.

"She told me about you as well, Mr. Kim HanChol. You were not a good friend to her."

JungHo saw with satisfaction how his enemy's face paled and lost its self-absorbed equanimity. So that was his weakness—the need to *appear* to be right. HanChol was the kind of man who could convince himself that he had always done the best he could. JungHo knew that this look of sorrow was just one way he protected his own self-regard. The best revenge against HanChol would be shaking his conceit, and that wasn't going to happen just by pummeling him with fists.

"The likes of you don't deserve to breathe the same air she breathes. Never, ever appear in front of her again, you hear me?" JungHo snarled, taking a step closer to his rival and barely resisting the urge to spit on the ground. HanChol hadn't moved an inch all the while, like a lizard that has sensed a predator and decides to play dead until the danger passes. He did not look so fine now—only cowardly, just as JungHo intuited. If only Jade knew!

"Boys, make sure Mr. Kim HanChol here gets whatever he needs," he said, turning around. YoungGu snapped to attention and sent his underlings off in all directions in search of food.

"And don't accept any payment from him."

He knew without looking that HanChol, with his tiresome nobleman's rules, was humiliated by having to accept the generosity of someone who clearly despised him. And no matter what happened in the past, ultimately it was he, JungHo, who was going to see her this evening. She needed *him*. The pleasure of revenge was so great that he felt as though he were a furious star, aligned perfectly in a constellation.

• • •

JUNGHO MANAGED TO BARTER THREE of YoungGu's potatoes for a yellow melon on the way to Jade's house. He had hardly finished knocking when she appeared and opened the gate for him. She accepted the heavy linen bag from him with both hands, opened it, and gasped.

"Barley, potatoes, anchovies . . . And what's this? A *chameh* melon! I feel like I'm looking at a mirage. JungHo, what would I do without you?" she said, ushering him inside.

"I only wish there's something more I can do. How is Aunt Dani?" he asked, taking off his fedora.

"She's still struggling with fever. I think it's the shock from the raids, and this steamy weather isn't helping, either. She hasn't had much to eat in months and has lost too much weight." Jade blushed. She herself had become gaunt, and there were dusk-like shadows under her cheekbones that he hadn't seen before.

"Did they take everything?" The police had been raiding people's homes to collect not just rice and jewelry, but also metal pots, pans, clothing irons, furnaces, fire pokers, and the like. Without discrimination they were all melted down and remade into artillery, ships, and airplanes.

"Almost. In the garden, I dug a hole under the cherry tree and buried a few of our most expensive jewelry. But what use is a diamond necklace or a gold comb when the rice is half mixed with sand and there's nothing to eat?"

"Jade, don't tell even me where your secret hiding place is! Be careful around your neighbors and friends. That's just for you and Aunt Dani to know." JungHo berated her, and a sweet smile warmed her face.

"But, JungHo, you *are* my family. You've been bringing us good rice for months. I trust you." She grinned, and little crinkles appeared under her eyes. It made her look her age—she was thirty-three, and more than twenty years had passed since he first saw her. And yet he thought she looked beautiful now in her waning, perhaps even more so than when she was a young courtesan in full bloom. Even the shadows on her face drew him in.

"Just hang in there. This can't last forever. Japan greatly underestimated how big a country China is. The world has turned its back on them after what happened in Nanjing. Rape, fire, killing pregnant women . . . What they did to us, they now do to the Chinese. Our Independence Army and the Chinese troops have already joined forces in Manchuria. My mentor says Japan cannot win this war," he said. Jade nodded firmly, as if her assent would help that prediction come to pass.

"Actually, that's what I came to tell you." He took his hat by the brim and turned it around in a circle. The air in the room was heavy, like a fourth drink. The second hand of the clock ticked away the silence to the beating of his heart.

"I was chosen to go to Shanghai on a mission," he said, almost like an afterthought. But it was hard—much harder than he'd anticipated—to feign nonchalance.

Among the many things he'd never learned how to do, letting go was the most difficult. But he resolved to do what he'd always done: act first and think later. To gain courage, he raised the heels of his hands and pressed them into his eyes a few times.

"I'm not going to be back for many months," he said. They both heard more clearly what was *not* being said—that he was likely not going to come back at all. A mutual understanding overtook them. The ticking of the clock slowed and then disappeared into oblivion, and JungHo felt satisfied that sitting here together in sorrow was the just compensation for all his years of waiting. It was hot and humid and death lingered in the dark corners of the room like purple shadows of a long summer sun.

"I'd been waiting for years for my mentor to entrust me with a mission," he said with a faint smile. "But now that the time has come, I feel a little—a bit sad."

"Oh JungHo, I'm so worried for you," Jade said, discreetly sponging her eyes with a finger. She was determined to seem brave, so JungHo pretended not to notice.

"You have been my only friend these past years, with Luna in America and Lotus missing . . . I don't know what I'll do when you're gone." She sighed, then rushed to the kitchen, shouting, "Will you at least stay for dinner? I will cook something."

JungHo stayed in the sitting room while Jade busied herself with preparing the barley he'd brought. Dani was sleeping, so she left a bowl of porridge next to her cot before setting the table for JungHo and herself. The soldiers had taken away Dani's polished bronze bowls, spoons, and chopsticks, so Jade had to make do with wooden bowls and utensils that not even her maids would have used before the war. Watching her fuss over the dishes, JungHo imagined that they were married and that this was just one of their ordinary meals in their ordinary lives. The fantasy was so pleasant that he couldn't help but say it aloud.

"Jade, it's as though you're my wife fixing me dinner." The moment he heard the words, he was terrified of repulsing her. But surprisingly, she smiled.

"It's hard being a bachelor. A man needs a woman's touch." She crinkled her eyes, pushing a bowl of radish kimchi closer to him. "Eat."

They chewed slowly to prolong the light dinner, talking of the war and Dani's illness.

"One of our comrades is a doctor. Before I leave, I'll drop by his clinic and ask him to visit Aunt Dani," he said, putting down his spoon.

"All I ever do is cause you trouble and ask for help." Jade knit her brows. "I've done nothing for you."

"There was never any need for you to do something for me," he said with a shy smile. That was the truth. At some indiscernible point—years ago already—JungHo had given up the idea that she could love him the way he loved her. It had happened without him even realizing, which was probably for the best. He'd made all the most important turns in his life based on a wish that was long gone, but to go back was impossible. And what good would it do to deny his past? Somewhere inside him flickered the intuition that this happened to all people to varying degrees, and that helped him make peace with his lot. But what she said next blew apart that peace with the force of a summer storm.

"Would you like to spend the night?" she asked.

• • •

SHE WOKE UP WITH his arms tightly wound around her body. Even deep in sleep, he didn't seem to want to let her go. There was a trace of a smile on his lips.

Had this been HanChol, she would have stroked his hair and kissed him in his sleep. With JungHo, she had only the deep desire to be alone again. She didn't regret asking him to spend the night. It was right that she should give what meant so much to him, which cost her so little. And yet, she felt so uncomfortable in his arms that her best efforts to stay still were in vain.

"You're awake already," JungHo whispered through half-closed lids.

"Keep sleeping. I'll fix some breakfast." She started to rise, but he pulled her back.

"I'd rather hold you a bit longer. And I want to talk to you."

She was even more uncomfortable now that the room was becoming lighter and she was still naked next to him, but she stayed.

"Jade, you know how I feel about you," he began, his eyes now wide. "I have loved you for a very long time. More than you know. Do you remember the day when you were in a parade, all dressed up in costume? That's when I first saw you. Even then, as young as I was, I felt like my life would change."

Jade did remember the parade, but of course had no recollection of seeing JungHo among the hundreds of spectators.

"After Dani told me to stay away and we lost touch, I used to look for you everywhere I went. When you were going to the cinema with Lotus, my eyes found you in the crowd like the sun was only shining on you." JungHo's face was suffused with that imagined light from so many years ago.

"How bizarre! Why, out of all the people you see in Seoul."

"I know . . ." JungHo smiled. "I would just spot the most beautiful girl, and then realize a second later that she's the same one as before." He took her cheek tenderly in his palm and she tried her best to enjoy it.

"You know, my favorite color is blue," he said with a distant look in his eyes, as though trying to recall a long-lost memory.

"I always loved looking at the sky, ever since I was little. So blue things just catch my eye—whether it's a tie, or a woman's dress. The way I kept noticing you, loving you, it's because you're my blue." He looked at her shyly, as if relieved and proud that he'd shared this thought with her.

Jade was touched, but also troubled by the unmentionable fact that *he* was not her blue. There was only one man who was her blue, and he no longer loved her and wanted nothing to do with her. She wished with all her heart that JungHo would stop talking.

"You're the only reason for everything I've done in my life," he said, turning over onto his right side to face her. "Jade, listen carefully. I'm going to tell my mentor that I can't go on the mission. Before, I had no reason not to go . . . But now, I want to stay here and have a life with you." He interlaced his hand with hers and squeezed.

Jade's heart started racing and her cheeks tingled with a current of overwhelm. "But you've already promised him. How can you go back on your word?" she asked, pulling imperceptibly away from him.

JungHo widened his eyes, and said in an eager voice meant to reassure her: "Comrade Lee is the most compassionate, humane person I know. He's never stopped anyone from leaving, for any reason. He has never acted as if he owns me."

She breathed slowly, struggling to contain the cruelty of her own words. But when she relaxed her grip, they rushed out of her mouth like hounds. "But the mission is bigger than any one of us."

She had no time to reflect on her words before they escaped, so they felt like mere meaningless sounds at first. But she realized their full horror as JungHo's loving face turned to stone. It wasn't just that he was very still and cold—what she'd found endearing about him, recognizably and uniquely JungHo ever since they were little, was extinguished at once with her utterance.

"After everything I've done for you," he said with difficulty. Jade saw before her eyes their life together: JungHo shouting at her to jump from the tree so he could catch her; flying out of her house to find a midwife for Luna; holding hands with her the night the war began; standing at the gates with sacks of food when all hope seemed to be lost, so much so that sometimes it felt like all she needed to do to summon him was look at the door. He was also seeing these memories in his mind, she realized—and the more he saw, the more he despaired.

"And I would have done even more—given up everything—to keep you safe." His darkly burning eyes made her struggle not to flinch.

"That's not what I meant to say. Of course I want you to stay," she said, so weakly that even she had trouble believing herself.

He said nothing; he seemed to have finally realized that he had spent his life loving someone so unworthy. He rose and dressed in silence, his face contorted with hatred. Then just before reaching her door, he turned back.

What happened next made her see who he really was for the first time—someone she'd only guessed at from his mysterious occupation. JungHo lunged toward her. Too terrified to cry out, she cradled her head in her arms and cowered, but his body flew by her. He fell onto the cot, attacking it like a madman. When the cot seemed dead enough, he grabbed the nearest object—a hand mirror—and hurled it at the wall, where it exploded into pieces. Ignoring the glistening shards of glass spraying over them, he buried his head in the comforter and screamed—just a sharp monosyllable, an inhuman howl. Thus spent, he lay prostrate, panting, his back rising and falling with his breath.

Jade felt herself sobbing, because his body looked so familiar and yet so alien to her. It was as if something invisible that had constellated them together since childhood had been severed, and she could no longer reach him even while sitting just an arm's length apart. She wanted to find a way to calm him, to make him understand how much he *did* mean to her. But before she could say anything, he pressed himself up to kneeling and with his head still bowed, exhaled deeply. There was no trace of violent rage left in him, just starry flecks of mirror clinging to his clothes and hair. A few more minutes passed in silence. When he finally lifted his head, she saw that his expression was cold and determined. Only his eyes were unusually bright and full like melted snow.

He stood up and put on his hat in the manner of someone leaving the funeral of a distant connection—dryly somber with an air of finality.

"I said to you once that no one would care if I died. Remember how you said *you* would?" Without waiting for her to reply, he dipped his hat and walked out of her house for the very last time.

• • •

IN JULY, MAJOR GENERAL YAMADA came home on leave from the campaign in China. His wife, Mineko, greeted him coldly. Though she'd begun their marriage in innocence and good faith, she'd become disappointed, then tired, then enraged by his complete lack of presence. She was barely moved to see him considerably aged. There were now deep grooves on his once-elegant forehead. He'd lost two fingers on his right hand, which he kept encased in a glove even in the sweltering heat. She might have felt pity for a stranger wounded in battle, but not for her husband, who had dedicated his entire life to war and conquest.

The morning after his arrival, Mineko sat down to tea with her husband and asked for a divorce. She was three months pregnant, she explained. If he would be decent enough to set her free, she would marry her lover and move back to Japan.

Yamada didn't say anything, not because he was angry or indignant but because he'd lost the desire to speak. He stared at Mineko, who was in a pink dress similar to the one she'd worn at their first meeting. It occurred to him then that they had been married sixteen years and were still strangers at heart. They had had nothing to say to each other, until this moment.

"I will have to speak to your brother about this," Yamada replied, putting an end to their discussion.

An hour later, he was sitting in Ito Atsuo's reception room. It was not the same one where he had looked at the porcelains and the tiger skin, so many years ago. Ito had built himself a fine Beaux Arts mansion at the foot of South Mountain, said to be one of the most beautiful houses in all of Korea. The room was decorated in French style with Louis Seize chairs and gilded drapes, and though there were a few celadons above a mantelpiece, the tiger skin was nowhere to be found.

"Genzo, how many years has it been? When did you arrive and how long will you be staying?" Ito strode into the room, looking barely aged since they last saw each other.

"Almost eight years. You look exactly the same," Yamada said, shaking Ito's hand.

"Do I? Even so, it hasn't been easy for me. Sit, sit . . . Let's talk about you first though. I heard about your hand, you war hero!"

Yamada sat down on the deep-seated chair and smoothed down his thighs, smiling awkwardly. "Hardly. There were many others who lost their lives. Farm boys, butcher's boys, and heirs to old and respectable families. Some were truly fearless, others were only worried about surviving. But in the end, they all died screaming. Death is a great equalizer."

"But surely you were in the thick of action. Not playing cards or drinking back at the camp!"

"It's not because I'm brave that I lost two fingers . . . It was only a matter of chance."

"Perhaps you're right. Still, you've made a sacrifice, as all men ought to. Even I've had to donate all of the iron and gold mined from my ores in the past six months. As you can imagine, that has been a staggering loss. But as an obedient subject of His Majesty the Emperor, I am glad to play my part. And, of course, I'll receive the rewards for my loyalty once this war is over. Indochina has far more ores than Korea, and Burma is rife with rubies. And within a year, we'll wrest India from Britain's grip. I will be richer than a rajah!"

Ito smiled triumphantly, but his brother-in-law remained silent. The quick-witted servant took advantage of the lull to step between them and lay out the coffee and biscuits.

"Coffee is rarer than gold these days. Drink up, my friend," Ito said.

"It's not going to happen," Yamada muttered, ignoring the steaming cup on the saucer. "The war. We can't win."

"What are you talking about? You were in China. We've conquered that giant beast—the great, decaying, toothless dragon. We've taken Indochina from France, and—"

"You speak that way because you know only what the newspapers are allowed to print. You haven't seen what I've seen on the front lines. We don't have enough oil, iron, rubber, or food to keep this war going. It's us up against Britain and France, and if America gets involved . . . They have hundreds of planes and ships for each one of ours, and thousands of soldiers for each one of ours, do you understand that?"

"Germany and Italy will fight with us if America gets involved."

"Germany is busy fighting Russia, and Italy is nothing without Germany . . . It's fine if you don't believe me."

"If you were not my brother-in-law, I would think that you have sacrilegious ideas in your head, Genzo. This is unbecoming of a general of His Majesty's Imperial Army," Ito warned.

"So be it. I am no longer your brother-in-law, so have me arrested if you desire." Yamada shook his head in ambiguity, more disdainful than melancholy. "Mineko asked me for a divorce. She is with child and wants to marry its father and move back to Japan."

It was Ito's turn to shake his head. He put down his cup and leaned back in his chair like a doctor about to announce some unfortunate but essential fact. "You can't divorce her. I'm sorry, it's not ideal, but you have to think about our families. We could arrange to have a distant relative adopt the child, if you wish."

"I'm afraid it's no longer up to you, Atsuo. I've already made up my mind to divorce her even if it's the last thing I do before I go back to war," Yamada countered. He felt so strangely uplifted by saying this out loud, he nearly wanted to say it again. "You know, Atsuo, I've never really felt free. But in my youth, I thought that constriction was good, beneficial. I saw the world as a system laid out by intelligent and important people, and I was going to be one of them. But now I realize what a fool I've been. That system is nothing but that which brings destruction."

Ito had never heard Yamada speak this way, and was almost worried that he would start acting violently. But Yamada got up calmly in the next moment, pulled down the hem of his uniform jacket, and extended a hand.

"We probably won't see each other again, so this is farewell."

"Genzo, of course we will. Just because of Mineko . . ." Ito started to feel quite sad in spite of himself. "With anyone else I wouldn't care, but I don't want us to part this way."

Yamada smiled, and it was a carefree and genuine smile that Ito had never seen before in his friend. "Fine, Atsuo. I'm being redeployed to China. No idea when I'll come back . . . But be well until we meet again."

22

ZOO ANIMALS

1941

THOUGH JADE DID EVERYTHING SHE COULD TO NURSE DANI BACK TO health, her conditions became worse as the summer wore on. Without telling the older woman, Jade had already dug out and sold most of the jewelry under the cherry tree to pay for medicine and food. A few doctors had come and gone without improving Dani's fever and consumption. Among the handful of trinkets that remained, Jade only resolved to keep the diamond necklace until the last. Her gold comb was enough to convince a Western-trained doctor to pay a visit.

"There are sores on her back," Jade whispered as she helped turn Dani to the other side.

"Yes. Typical for the last stage of syphilis," the doctor pronounced, pushing back his glasses. "She must have had a long latency. It's probable that she contracted it when she was still active as a courtesan . . . Syphilis also causes infertility. She has never gotten pregnant, has she?"

Jade looked in fear at Dani's sweat-streaked face; her eyes were closed, her mind was in feverish dreams.

"The other doctors said nothing about syphilis," Jade protested quietly.

"This disease can look like many other things, until the very end when the sores come out. Be careful not to touch them, they are very contagious. As for the prognosis, it's hard to say how long she has left. Tomorrow, I'll send my servant with some arsenic she can take to ease the symptoms."

After the doctor left, Jade went to the kitchen to make whatever she could for dinner. In the pantry there was just a cup of barley left and some dried seaweed she could dress with a half thimble of oil and vinegar. Mindlessly, she pulled out the knife and the cutting board and then realized there wasn't anything that even required chopping. Still, she grasped the handle of the knife with her bony hand, fighting the tears clouding her eyes. She was remembering how she'd cut her hand all those years ago on a hot summer night. If the knife sliced just a few inches above that scar, all her sorrows would be over.

She laid down the knife and prepared the simple barley porridge.

When she went back, Dani was in an increasingly rare, clear, and calm mood. "How ever did you manage to make dinner again?" Dani asked as Jade set down the tray next to her.

"We still had a bit of barley left from when JungHo visited," Jade lied; that supply had run out a long time ago, and the barley was from the black market. "Also, don't worry about where I get the food. You just worry about getting better."

"I'm such a burden on you," Dani said. She was trying to swallow the porridge that Jade was spooning into her mouth without dribbling. But even the control of her facial muscles cost her tremendous effort, and a glistening drop slid down the side of her mouth. "I am like an old, senile woman," Dani said, smiling painfully.

"You will never be an old, senile woman," Jade said. "You will always be beautiful. None of us, not even Luna, could ever compare to you."

"You're just being kind. But more than kind . . ." Dani blinked, and a tear escaped from her still lovely eye. "Do you remember? In PyongYang, when my sister Silver asked me to take you in, I refused at first. This girl doesn't have a personality, she's so bland and boring, I told her. But she said you were a good one. She was right; I was wrong."

"I was happy to go along with whatever Lotus suggested. She was the vivacious one. I was shy," Jade said.

"But in hindsight, you're the strongest one of all of us . . . Even after I die, and after the war is over, you'll survive—and hopefully, find a good man and settle down."

"You won't die! Why are you saying such things," Jade protested, though she couldn't stop the tears from flowing.

"I heard the doctor—I wasn't asleep," Dani whispered in a fading voice, straining to turn her face. Jade rushed to lower her head down onto the pillow.

"Shh, you must rest now. Don't tire yourself out by saying such useless things."

"Don't pretend it's not true, because I don't have a lot of time to waste. Listen to me carefully, Jade. Just two things . . ." She closed her eyes. "First, I want you to have my diamond necklace. No matter what, hold on to it. Don't sell it right now—use it when there seems to be no other recourse. Of course, this whole house and everything in it will be yours too when I'm gone. But that necklace is itself more valuable than everything else combined, remember that.

"Secondly, I'd like to see two people before I die. They are the only two men I've truly cared for in my life. Will you help to bring them here? I don't think I can even write a letter anymore."

The next day, Jade wrote and mailed out two letters: one to Lee MyungBo's home address, and the other to Kim SungSoo at his publishing house.

• • •

MYUNGBO RETURNED HOME LATE that week after meeting with his comrades in the Coalition. It tied together groups from all points of the political spectrum under the one banner of independence: the Anarchists, the Communists, the Nationalists, the Christians, the Buddhists, and the Cheondoists. He was one of the senior leaders of the Communists, but among their ranks there were those who saw the struggle as primarily between the bourgeoisie and the proletariat, the rich and the poor, and not between Japan and Korea, as MyungBo had always believed. The Anarchist credo was that any social order was destructive and oppressive. The Nationalists were the conservatives and some of them put more faith in America than in Korea itself. They also opposed the Communists almost as often as they fought the Japanese. Then some of the Christians were Pacifists, although a few of them had gladly assassinated Japanese generals and governors before putting a gun to their own heads. All the groups believed that Japan would send every Korean man to the mines and every Korean woman to the military brothels rather than admit defeat; their opinions diverged on what they could do to implode Japan from within before that point.

When he returned home, MyungBo found out that there was a letter from Dani—and that his wife received it herself from the postman. It lay unopened on top of his desk, but he blushed to the roots of his ears at the thought that his wife, a perfectly sensible woman, would have noticed the neat, feminine handwriting on the envelope. His wife was an old-fashioned gentlewoman who had been taught that a woman's jealousy was a crime graver than a man's philandering. If he had brought home a second wife, like so many men of his stature, she would have accepted it without objection. Nevertheless, MyungBo had never deceived her even in secret. It annoyed him that he'd been faithful all these years only to be implicated in something unsavory and beneath his nature. But that he'd felt real passion for Dani at one point was not forgotten. He opened and quickly read the letter, which was dictated to Jade and devoid of any mention of a serious illness. It didn't take long for him to decide to ignore it.

Unlike MyungBo, SungSoo read Dani's letter with some warm feeling. Glossed up though he was—for his life hadn't hardened his exterior as much as sealed it like a glistening, poreless surface—SungSoo could still occasionally recall himself as a young man and fall into a reverie about his lost innocence. Pleasant, spring-scented memories flooded him upon seeing Dani's letter. He could not fail to acknowledge that some of the most formative moments of his life had involved her. In fact, anytime he wrote a story or a novel, some trace elements of Dani always made it onto the pages. She was the ink of his thoughts. She had been extraordinary in every way.

But the idea of seeing her again didn't immediately appeal to SungSoo. Dani was fifty-six years old. He now sought the company of courtesans who were younger than his own daughter. If he saw Dani again, he would have no inclination to rekindle their relationship. Rejecting her would hurt not only her feelings, but his own as well. He was loath to see her ravishing beauty diminished and her attractive spell broken. So he wrote back that he only had the fondest memories and the best wishes for her, but that their lives had gone their separate ways so long ago. Of course, if she were in financial hardship, he would try to help her as much as possible. All of this was expressed in the most elegant and courteous fashion, and afterward he reread his own letter with the characteristic satisfaction of writers who take pride in their own work, even correspondences.

• • •

"PLEASE WAIT HERE," a young male assistant said to Jade, gesturing at the hard-backed chair outside the office. The auto garage was one huge space filled with cars, military trucks, stacks of tires, parts, and technicians moving rhythmically among the miscellany. Off to one side, a pair of Japanese officers were dropping off their armored truck and explaining something to a mechanic. There was a small, walled-off section in a corner that served as an office; beside its door, a few chairs served as a waiting room of sorts. Jade sat down carefully and watched, mesmerized at the speed with which HanChol's employees worked. There were at least thirty on the floor—mostly young men but some with salted hair.

Ten minutes or so had passed when the door opened and Jade sprang to her feet. A woman emerged from the office, followed by HanChol himself. Jade stopped herself from calling out his name and stayed rooted in her spot, suddenly wishing she could disappear. But HanChol's face lit up in recognition.

"Jade!" he said in his low voice as the woman beside him looked on curiously.

"How have you been?" Jade asked, and the young woman cleared her throat.

"Miss Jade, this is Miss SeoHee—SungSoo *sunsengnim*'s daughter. Miss SeoHee, Miss Jade is a very old friend."

Though a bit shorter than Jade, the young woman was gracefully built with slender, stemlike lower legs below a maroon skirt. Her nose was imperfect, but her large and wide-set eyes gave the impression of fresh beauty.

"I feel as though I recognize you . . ." SeoHee said. "You're the actress in *One Lucky Day*! I went to see it at the cinema when I was in middle school."

Jade bowed lightly in acknowledgment. She hadn't been in any new films since 1936 but many people still remembered her. The only movies being made these days were propaganda films. Those days spent on set and at cafés were so faded that she sometimes felt as though she'd dreamed the whole thing.

"It is very nice to meet you," Jade said, and SeoHee laughed.

"Your voice is very different from what I'd imagined. I've only seen your silent films . . . Well, how do you two know each other?"

"When I was a student, I used to make money by driving a rickshaw. Miss Jade was one of my best clients," HanChol stepped in. "We'll have some catching up to do."

"Of course. I will get going then. It was nice to meet you, Miss Jade," SeoHee said, gazing confidently with her shining black pools of eyes before taking her leave.

Drawing a deep breath, HanChol opened the door to his office, and they both walked inside. A bare lightbulb hung from the ceiling, casting an orange light over the large wooden desk piled high with ledgers and books. HanChol sat down behind this desk and spread his hands, palms down, on the papers.

"How have you been?" he said at last. "It's been such a long time . . ."

"Seven years," Jade replied. She always had an awareness in the back of her mind of how much time had passed since she'd last seen him. "I heard about your companies, they're the talk of the town. I was happy to know you're doing so well. Didn't I tell you how successful you'll be?"

"This is nothing much. I'm only just beginning," HanChol said, smiling.

"You didn't even know how cars work, and now look at you. This repair shop, so many employees all working under you. I could never have figured out something so complicated."

"Cars are not that hard to understand if you take the time to study each part. That's why I like them—their simplicity. Arithmetics, accounting, these are all simple matters. It's dealing with people that gets complicated." He wore a weary smile that reminded her of those early years when he'd had nothing.

"You haven't changed at all. You still look the same," Jade said. In truth, HanChol had aged. Subtle lines were forked along his forehead; the peaks and valleys of his face had become sharper, setting his handsome features into high relief. He had acquired a more distinguished appearance through aging, as often happens to men between the prime of their youth and a true middle age. He wasn't wearing a tie, and the loosened collar revealed the top of his strong chest.

"You haven't either," HanChol replied. "But why have you come today? Is it because you need food or money? Because if that's the case, I will do everything I can to help . . ."

"No, that's not why I'm here," Jade protested, thinking she would rather starve to death than ask HanChol for food. It devastated her to hear him say that out loud.

"I'm here because my aunt Dani is very sick. She is dying."

"Oh, I'm so sorry to hear that." HanChol exhaled, shaking his head. "I know she raised you up."

"Before it's too late, she wants to see someone who meant a lot to her in the past. Kim SungSoo *sunsengnim* . . ."

When the news of HanChol's thriving businesses had first reached Jade, she had learned that Kim SungSoo was his first employer and benefactor. After turning the publishing house around as its business manager, HanChol had then opened the garage with an initial investment from SungSoo. When Dani told her about SungSoo, Jade finally realized that HanChol's mentor was one of Dani's great loves.

"I've already sent him a letter dictated by Aunt Dani. And he wrote back saying that if it's money she needs, he'll try to help, but that he isn't up to seeing her face-to-face."

"That's unfortunate. He is not a bad person, you know . . ."

"I understand. He probably doesn't know how much peace he would bring her, how much it would mean to a dying woman. That's why I've come to you. You are so close to him—would you speak to him about this?"

HanChol's first impulse was to say no, but Jade's expression of luminous sorrow gave him pause. Her face had thinned and her ivory skin, glittering with sweat, was pulled closer to her bones. There was a new haggardness to her appearance, and when she proudly held her chin up, he could see the subtle horizontal lines skating across her sensitive throat. If he had to describe how she looked, he would have said: like a song your mother used to sing. Or an unopened letter from someone you loved a long time ago, found in the back of a drawer. Or an old tree that suddenly comes to life one spring, its black branches aflame with flowers, as if saying *I, I, I.* But what moved him wasn't just the remnants of the past. What was he seeing now that he hadn't seen before? It was something mysterious and close to her true self. He couldn't deny that he still found her alluring, even intoxicating. Her bare lips were the color of young girls' nails tinted with touch-me-not petals.

"I can't promise anything. He has his own mind about things and it's not really my position to tell him what to do," he said. "But I will try my best."

"Thank you. Thank you so much." She sighed in relief. "Well, I won't keep you away from work any longer."

"Let me walk you out."

Without speaking, they made their way through the garage and out the entrance. HanChol was intending to walk with her just a little and then go back inside, but the brilliant twilight forced him to stay. The bloodred sky and the long purple shadows made it difficult to say goodbye.

"How are you getting home? It's far from here."

"It's not that bad . . . And this weather is good. It's not so hot and humid anymore."

"I want to see you get in safely," he said, protectively grazing his hand on her upper back for a moment. Jade was relieved to discover that something familiar had returned to the crepuscular air between them. Did he still love her? She dared not say. Did she still love him? She had never stopped. The answer was Always.

They started walking south along the ChangGyeong Palace, the green-black branches of zelkova trees leaning over the walls.

"This reminds me of when I was young. My friend JungHo took

me to see Giant the elephant. We climbed on top of a tree to see him for free, then got chased away by a guard." Jade smiled. "Have you ever been?"

HanChol had not.

"They have so many animals—lions, a hippopotamus and her baby in a swimming pool, camels, zebras, and elephants. Korean animals too. The crescent moon bears and the tigers."

"I've never seen any of those except in photographs. Not even the Korean ones. There are not so many bears or tigers left in the wild now."

"I know. And I heard they have almost nothing to feed the animals at the zoo since the war. Poor things—not knowing anything that's going on, waiting in their cages, wondering if anyone will come help," she said, turning to face him. "Why won't anyone help them?"

"Someone will, Jade. The zookeepers . . . they'll find some food for the animals. You just focus on taking care of yourself and Aunt Dani." HanChol nudged her waist gently, recognizing the curve under the muslin blouse. As soon as they were facing each other, they could no longer pretend at indifference. He wrapped her in his arms and squeezed the bony frame as hard as he could. A familiar happiness coursed through them, and suddenly the world seemed less terrifying.

"If I die, will you please remember me?" Jade asked, her cheek pressed against his chest.

"You're not going to die. I'll make sure you're safe. Come on, let's go home."

Those last three words—among the sweetest words one can hear from a lover. There were no lights in the house when they arrived, hand in hand. Without going to see Dani, Jade led HanChol to her room. She was surprised by their urgency, how much they wanted to feel each other after all the years of absence. But when they were fully naked, HanChol stopped touching her just so he could gaze down at her whole body. She didn't feel shy because she knew he would only see her as beautiful, even now when her jutting ribs and pelvis held dark blue moon shadows in their hollows. He softly touched the sharp bones above her breasts, before lacing his hands with hers and kissing her in the mouth.

It was the deepest part of the night when they were finished and lying in each other's arms.

"I've missed you so much," she said then.

"I've missed you too." He gave her another kiss.

"So what now? Where do we go from here?"

"What do you mean?" HanChol asked, furrowing his eyebrows.

"I make you happy and you make me happy. When life is so short, why do we keep wasting time like this?"

"Ah, Jade." HanChol sighed, and Jade felt his arm slacken around her a bit. "I'm getting married in two weeks," he said.

Jade's heart started to hammer uncontrollably. "What do you mean? To whom?"

"Miss SeoHee."

"She's basically a child! And you're telling me this, when we're still lying naked together in my bed?"

"She's twenty-three, which is well past the age when most girls like her get married. And I'm sorry if I've offended you—" he said. Jade was pressing herself up and away from him. "But I didn't plan on seeing you today or coming to your house, did I? It was you who showed up unannounced. And yes, I was attracted to you and acted on it. Was that wrong of me? Perhaps to SeoHee, although in the grand scheme of things, I don't think it matters. But I didn't lie to you. If you'd asked me earlier I would have answered the same way, we wouldn't have slept together, and that would have been the end."

"The end? The end!" Jade was sitting up, her black hair lapping around her gaunt shoulders. The ease with which he pronounced those words shredded her insides.

"Do you even care for this girl? You like her young and pretty face? Or is it about her money? You prefer her to me because of her rich father . . ." She balled up a bit of the comforter and squeezed so that the veins popped on top of her withered hands.

"Don't. Please don't," HanChol said quietly.

"I loved and ached for you every single day, all these years. You know this is true because you feel it, this constant warmth and light inside your heart, everywhere you go. But I will try my best to stop loving you now. One day you're going to realize that the sun isn't shining inside you anymore and you'll know I no longer think of you." She got up and pulled on her threadbare clothes. Shrugging into her blouse, she turned around.

"When I come back, you won't be in my room anymore. And just one more thing—for every bit of love you've given me, you've also caused me an equal amount of suffering. So I have nothing left, in all senses of that word. Please see yourself out," she said, then stepped out of her room.

Jade walked quickly to the garden and sat facing the weeds for a while. When she came back, her cot was empty but still dented in the shape of HanChol's body. She lay down fully clothed and quickly fell asleep, as though her body knew that it was the only thing that could help her.

About an hour later, just before sunrise, Jade woke up and immediately went to her aunt's room. Dani didn't answer when Jade called her name and sat down next to her.

"Wake up for a moment and drink some water. The heat's finally broken and it's a beautiful morning . . ."

There was something about the way that her words scattered unheard that reminded Jade of the white seeds of plane trees. In the summer, when the sun shone just a certain way, the fluffy particles sparkled like stars in the air, each seed tracing a resolutely different path, although the wind blew only in one direction. Jade once watched for a long time to see if they came down to the ground; and they did not, they just kept floating between the earth and the sky. It was the way her words hung in the air like seeds that let her know that her aunt had died.

23

THE BEGINNING OF THE END

1944

AFTER THE MORNING MEETING AT THE PROVISIONAL GOVERNMENT ended, JungHo descended the staircase and walked out into the courtyard. As he blinked a few times at the alabaster light, one of his comrades caught up to him.

"Brother JungHo, are you coming with us to play tennis?" The comrade was a son of an academic family, the end of a long line of white-bearded scholars and ministers. Unlike his progenitors, he was more of a physical type, a star athlete back in high school. He was only twenty-two and constantly raring to do things, which was all in keeping with the directive that they spend plenty of time exercising. Sometimes he even looked disappointed that he had to sleep at night. At thirty-eight, JungHo both envied and doted on that puppyish energy.

"I can't today. I have to get the soles of my shoes fixed," JungHo said with a smile.

"Next time, then." The young tennis player bowed to him and hurried out of the courtyard.

JungHo followed him out a little more slowly. The Provisional Government was housed in a dark, three-story building accessible through an alley; once outside the courtyard and on the main road, the restless light and sounds of the French Concession took hold of him more fully. JungHo had the impression that the red brick buildings here were redder, and the plane trees lining the boulevards greener. The long-limbed and slender-hipped women strolled in skintight cheongsam, saying something unintelligible in throaty Shanghainese. There was a kind of music in their steps, and in the air scented with cooking oil and tea. In spite of the Japanese flags fluttering ominously on the buildings, people here seemed far less tormented. MyungBo had said that the Chinese were accustomed to war and dynastic changes, much more than the Koreans were. They had less concern over which master they served, he'd explained. Within the boundaries of the French Concession at least, the impact of the Japanese occupation was less felt than in the rest of the city.

The cobbler was located just a few blocks east, on an alley even darker and dingier than their own street. The Chinese owner greeted JungHo in Korean and took away his shoes to the back to be resoled. JungHo sat on a chair and waited in his socks; those were the only pair of shoes he'd brought to Shanghai. He even played tennis in them.

After a while, the cobbler brought back the shoes, resoled and shined.

"These look as good as new," JungHo said, lacing up his shoes.

"*Ya ya*. See you next time." The owner smiled and bowed to him. JungHo bowed back.

JungHo let his feet lead him to the dock, thinking of those words *next time*. It occurred to him that he probably wouldn't ever need to resole his shoes again. His shirt, his trousers, his hat—everything he owned was all he'd ever need. But how much more tender were those words, *next time*, knowing that there won't be one? How much more did he look into people's faces with compassion and forgiveness? The slow-burning rage he'd felt in Seoul had been washed away and all that was left was a sense of being free.

He slipped past the cars lined up by the dock and walked along the wharf alone, watching the seagulls float like skilled sailors of the sky. Every day he came here and every day, he saw something different in the color of the sky, in the crying of the birds, in how the light glittered on the Pacific Ocean. It was achingly beautiful how new the world was each day, and he only wished that he could have realized it a little earlier.

JUNGHO HAD GONE TO SHANGHAI with three other men. One of them had shot and killed a Japanese general at a train station and then was tortured to death in prison. Another had walked into a police station and thrown a bomb hidden inside a lunch box, and was shot on the spot when it failed to go off. In January, the third comrade—the young tennis player—disguised himself as a cook at a military banquet, opened fire in the ballroom, and screamed "Korean Independence *manseh*!" on the rooftop, before getting swarmed by dozens of soldiers, his entire body perforated by bullets. JungHo hadn't seen this, as they strictly adhered to their own assignments; instead, he had heard about it from others who read the Chinese newspapers. JungHo tried to imagine his comrade in death, but he could only picture him laughing breathlessly after scoring the match point.

It was now JungHo's turn.

His assignment was to assassinate the deputy governor-general as he made a stop in Harbin, a thousand miles north of Shanghai. The governor was touring Manchukuo, a puppet state ruled in name by the last emperor of China but de facto a Japanese colony. Swallowing such a large territory was proving thorny: the Han Chinese and ethnic Manchurians had formed a guerilla army in Harbin, and Koreans for their own part had been attacking there for decades.

The security, therefore, was seemingly impenetrable. In the weeks leading up to the governor's arrival, there were Japanese soldiers stationed at every place of note, from squares, banks, and post offices, to even large shops and popular restaurants. JungHo was to shoot the governor while he was making a speech in front of thousands of spectators and hundreds of officers. There was no question of whether JungHo would survive; the only question was whether he would succeed in his mission before getting killed. In case he missed, JungHo would be accompanied by a backup sniper who had just recently joined his group. He was twenty-six years old and spoke slowly with a bad stutter. JungHo had never seen him hit the bull's-eye during target practice.

The night before the mission, JungHo took his backup out for a walk.

"It's fre-fre-freezing outside," the younger man said quietly.

"It will clear our minds, Comrade Cho. Better than sitting in that tiny, stuffy room," JungHo said, clasping Cho on the back encouragingly. They crossed the town center and made their way to the little clearing by the Songhua River, a popular spot for lovers seeking to hide from prying eyes. There was no one there now, however. Cho's teeth were rattling as he tried to retract his neck into his coat collar like a turtle. JungHo was also shivering, but the formidable cold in Harbin reminded him of his childhood in PyongAhn. It invigorated him and soothed the restlessness from being cooped inside the overheated room. Even all these years later, he didn't like being indoors for very long.

"Now I can breathe. I was getting antsy about tomorrow," JungHo said. Cho made no reply and just stood there, creating white puffs in the darkness. "Remember, you don't have to do anything if all goes according to plan. And if I succeed—and they take me—you don't try to help or anything. You understand me?" JungHo looked sharply at Cho, and he nodded.

"You're a quiet fellow," JungHo said wistfully. He missed the warm, muscular, familiar closeness he'd had with his underlings who used to call him Chief. He didn't feel that with anyone in

Shanghai or Harbin, not the way he once did with his blood brothers YoungGu and Loach. "Do you have family to go back to?" he asked.

"N-n-n-no."

"What about a sweetheart? You don't have a girl back home?"

Cho shook his head. He did look a little too simple or too quiet to have anyone care for him, and JungHo sighed.

When JungHo was a child and his father was still living, there was a strange wedding in his village. It was like a normal wedding except that it was held at night by the torchlight. As usual, all the villagers were invited, and he too joined with the other children in following the groom's horse to the bride's house . . . But there was no groom wearing a blue robe and a horsehair hat on the saddle. He had died a bachelor five years previously from smallpox. To calm his spirit, the bachelor's parents had reached out to a family of a recently deceased virgin with a wedding proposal. At the bride's house, her relatives and neighbors were murmuring around the table laden with food and wine. Everyone acted as though they could see the ghost bride and the ghost groom, praising her beauty and teasing his eagerness. Hearing their whispers made JungHo feel as though he could see the girl blushing with pleasure and the young man trying not to laugh at his mates' heckling. Once the ceremony was finished, the couple was led to their marriage bed; and the villagers swore that as soon as the chamber's door was closed, torchlights in the courtyard all went out. This was taken to mean that the ghosts truly liked each other and that they could finally rest, for a soul that's never been married couldn't move on to the next world.

No one would hold a ghost wedding for JungHo's bachelor soul, however. He began wondering how Jade was doing and then stopped himself abruptly. So much had happened in China that he'd had little chance to brood, and this had been good for his recovery. He told himself in no uncertain terms that he hated her and that he looked forward to never seeing her again, in this life or next. The wind roared into his ear in agreement.

"Come, let's go back now," JungHo said, but Cho shook his head obstinately, rooted to the frozen ground.

"My family was bu-bu-burned after the March. Th-th-that's why I'm he-here," Cho said in a burst of speech that he'd been composing in his head for some time.

JungHo looked at him, and felt sorry for thinking that Cho was simple. Or perhaps he *was* simple, but calling him so wasn't entirely honorable. MyungBo would say so.

"Tomorrow, you'll get your revenge. Then you'll go back home, marry a pretty girl, and have lots of children. Now let's go eat the best meal of our lives," JungHo said, patting his young comrade in the back. Off in the distance the clock tower struck ten times, and JungHo held on to the misty halo of sound after each stroke.

• • •

THE SUN ROSE WITHOUT INSISTENCE; it was a visitor in the North, and as such always hurried away to its true home in the South. Under the monochrome sky, hundreds of white flags flashing their red dots were crisscrossed between the buildings. JungHo was standing among thousands of spectators filling up the length of Central Street like frosted trees in a birch forest. It was silent save for a military band playing a march on the stage, next to the podium where the governor would later speak. JungHo found Cho's pale face some thirty yards to his right and gave the slightest nod.

The band wrapped up the song and the crowd's energy shifted to the right side of the stage. JungHo could feel his hair standing on edge underneath his fedora, and his heart was pounding so much that he was sure it was rattling the pistol in his inner pocket. But his colleagues had already completed their missions and shown him what to do. He too would kill himself cleanly before they got to him. He only worried that he would miss and that his death would mean nothing.

As the images of his impending end reeled through his mind, a bird—some sort of heron—flew into his line of vision over the tops of the buildings. It was obscure and fleeting, like the death omens he'd seen and resisted in the past; but he knew instinctively that it was, in fact, an opposite force. It reminded him of his father, the famous marksman who could shoot a quail from a hundred yards away. His father's father had once shot and killed a tiger with nothing but a bow and arrow. The same hunter's gift ran through his veins as clearly as his name was Nam JungHo. The cigarette case, also in his inner pocket, was resting just over his heart.

A weathered old man covered in medals walked onto the stage, surrounded by his entourage. It was unmistakably the governor, judging by the purplish birthmark on his left cheek. JungHo had carefully studied his photographs, since the Japanese sometimes used doubles of important officials to appear in public. A wall of officers surrounded the governor almost completely as he took to the podium. The only way to get a good aim was to stand directly in front of the podium, and to do that JungHo would have to push his way through the crowd, attracting attention to himself. Seeing the guards scanning the crowd and standing ready to shoot, JungHo stayed rooted in his spot.

The governor finished his speech and there was an applause. JungHo had hoped that there would be an opening as the governor left the stage, but the wall of officers kept its formation around the leader and started moving away. He was running out of time, they were going to get offstage unharmed.

JungHo took out his pistol, aimed, and fired.

An officer keeled over with a scream, and the wall was breached. Others onstage instinctively threw themselves on the ground, and one of the guards tried to shield the governor with his own body. JungHo aimed at that guard and fired; the bullet went clear through his forehead and he was felled like a tree. People were screaming around JungHo, pushing to get out of harm's way, but with so many bodies pressed together no one knew exactly where the shots were coming from.

Another shot was heard, and it wasn't from JungHo's gun. No one fell onstage that time. He looked to the right and caught a glimpse of Cho, gripping his pistol with both hands and shaking badly. Another guard was dragging the governor by the arm, taking him offstage. JungHo fired again and saw the old man fall down, clutching his chest.

"Go, Cho, Go!" JungHo shouted to his right. People around him had flattened themselves to the ground and he'd lost his cover. He ran without turning back to see if they were following him. He could hear shouts, screams . . . Above it all, someone yelled "K-Korea *man-seh*!" followed by another gunshot. JungHo stopped in his tracks and turned his head toward the sound. Then there it was—the voiceless whisper in his ear, urging him to flee. He obeyed, changing direction and sprinting to his right. Soon he was shielded by hundreds of spectators on all sides.

Near the edge of the crowd, there was an open space of roughly twenty yards in front of the entrance of a department store. As he was hesitating, JungHo felt a hand on his elbow. In a flash, he aimed his pistol at the man behind him. The green-eyed man said something in his plangent language, taking off his fur hat and pressing it to JungHo's chest. A Russian. JungHo ducked under people's heads and took off his fedora. He threw it on the ground, stashed his pistol in his inner pocket, and put on the fur hat. He resisted the urge to run and crossed over the empty street calmly. About fifty yards away, he could see a clutch of soldiers running into the crowd, screaming orders. When he pushed the rotating glass door into the department store, he knew he had made it. He exited out the back entrance onto a side street and crumpled down on the icy stone stairs. "I'm sorry, Cho, so sorry," he said repeatedly to himself, choking from dry, hoarse cries as though even his tears had frozen.

• • •

IT WAS A BALMY, EARLY-SUMMER evening when JungHo came back to Seoul. He was more gaunt than ever before, and his old suit jacket was loose on his shoulders. The Great South Gate still stood in its place, but everywhere else had changed. More Japanese flags were hanging from every building and flagpole, yet the streets were eerily deserted and there were no cars or trucks in sight. JungHo knew that there was no more oil anywhere in the city. Japan was pouring all its resources into fighting the United States in the Pacific, and boiling pine roots and cones down to create fuel. This sappy liquid gummed up the engine like taffy after a few hours. As a gasoline-saving strategy, fighter pilots were ramming their planes into American warships instead of flying back to base. The rumor was that in black-green jungles and insidious islands the Japanese troops were fighting to the last man with sharpened bamboo spears. At night, animals of the forest feasted on their flesh.

He had an hour and a half of walking from the station to reach MyungBo's villa. It was past eight thirty, and there was still a gauze of gray twilight left behind by the sun on the western horizon. JungHo hadn't eaten anything all day and despite his ability to withstand great physical distress, felt the last remaining strength being drained from his body.

He decided to take a break and leaned against a ginkgo tree. It was calm rather than windy, but the air was cool and fresh. The nearly full moon was rising in the opalescent sky. It was particularly bright and beautiful over a lightless city. Out of habit, JungHo touched the silver cigarette case in his inside pocket. It gave him a sense of comfort, as always. But at that moment, he heard a voice call out from behind him.

"Raise your hands slowly and step away from the tree."

JungHo pulled out his hand from his jacket and walked sideways out of the tree's shadow.

"No sudden movements. Don't try anything stupid," the voice said, coming closer to him from the back.

JungHo wasn't carrying a gun with him. If he'd had one, he would have jumped back toward the tree and shot his interlocutor, then fled through the network of narrow alleyways untouched even by the moonlight. But all he had now was a knife hidden on the inside of his waistband, and that would be useless against a man behind him with a gun. He could hear two pairs of feet approaching him; one of them finally reached him and roughly whipped his arms behind his back before cuffing his wrists. When that was done, an officer wearing a thin, slanted mustache came into his view.

"What is this for?" JungHo asked and then immediately regretted his weakness. He'd intended to maintain a stony silence.

"Running away in the middle of the night . . . Avoiding conscription, are we?" the first officer said in Japanese, but based on his features JungHo surmised that the man was in fact Korean. The other officer, who had actually handcuffed JungHo, looked no older than sixteen and almost afraid of his own captive. JungHo kept his mouth shut this time.

The three of them walked in near darkness to Jongno Police Station. They arrived at eleven, and JungHo was uncuffed and thrown into a cell filled with men, sleeping on their sides. No one said a word to JungHo except to grumble at the lack of space. He sidled up to the only spot of empty floor remaining, next to an overflowing chamber pot. The only posture he could maintain was sitting upright and hugging his knees in front of his chest, and in this position he spent the night and most of the following morning.

By noon, some of his cellmates started getting taken out, one by one, until JungHo could sit with his legs stretched out in front of him. His head was pounding and his throat was burning as if he'd swallowed a fistful of sand. JungHo tried to remember all those other times in his life when he'd gone even longer without water or food or lying down, but he'd been younger then. In the past, he'd also had the conviction he needed to live longer, see something through. Now, however, he felt as though he'd already seen it through—whatever *it* was. To end his own suffering did not seem like such a bad choice.

Just as his thoughts were turning to the knife still hidden in his waistband, an officer came around and picked him up for questioning. But instead of a solitary room as JungHo had imagined, he was taken to a large courtyard where three army officers were seated at a long table. The prisoners were filing in front of them in one long line, and then being taken across the courtyard. When JungHo reached the table, the decorated general in the center looked at him with an almost bored expression.

"Name and date of birth," the general said, pointing at a piece of paper with a hand that was missing the last two fingers. JungHo wrote down his name and birthdate, stamped his thumb with red ink, and went to join the others standing in the courtyard.

The sun made its arc across the sky and the shadows in the courtyard moved with it. The men burned in its spear-like rays without daring to follow the shade. JungHo's throat tasted of ashes, but he closed his eyes and kept himself empty of any thoughts, especially those of water. By the time the light had turned bloodred, there were hundreds of men in the courtyard, standing in silence.

The three officers got up from the table and walked over to the men. The general, with the grim look of someone doing something purely out of formalities, stepped forward and spoke in sharp, clipped Japanese.

"You have each been blessed with the opportunity to defend our empire from the grasp of Western Imperialism. Some of you will fight in the Pacific against the arrogant America, and some of you will fight in Manchuria against the hateful Russia. No matter what, dying for His Majesty the Emperor is the highest glory that can be attained by his humble subjects, an honor for which you must all be grateful."

The general stepped back and let his adjuncts take over; they barked orders to strip down into undergarments. All around JungHo, men hurriedly took off their clothes and folded them into a bundle at their feet. Most of them, who didn't understand Japanese, merely followed what the others were doing with a dazed and questioning look. They didn't fully grasp that they were being shipped off to the jungles or the steppes to fight with nothing but bamboo spears, and their eyes absurdly reflected equal parts fear and hope. JungHo alone stood still in his sweat-soaked jacket and pants. He actually felt a lightness of heart, realizing that this would all be over soon, and that he may even be able to kill a few high-ranking officers before slashing his own throat.

"There, you son of a bitch!" One of the officers noticed JungHo in his clothes and shouted at him. "Step forward!"

JungHo stood in his spot, but the men around him stepped away from him, creating a pocket of empty space. The officer pulled out his gun and aimed it at JungHo's head.

"Take off all your clothes immediately, or I will blow off your head like a melon," the officer said.

JungHo decided to take off his jacket and lure the officer in. When he shrugged it off of his shoulders, something small and shiny tumbled out from the inside pocket—his silver cigarette case. Reflexively, JungHo bent over to pick it up, and the officer strode toward him, the gun still leveled at his head.

"You dumb son of a bitch! Leave that there!" the officer cried out in a rage. JungHo still reached for the cigarette case, as if he didn't understand or care. The moment his hand closed in on the case, the officer stepped on his wrist and dug into the ground.

"You dirty, stinking pig!" the officer screamed. The veins were popping out on the back of JungHo's fist as he held on to the case;

but after a few seconds, he released his grip. The officer stepped off his wrist and kicked the case far behind him, smiling contemptuously. He had lowered his gun in his moment of satisfaction. His voice too was husky from thirst, and fat drops of sweat rolled off from under his visor and fell on the dust. After swiping at his brow, he gave JungHo a leisurely kick in the stomach, just as animals toy with their kill before eating. JungHo crouched low and felt for the knife inside his waistband.

"Stop!" a voice called out from a distance. "Leave him be." It was the general. He was striding toward them with something that glinted red in the last rays of the sun—the cigarette case.

"Where did you find this?" he said, holding up the case in front of his face, standing closely enough that JungHo could easily kill him.

"My father gave it to me," JungHo found himself answering.

"Your father?" the general repeated, frowning and apparently deep in thought. "Where are you from? And what is your father's name?"

"I'm from PyongAhn province. My father's name was Nam KyungSoo."

The general turned the case over in his hand that was missing the last two digits. The man was completely vulnerable—but as JungHo felt for the handle of his knife with his thumb, the general lifted his head and fixed his gaze on him.

"I gave this to your father . . . We met by chance in the mountains, almost thirty years ago. He saved my life. I told him then that he can show this to anyone if he ever gets into trouble. Little did I think it would be me," he said. "I never thought I'd see this again."

JungHo couldn't understand anything except that somehow, this man had known his father and even gifted a token—the same heirloom he himself had cherished his entire life. All thoughts of killing the man vanished.

"My first instinct was that you've somehow stolen this, but you are telling the truth."

"Why would you believe me?" JungHo asked in confusion.

"Because you look exactly like your father," the officer said, running his finger on the engraving. "See, there. My name . . . Yamada Genzo."

Yamada turned to his adjunct, who had suddenly become meek. "This one, I'll handle myself. Take the others to the camp," he said. "Try not to kill them all before they even reach the front. We need bodies." The adjuncts nodded and started rounding up the men, and Yamada motioned to JungHo.

"Follow me," he said, leading the way outside the courtyard and into a corridor, then a small office with a window opening out to the streets. Once inside, Yamada gestured at a chair against the wall. He poured a cup of water from a jar and handed it to JungHo.

"Drink," he said, and sat down behind a desk. JungHo collapsed onto the chair and at the same time, gulped down the water in a single swig. He himself refilled his cup and drank while Yamada busied himself with writing something.

"How did you meet my father?" JungHo asked once he was done with his third cup.

"We were hunting and we got lost. I found your father in the woods. He was too weak to make it down on his own, but I gave him my food and he recovered. Later on, when we were making our way down . . . A tiger tried to attack us, but your father somehow drove it away. He had nothing—no weapons, just his bare hands. I still don't understand how he did it." Yamada looked up from his papers and shook his head. "He was a small man, like you."

"He told us the story of the tiger a few times, but he never mentioned meeting any soldiers . . ." JungHo wondered whether his father left that part out because he was ashamed to have helped the Japanese, even by coincidence. "So is that why you gave him that case?" JungHo asked.

"You could say that." Yamada sighed. "Now listen very carefully. I've written up a letter saying that the bearer of this paper is on a special mission assigned by General Yamada Genzo, the commander of the Fifth Army. Take this and go somewhere safe. If anyone from the military questions you or tries to take you in, show the letter and they'll release you. It's very important that you don't get caught again, you understand? If you get sent away, you won't come back. The Germans have surrendered long ago, we're alone against America to the south, and Russia is coming for us from the north. The war will be over soon, but not before we lose every single troop in our armies. That's already been decided."

Yamada put his red seal at the bottom of the letter, put it in an envelope, and handed it to JungHo along with the cigarette case.

"You should keep the case," JungHo said.

"No, it's yours," Yamada said with the faintest trace of a smile. For a moment he looked more whole, like someone remembering a funny episode from childhood; then the light in his face faded and he assumed his usual dry air. "You should leave now. Good luck." Yamada opened the door and stood aside. JungHo stumbled to his feet and left the office, not even knowing the exit out of the building but slouching like an animal toward the hint of fresh air and the way to freedom.

• • •

JADE SAT IN A DAZE, facing the garden, wondering how the trees alone went on, indifferent to everything. She had finally sold all her jewels, clothes, furniture, and linens, and there was nothing in the house that was of any value save for the diamond necklace. It was still buried under the *aengdoo* cherry tree, which bore the only reliable food Jade had for a month in early summer. There came a point with hunger when even breathing became exhausting. Everywhere, people who used to be perfectly well before were quietly starving to death, too ashamed to draw attention to their calamity. Jade also thought of simply lying down and never getting up again, but some hidden energy roused her from her stupor. She listened to a voice in her head saying, I want to live. That she was hearing things didn't faze her, because she was past the point of surprise. It only reminded her of what JungHo said once about being given a clear choice to either hold on to life or let go. He had told her he'd refused death every single time.

She went back inside her room and put on a worn blouse and skirt with shaking hands. The effort of dressing made her keel over several times, clawing at the wall to steady herself. But she pulled her hair—now grown long again—up in a chignon, pressed a blue hat on top of her head, and walked out to the streets.

She wandered the boulevard in Jongno, looking for a for-hire sign in the shop windows. There weren't any flyers on the storefronts, and she couldn't muster the courage to walk in and ask if they had an opening. After about an hour of searching, she swore she would go inside the next store, which was an upscale women's dressmaker. The bell chimed as she opened the door, and the pretty shop owner greeted her with a smooth smile. "Welcome. How can I help you today?"

Jade tried to say why she'd come in, but found it beyond her power. It was clear the owner didn't need help around the small shop; and she already looked annoyed that this penniless woman was taking up her time.

"I'm okay, thank you," Jade mumbled, heading for the door.

As she was nearly running out of the store, she bumped into a man by accident. She lowered her head as an apology; but instead of sliding by, the man grasped her wrist and smiled at her.

"I never thought we'd meet again," he said. It was Ito Atsuo. Save for some strands of silver at his temples, he hadn't changed much from his younger years, still handsome and sharp and agile in his white linen suit. Jade couldn't find any words and felt as though she'd break down sobbing if she tried. Instead, she exerted all her strength to maintaining her steely gaze.

"You don't have to cry because you're so happy to see me," Ito said lightheartedly, all the while noticing how thin and bony she'd become. Locks of limp hair escaped helplessly from her chignon and fell around her neck. A husk of the woman she'd been. "Well, what were you doing? Headed somewhere?"

Jade shook her head.

"Good. Come with me, I was about to go to dinner."

It was a damp midsummer evening. The clouded twilight blindfolded the world in a soft gray haze. They made their way to a Japanese restaurant nearby, where the windows were fogged with condensation. Jade sat silently while Ito ordered more than enough food for four people. She didn't understand how the restaurant still had anything to serve, though people like Ito evidently had no trouble keeping on as before. Seated across from him, Jade worked away on her grilled eggplant without further pretense or embarrassment. No matter how much she ate, she felt she could keep going. Only the onset of nausea forced her to reluctantly slow down; she was terrified of vomiting up the precious food.

"Do you know, it's been twenty years since we first met. You were seventeen," he said, taking spare bites of the fried fish. He held his elbow high, archly straining the shoulder of his fitted jacket, emanating a princely indifference to food even while eating with pleasure.

"I was a child. I didn't know anything," she replied, putting down her chopsticks.

"That's true. An obstinate, arrogant little girl. You thought you were smarter than you really were. Like most pretty little girls." He smirked, and Jade blushed. "But you were a fighter. That's why you were different. You bit me once, do you remember? But life has taught you many things since then, I assume."

"I've lost everyone I once loved or cared about." Jade's voice was breaking. "I don't have anything left to fight for."

"Ah. That doesn't matter. You fight until you die—that's what this is about." Ito sipped on his cup of sake. "The war is going very badly. Truthfully I didn't foresee this coming, but we're going to lose. The Americans have all but wiped us out in the Pacific. But the Japanese army will keep fighting until the last remaining soldier is dead."

"And you? You're not afraid?"

"Afraid? No. What for? Every man has to die at some point. I have killed enough people to know that one day, my turn will come. But dying prematurely is the business of small men. And I have a plan." He leaned in close and lowered his voice. "When Japan loses the war, Korea will gain its independence. And that would mean terrible things for the Japanese living here. I'm going back before that happens." He poured himself another cup of sake.

"You're going back to Tokyo? What about your mines?"

"No, Nagasaki, where my family is originally from. We have a beautiful mansion on the side of a mountain, overlooking the sea. I haven't been back since my father passed away and it's about time I returned. And the government took my mines a long time ago to pay for the war. Fortunately, by that point I'd already invested most of my cash in art and Koryo porcelains. I have acquired over a hundred pieces, each worth at least ten thousand won but some that are many, many times more. They're worth more than the ores at this point, which had begun to run dry anyway. So that's what I'm taking with me."

He sat back in his booth, glancing contentedly at Jade and seeing not her, but his immaculate collection and his similarly immaculate plan. Then, as if remembering something he'd forgotten, he checked his gold-faced watch.

"It's quarter after nine. I have somewhere to be," he said, summoning the waiter and instructing him to pack the rest of the dishes still untouched on the table. "I'm on my way to the ChangGyeong Palace Zoo. That's near your house—I could drop you off."

26

HOURGLASS

1964

IN KIM HANCHOL'S HOUSE, EVERY SINGLE DAY BEGAN WITH A FAMILY breakfast at 6:00 A.M. That was when he sat down at the head of the dining table, while his wife laid out the individual bowls of rice, soup, blanched and dressed spinach, young fiddlehead fern, gingery radish, mackerel simmered in soy sauce, egg roulade, kimchi stew, and the like. His two daughters helped their mother set the table with silver spoons, chopsticks, and cups of barley tea. His three sons sat near him in respectful silence and waited for the female members to sit down. No one began eating until he said, with firm benevolence, "*Ja, mukja*"—here, let's eat.

After breakfast, the housekeeper cleared the table while his wife fetched his coat and briefcase. He only called her *yeobo*. To others, he referred to her as "my wife" or "my children's mother," and was almost never reminded of her name, SeoHee. They'd been married twenty-three years and it was impossible to think of her as the shiny-haired sixteen-year-old she'd been when they'd met. Underneath her tidy apron, her breasts sagged and her stomach strained uncomfortably against her skirt. Only her slim and straight calves with their tiny ankles had retained their girlishness. She knew this and wore knee-length skirts even in the coldest days of the winter.

"*Yeobo,* come home early," she said as he used a shoehorn to slide into his shoes. It was just her normal greeting, and didn't mean he needed to actually come home earlier.

"I know *yeobo,*" he said as usual, wrapping her in a brief hug before walking out.

The graveled path leading out from the front door of the house was covered lightly in frost. HanChol was reminded of something as his feet crunched on the ice, but couldn't remember what, exactly. It was still quite dark at 6:30 A.M. and he found his way carefully to his car. The windshield had frosted over too; HanChol brushed it away with his gloved hands and got into the driver's seat.

Of course, he was well able to afford a chauffeur. After the Korean War ended, he had won numerous construction deals to rebuild entire neighborhoods in Seoul. That led to more contracts even in other cities—the whole country needed to be resurrected. Then his father-in-law passed away, leaving his vast fortune to HanChol. In just over ten years since the war's end, HanChol had become one of the richest people in the South. But he still preferred to drive himself. He didn't want to become one of those lazy men that he so disliked as a rickshaw driver, many years ago.

His was the only car on the road to InCheon, a dark gray line between light gray seas of fallow barley fields. The moon was still stenciled over the western sky when he arrived at the factory. His chief of staff met him at the entrance, his baggy bomber jacket and twill pants giving him a scarecrowish look. They went over HanChol's schedule for the day; there was an interview with a magazine reporter at 2:00 P.M. and a dinner meeting with a lieutenant general, who was a trusted confidant of President Park.

"Did you make a reservation?" HanChol asked, taking off his gloves and stuffing them in his pockets. Inside the factory, there were already dozens of workers moving efficiently over the assembly lines.

"Yes, it's at nine P.M. at MyungWol," the chief of staff said courteously but without overeagerness. HanChol appreciated that about this young aide; he liked to see some dignity and spine in his subordinates.

"Good, good." HanChol nodded. MyungWol had been rebuilt after the Korean War in the Western style. Instead of sitting on the heated stone floor covered in golden wax paper, the guests now lounged on ornately carved Italian chairs under crystal chandeliers. The courtesans in braided chignons and voluminous silk skirts were also gone. Now the women, called hostesses, wore tight, low-cut gowns and hair improbably rolled and lifted above the crown.

"What happened to the crankshafts? They were supposed to be here on Monday." HanChol made his way across the factory floor, his aide dutifully following behind him.

"We got the shipment in last night," the aide answered, and they walked in silence the rest of the way to the workstation where he would be briefed on the latest prototype.

HanChol only frowned to signal his displeasure—his suppliers were all too prone to late deliveries. In the past, he would have snapped at his aide and considered punishing the subcontractor with reduced orders. But these days he was far less given to impatience over such delays. He had learned that if something was meant to happen, it would happen no matter what, sooner or later. The reverse was also true, so frightfully true. This made him act generously to those people who would not *happen* on the scale that he had, no matter how much they tried. People like his suppliers, employees, his quietly diligent aide. As a matter of fact, most people he knew fell into this category, except his military and political connections.

At the station, his engineers were waiting to show him the most recent tweaks to the engine, and seeing its gleaming iron pistons and cylinders, all so perfectly formed and in sync with one another, resting in immaculate silence and contained energy, HanChol had the distinct impression that he was looking inside his own heart.

• • •

JADE HAD SLEPT only a few hours that cold December night. When the sky began to get lighter, she wrapped herself in a thick sweater and stood on the portico, waiting for the sunrise.

The day before, the fellow teachers at her school were gossiping in the faculty lounge about the latest batch of arrests. Jade usually stayed out of these conversations. The others were well-born women who had studied piano and ballet in England, France, and America. Jade knew that they sometimes mixed in foreign phrases so that she wouldn't understand what they were saying.

"Five assemblymen, on charges of communism and espionage. One has even been accused of being sent by Kim Il-Sung to assassinate the president . . ." The piano teacher arched her eyebrows, folding the newspaper in half. Ever since a North Korean spy had crossed the border and made his way to the Blue House a few years back, even longtime politicians were being exposed as impostors and secret agents.

"But I doubt that it's true. How many more people have to be arrested before this stops?" she finished under her breath.

"You shouldn't say that," the ballet teacher whispered, looking anxiously over her shoulder at Jade. "At any rate, one of them was definitely a member of the Communist Party back in the colonial period—this Nam JungHo fellow."

"What did you say?" Jade blurted out loud from her corner, and the piano teacher passed her the newspaper.

"Anyone you know?" the ballet teacher asked, folding her arms below her chest and feigning kindness.

"No, not really," Jade said. She merely glanced at the paper and put it down. But all the strength was drained out of her body, and she exerted the entire force of her will to appearing normal the rest of the day.

As soon as she got home, she undressed and lay under the covers. She hadn't heard from JungHo since they had brought Lotus home together. She had thanked him warmly and asked him to come to dinner, and he had declined with cool politeness. After that, he never again showed up to check on her. It was clear that he no longer wanted anything to do with Jade. Yet, he had been her truest friend over the years. He'd saved her life more than once, and in more ways than one.

Jade only knew one way she could save JungHo now. She would have to ask help from the most powerful person still connected to her—she'd have to talk to *him*. As the sun warmed the frozen courtyard, she was remembering how she'd told him long ago that she believed in his success before anyone else. She hated herself for having been so naive and good-intentioned; she hated life for proving her right.

• • •

AROUND NOON, HANCHOL DROVE BACK to the office in Seoul and had a quick lunch. He asked his chief of staff about the itinerary of his upcoming business trips to Hong Kong, Bangkok, and London. Then it was time to look over bank documents. While he was cross-checking the statements to the bookkeeping, the chief of staff poked his head in and announced that the reporter had arrived.

HanChol raised his head from the files and was mildly surprised to see that the reporter was a woman. She had short, poofy hair and her small lips were painted a very pale beige. Below a tan turtleneck sweater, she was wearing red wide-legged trousers.

"Please, have a seat." HanChol showed her to the sofa, and sank down on his own club chair across from a glass-topped coffee table. The reporter sat, crossed her legs, and laid her notepad on her lap.

"So, Chairman Kim, it's an honor to meet you in person," she said, blushing slightly across her rather pointy nose. "I studied your companies in my economics class in college."

"That makes me feel old." HanChol smiled.

"Oh no, that's not what I meant." The reporter opened her eyes wide. "I'm excited to hear about how you made this happen in such a short time. To rise out of the destruction of the Korean War and actually become even more successful . . . And creating the first-ever automobile manufacturing company in Korea. Have you always known that this is what you wanted to do?"

"Yes, I would say so." HanChol cocked his head thoughtfully. "When I was in my teens, I worked as a rickshaw driver to pay my school fees. Then I moved on to working at a bike repair shop in my twenties. Even then, I knew I could figure out how cars work and how they're put together. No one would have believed me then. But life has a way of working out if you just believe in yourself."

"That's incredible," the reporter gushed. "So, it's about vision, it's about confidence."

HanChol nodded, brushing his hair back from his forehead. He still had a full head of hair, only it was more white than black.

"My next question is, how can someone have confidence? It seems like some people are simply born with a stronger sense of self-esteem, doesn't it? Were you always so sure of your own abilities?"

"Oh, confidence isn't something you're born with. If you have it from the beginning, it means you're a fool," HanChol said slowly, organizing his thoughts. "There are just two things in the world that give you true confidence. One is overcoming difficulties on your own, and the other is being deeply loved. If you experience both, then you will be confident for the rest of your life."

HanChol was definitely not a sentimental man, but even so, he couldn't help feeling a bit wistful about the past. Out the window, a cold and dry gale was whipping through the new buildings, those cylinders and cubes of concrete and steel. The slender brown trees danced, and men and women pulled down their hats and wrapped their coats more tightly around them, leaning forward as they walked against the wind.

The reporter continued to ask him about his beginnings, how he started his own auto repair shop in the colonial period, his marriage and family life, his first contract with the American Army after World War II, how all of his companies burned down during the Korean War, how he rebuilt them from scratch, and what his plans were, now that he had achieved all the dreams of his youth.

"My plans? I don't have any, except asking you out for dinner tomorrow," HanChol said. "Meet me at Silla Hotel at seven P.M."

The reporter flushed brightly but gave him her phone number before walking out of the office, her high-waisted trousers riding up her firm, heart-shaped ass. When the door closed, HanChol was tempted to masturbate—but he sighed and started reviewing the loan agreement for the construction of a new factory in SongDo.

There was a knock on the door; it was his chief of staff.

"I beg your pardon, some old lady is here to see you without an appointment. I tried to turn her away but she says that you know each other from long ago."

HanChol looked up from his documents. There really wasn't much time to entertain distant relatives and hangers-on. But if it happened to be some estranged aunt, he would send her away with a little money.

"Bring her in," he said with a sigh.

A moment later, the door opened again and his heart started pounding as he recognized her familiar form. Her hair pulled back into a bun was a slate gray, and her narrow forehead was deeply creased. Her lips, which had once been so ripe and voluptuous, were now thin and shriveled. But her eyes still looked the same with their peculiar brightness, and her silhouette with its unusually erect posture was as graceful as he remembered. He found it hard to breathe.

"Jade," he called out softly. Not knowing what else to do, he walked over and held her hands in his own. She was quietly processing him in turn. His arms, shoulders, and chest had leaned out while his stomach had become round and soft. His hairline had receded an inch, and his skin had the muddy bronze tint of old men. But what she had most liked about him, his smile, had remained the same.

"I'm sorry to barge in on you like this." Her voice trembled.

"How in the world did you find me?"

"The phone book." She let his hands drop and cast her chin down, as though ashamed.

"Hey, hey—I'm so glad you came. Please sit down," HanChol said to her, then ordered his chief of staff to bring coffee. They talked softly about the weather and the coldness of this winter until the aide reappeared with two cups of hot coffee and a plate of cream roll cake.

"So, how have you been all this time?" HanChol asked.

"I've been well, in my own way. Since independence I've been teaching at Koryo Arts School for Girls. It's been good—although every year, fewer girls choose to specialize in traditional dance. But I'm grateful to have the job."

"And what about marriage—family?"

Jade shook her head in embarrassment. This was a particular humiliation that she hadn't foreseen. "I don't mind that I never got married. But I wish I could've had children," she said simply and honestly.

HanChol felt sorry for her and didn't know what he could say that wouldn't sound obnoxious. He replied, "Yes, I understand."

"And you? I read about you all the time in newspapers and magazines. I even saw you on TV once! It seems everything has gone for you in the best way possible."

"I've had ups and downs like everyone else, but it turned out okay for me."

"And what about kids?"

"I have three boys, two girls. The oldest is a third year in college, and the youngest is just twelve."

Jade smiled. "How can anyone not be envious of your life? I always said you will be the most successful man in Seoul, and you've surpassed my prediction."

"Jade—" HanChol took a small sip of his coffee. "You know, I owe a lot to you."

It was Jade's turn to sip on her coffee, which was really to hide how her eyes had suddenly filled with tears. "Yes, I know," she croaked unevenly behind her cup.

HanChol reached over and touched her arm gently. She put her cup down on the saucer and sponged the corners of her eyes with a finger, carefully avoiding her eye makeup.

"I'm so sorry about how I hurt you," he said.

"That night when you came over for the last time," Jade began shakily. "Aunt Dani passed away. I almost died of guilt, but then it was the war, so maybe I was just dying of hunger. How I survived that, I don't know exactly."

HanChol withdrew his hand from her and looked down at his lap in silence.

"I'm truly, truly sorry," he said at last. "I wish that there was something I could do to beg your forgiveness . . ." Without looking up, he sensed she was now crying openly by the sound of her sharp breathing.

"There is something you can do for me," she managed to say between hiccups.

"I'll do anything."

"Do you remember Mr. Nam JungHo? He helped me with a lot of things when we were young. If I needed anything, he was always there," Jade said. HanChol remembered the man—short, wiry, a bit savage and uncouth. There was an incident during the war when JungHo rudely offered him free food in front of all his cronies, just to show who had the upper hand. But HanChol didn't hate or even scorn him, having never given him too much thought.

"Before Aunt Dani died, JungHo used to come by with sacks of rice when no one had anything to eat, and he helped me find Lotus after she went missing. He's been arrested," Jade continued.

"On what charges?" HanChol asked, though he more or less already guessed at the answer.

"Espionage, Communist activity. He was a member of the Communist Party a long time ago, but I doubt that he's a spy for the North. You know it's not about what he actually believes or commits . . . This is just an excuse to get rid of any opposition. I know JungHo is innocent. I've never met any other man with such a good heart. You have connections to the regime—couldn't you put in a word?"

"What you're asking—it's very difficult. Even if I speak on his behalf, there's no guarantee that it will work. President Park has his own way of doing things. You understand that, don't you?"

"I know it will be difficult. All I'm asking is that you try," Jade said.

"Okay, I promise I'll put in a word."

When Jade got up to leave, HanChol rose with her. "Don't leave—stay with me," he wanted to say; the words were almost caught up in his throat.

"I hope I'll see you again," he said instead. "I once told you I wouldn't feel for anyone else the way I did for you . . . It turned out to be true."

"Ah, HanChol, me too." She reached over and squeezed his hand one last time. A hot tear rolled off and landed with a splash on his wrist. "Me too, a thousand times."

• • •

IN JAIL, JUNGHO HAD BEEN having peculiarly vivid dreams. In one, he was walking in the mountains when a tiger approached him and knelt down. He climbed up on its back and it went leaping over the blue hills, almost flying, shrouded in clouds. In another dream, he was crossing a beautiful, heatless desert. The sand was as fine as flour and sunset-pink, and the sky was a clear turquoise. He was looking for something—a well. Then, seamlessly as it always happens in dreams, the object of his search changed to Jade. Without warning the sand started pouring down from the sky like rain. It was painless, nothing got inside his eyes or nose, but he realized he would be buried if he didn't pick up his pace. He was running weightlessly in the sandstorm when he woke up, drenched in sweat.

The morning after that dream, he woke up and ate a bowl of murky porridge that was slid underneath his door. There were a notepad and a pencil among the few things that he was permitted to have in his cell, so he began practicing writing. Even though he'd campaigned and was elected as the representative of his district, JungHo still had trouble with his letters. MyungBo had once said that he wrote to his son from prison; JungHo had two sons, and wished he could say something to them as well. So far, he'd only managed to fill a whole page with the blocky characters of his own name. Then there was a sound of footsteps clanking along the hallway and the sliding of the peephole.

"You have a visitor," the guard announced.

"*Yeobo*?" JungHo started to say. His wife hadn't been to see him yet, but he supposed that she'd been tied up with the children.

"Turn around and put your hands together."

JungHo turned around and gathered his wrists behind his back, and felt the handcuffs clasp around them. He was led through the hallway and into an empty room, where he was uncuffed. There was a wooden table and two chairs in the middle of the room. JungHo sat down, folded his arms over the table, and buried his head low. He was overcome with fatigue and he was not such a young man as to keep his head stiffly up out of pride.

"JungHo," someone called out.

He looked up in disbelief. His eyes came into focus and took in the figure of Jade, both completely familiar and strange at the same time.

"Jade," he managed to say, still reeling from dizziness. "Is it really you?"

Jade nodded, sat down across from him, and held on to his hand. "How are you feeling?"

"I've missed you. It's so good to see you," he said shakily. He had so much to tell her, but now his mind drew a blank and all he could do was squeeze her hand.

"It's good to see you too. I always regretted what I said before you went to Shanghai. Please forgive me," Jade said, looking into his eyes. She'd always been this way, candid and kind—he remembered with a rush of fondness.

"No, that was my fault. I shouldn't have pressured you." JungHo felt like being direct with her because there wasn't much time left anyway.

"You know, you've been my truest friend and the best person I've known in my life." Jade tried to sound uplifting instead of sad. "I went to ask HanChol to put in a word for you. He's extremely well connected with the regime and the military. He'll do the best he can for my sake."

"Thank you—it means the world to me that you wanted to help me. I just don't know if it's possible . . ." He paused. Jade started to protest, but he shook his head and continued. "I had a dream last night where I was crossing a desert. It was a beautiful place with fine, soft, pink sand and a clear blue sky. Then the sand started to fall from above, like rain. It first came up to my ankles and then my knees . . ."

Jade gazed into his face with her dark, still-lovely eyes.

"I was trying to run out of there when I woke up. And then it hit me later this morning. I was inside an hourglass." JungHo smiled so that many lines appeared on the loose skin of his cheeks, grizzled with gray hair.

"JungHo . . ." Jade began to say, but he shook his head.

"Given the odds, I should have died a long time ago. I'm not afraid of anything that may come to pass . . . The only thing is, I wish I'd done some things differently in my life. Only now that I'm nearing the end, do I finally see everything so clearly." JungHo wrapped both his hands around Jade's smaller ones.

"What do you mean?"

"I never told you about the story of my father and a tiger, did I?"

Jade shook her head.

"It's an astonishing story my father told me before he passed. As a child I didn't know what to make of it, but many years later I met someone who confirmed that my father's account was true.

"This was about fifty years ago in PyongAhn province. It was in the middle of winter and we didn't have anything to eat, so my father went hunting in the mountains with a bow and arrow. He was hoping to catch some rabbits or a deer, but started tracking what looked like a leopard's paw prints.

"So he followed the prints all the way to the deepest mountains, and it ended at a cliff. There he came face-to-face with the animal—but it turned out to be a tigerling rather than a leopard. If he'd shot and killed it, we would have had enough to eat for a year at least. But he just turned around and started walking down the mountain. It started to snow, and he was already close to starvation. Finally, he fell down, thinking he would not get back up.

"He was nearly frozen to death, when a Japanese officer found him and revived him—this officer was the one who corroborated the next part of the story, when I met him by sheer chance decades later. He described my father perfectly and said I looked like him.

"As my father and the officer were making their descent, they realized that a tiger was following them. A gigantic one, judging by its footprint. All of a sudden, it came leaping out of nowhere, ready to attack. But my father drove it away just by shouting—it saw him, turned around, and ran back into the woods. A tiger like that should have killed my father with one jump."

"Why did it not want to hurt your father?"

"My father always thought the tiger was my mother, reborn."

JungHo looked into Jade's eyes, her only feature that still looked the same as when they were both young. He ached to discover that even inside the hourglass there was something untouched by time.

"I don't know if that's true—it's just what he believed, that she loved him so much that even in another life she wanted to protect him. Because, Jade, everything is *inyeon* in this world. It's true what they say, even brushing the hem of one's coat on the streets is *inyeon*. But the most important *inyeon* of all is that between husband and wife. That's what I regret . . . that I didn't get to be with you." JungHo smiled sadly. With everything they both knew, and experienced together and apart, he was no longer afraid of putting her off with this truest statement of his life.

"I'm sorry . . . I regret it too," Jade said, wiping at her stinging nose.

"If I were to come back in another life, I would find you and marry you. Even if I don't come back, and I'm stuck somewhere in the eternal twilight . . . or heaven or hell . . . I will float around, looking for you." JungHo laughed quietly.

"If you ask me again, I will say yes. I promise," she said. Drops of tears were turning into streams along her cheeks.

"Wait, hold on." JungHo let go of her hands and started fumbling with his pant pockets. "I want to give you something."

He held out something small in his hand. It was a silver ring of the rounded, *garakji* type.

"How ever did you keep this in here?" Jade whispered.

"Hidden inside my waistband."

"It looks exactly like a ring my foster mother used to have, back in PyongYang. Since then I've never seen another one like this. Where did you get it?"

"My father gave this to me before he passed away. It must have belonged to my mother . . . He loved her very much. Here, give me your hand."

JungHo slid the ring on her once-slim, now knobby finger.

"It's beautiful. Thank you," she said between sobs. "Do you know, this is the only ring I've ever received. I always wanted one just like this."

"I only wish I could've given this to you a lot earlier. If I could go back, I would give you all the jewels in the world . . ." he said, looking away behind her ear so that he wouldn't cry, so he wouldn't burden her with his tears.

27

THE WALK

1964

THE NEXT MORNING, JUNGHO WAS WOKEN UP BY HIS GUARD, WHO handcuffed him and led him to a door guarded by soldiers on either side. It was a dank room of concrete walls, and at the front there was a raised dais where a man in military uniform was writing something down on his notepad. He was one of those unremarkable, flat-featured men whose appearance is substantially improved by the addition of headgear, which was for him a camouflage cap. To his right, there was a secretary in front of a typewriter; to his left, there was an empty wooden chair. In the center of the room stood a stool, which was casting multiple faint shadows from the bare bulbs hanging on either side of the room. JungHo took his seat and looked stolidly at his interlocutor.

"Nam JungHo, you're here on charges of treason, espionage, collusion with the enemy, and antipatriotic beliefs. How do you plead?" the man in camouflage asked.

"Not guilty," JungHo said hoarsely.

"Listen, Nam JungHo. I read in the report that you were born in PyongAhn province. As was I—not sure if you can hear it in my accent," the man continued, stabbing his pen into his notepad several times for emphasis.

"I also read that you have two sons. One's fourteen, and the youngest is just ten. Wonderful age. I have children too, myself. So be very careful how you respond . . . I don't like tearing up a young family, but I have to do my duty to the country, and the case is stacked against you completely.

"If you plead guilty, you'll get sentenced to twenty-five years. But if you behave in prison, renounce your antipatriotic beliefs, and prove your reformation, you'll go on parole. You could be a free man after—say, ten years, max. If President Park feels up to it, you may even get out after five. At that point, your youngest will still only be fifteen. You'd be able to raise your family." The camouflaged man had the manner of explaining something patiently to a child. JungHo glared at his face.

"If you deny the charges, I can't guarantee any such leniency. You may never see your family again. Why be so foolish?"

"I never had any contact with anyone in North Korea."

"Nam JungHo, you have an extensive and widely acknowledged history of Communist and antipatriotic activity all your life. You were a follower of Lee MyungBo, the one-time head of the Koryo Communist Party. Do you want to end up like him?"

"I renounced all ties with him back in 1948 when he went to trial. I've been absolved of all of that." JungHo closed his eyes at the mention of MyungBo's name. In his mind, his mentor's gentle face flashed like a beacon and then vanished, leaving him alone in the darkness of shame.

"It's not so simple, Nam JungHo. You weren't just a follower—it seems you were almost a foster son to him. He personally taught you how to read and write. You lived in his guesthouse for years."

JungHo looked down at his knees, not understanding how the man in camouflage could know so much of such ancient history. Not even his wife knew how closely he was tied to MyungBo.

"Bring in the witness," the interlocutor said to his secretary, who stopped typing and opened a side door. Harsh light streamed in from this opening, so that it scattered the intricate pattern made by the two bare lightbulbs in the room. JungHo saw a new shadow in the shape of a manlike creature appear against the wall, behind the interlocutor, before the door closed and it faded away into darkness.

A thin old man had slinked into the room and was seated on the empty wooden chair. JungHo could make out just the slender spine and the narrow eyes shaped like sideways commas. Then he realized with a distant, dreamlike horror that it was his old friend Loach.

"Hwang InSoo, also known as Loach—when did you first come to know the defendant?" the interlocutor asked.

"I was twelve . . . So 1918," Loach answered, not looking at JungHo.

"The defendant lived on the streets, panhandling and stealing, until he became old enough to use his gang and rip money off the neighborhood businesses, correct?"

"That's correct."

"What happened after that?"

Loach cleared his throat dryly. "He met Lee MyungBo and became one of his Red cronies."

"*You* took me to him," JungHo interjected in disbelief, but Loach still resolutely avoided his eyes.

"Is that true? You left that part out in your earlier testimony." The interlocutor frowned in displeasure.

"No, it was JungHo who took me. I followed him, that's true—but why would I lead him anywhere? He was the chief, that was his title," Loach said calmly.

"So what happened then?"

"JungHo quickly became MyungBo's favorite, his right-hand man. They went to a lot of meetings together . . . My heart wasn't in it, so I dropped out. But JungHo was absorbed right into the Communist Party. He did everything MyungBo asked him to do, and went to Shanghai for some years. We lost touch during that time."

"When was he in Shanghai?"

"He left around 1941 . . . I'm not sure when he came back, he didn't let me know."

"It's possible, then, that he made contacts with the Chinese Communist Party during that time? The Chinese who invaded South Korea alongside Kim Il-Sung less than ten years later?" The interlocutor raised his voice with the excitement of a game show host.

"Yes," the witness affirmed.

"Why are you doing this, Loach?" JungHo cried out. Upon hearing that nickname, Loach finally stole a glance at his old friend.

"I do what I need to do." He breathed out the words so quickly and quietly that they were almost unintelligible to JungHo. The interlocutor acted as though he hadn't heard.

"Nam JungHo, we searched your house and have the proof of your antipatriotic activity after you came back from Shanghai in 1945." The interlocutor opened a portfolio and pulled out a yellow sheet of paper. He carefully unfolded it and began reading in Japanese. "The bearer of this document, Nam JungHo, is on a special mission assigned by General Yamada Genzo, the Commander of the Fifth Army. Do not impede his mission and grant him safe passage. *Tenno heika banzai*. Signed, Yamada Genzo, June __ 1945."

The interlocutor had a very fine pronunciation that hinted at Japanese military academy training; the parabolic fall of his sentences made clear how keenly he savored reading in that language.

"And this—a memento from Yamada, it seems." He held up something small and rectangular. It had turned sooty gray over time, but it was unmistakably the silver cigarette case.

• • •

JADE WAS WALKING HOME AFTER finishing the last day of school. She had a month and a half of winter break and was buoyed by a sense of relief and possibilities. She allowed herself to think back to the meeting with HanChol just as a writer dips her pen in ink—with habitual pleasure.

At the time, she hadn't had a chance to dwell on her emotions. As always happens with significant events, the feelings developed fully and took on new colors and scents as she relived the scene in her mind. She now saw that she hadn't been angry at him in his presence, even over Dani's passing. She was more surprised to discover that she wanted to see him again, to talk to him about the different paths that they had taken. It was hard to believe that they had once walked the same path, enough for her to have imagined that they might one day marry.

She took a turn onto a boulevard in Jongno. She wanted to stop by Café Seahorn for coffee, as she sometimes did by herself. The café was now a quiet place that strictly played music from before the Korean War. The red-leather booths were cracked and peeling, the umbrella stand was filled with canes, and the have-been patrons murmured in heated tones about art that had fallen out of fashion twenty or so years ago. They had a habit of quarrelling among themselves over misremembered history or perceived slights, but quickly forgetting or pretending to forget. There were so few of them left after two wars and countless struggles in between, that it wasn't easy to end relationships even with one's enemies.

The poet-owner was still there, and though his head was now gray he was the thing that had changed the least from Jade's younger days. He wore the same round spectacles and a well-pressed white shirt, and never noticed his clientele's aging or their star waning. He never married or had children, and people no longer bothered to spread rumors about why. Even his acquaintance with Jade had never deepened to friendship, and she was perfectly happy with that. When she walked in he always chatted amicably for just one minute and then left her alone.

Jade was startled out of her reverie by a crowd lining the boulevard on either side. She was annoyed; she'd wanted to walk in peace and quiet to her café. As she started to weave her way out toward a side street, people started shouting and jeering.

"Bastards! Sons of bitches!" they cried out.

Jade turned around and saw a line of about a dozen men, wrists bound and roped together like a string of dried croaker fish. Each man had a large placard hanging over his neck. I AM A THIEF AND I DESERVE PUNISHMENT read one sign. I SLEPT WITH MY FATHER'S WIFE read another. Not merely satisfied with booing, some people started picking up stones and throwing them at the men.

Jade nearly screamed out loud when she saw JungHo in the middle of the line. His sign, in a shaky, childlike handwriting, said: I AM A GANGSTER & A COMMUNIST & I DESERVE TO DIE.

"No! No!" Jade cried, pushing aside the waves of gleeful strangers. People hissed at her from all sides, but she made her way to the front and followed the train of men.

"JungHo!"

Somehow, above the din of the crowd, JungHo heard her and found her eyes. One side of his face was already purple and swollen, and the rocks still flew by him. One hit him in the back and some young men near Jade erupted in delighted whoops.

"Stop, you dogs!" Jade pushed the young man who was cheering the loudest.

"What the fuck? Old bitch," he muttered, not so loudly, and then disappeared into the crowd with his friends.

Jade met JungHo's eyes again. He gave her the tiniest shake of his head—*don't do anything.* Then he smiled, to let her know he was okay.

He was remembering at that moment the parade of courtesans, many years ago now. It was almost at this same spot he'd fallen for the beautiful young girl who threw a flower at his face—the first time he saw Jade. He had the delirious sensation that he'd been walking this road all this time; and all this time, she was there to meet him. He wanted to look at Jade again, but thought that might provoke her into doing something dangerous and heroic. He had to look away, even though it pained him not being able to say to her, I love you. The rope was tugged, another rock hit him in the ear, and the jeer of the crowd faded away. He began to walk again, one footstep at a time, toward wherever the road ended.

EPILOGUE

THE SEAWOMAN

1965

AFTER THE EXECUTION, I COULDN'T BEAR TO STAY IN SEOUL. I RE-signed from the school, came home, and packed all my things. I gave away almost everything to the neighbors and some of my pupils. Then I went to the garden and dug up the diamond necklace and the celadon vase. Wrapped in silk and hidden in two nesting boxes, they still looked the same as when I had last seen them. It was only I who had changed.

I took the train to Busan, watching the landscape change out the window. When I got off the train, the sun was setting in the harbor and a flock of seagulls landed noisily near my feet. Then I heard the ships blow their horns, just like the poet told me. I felt like I could breathe again for the first time since that day. But this still wasn't far enough from Seoul, and the next morning I got on a ship to Jejudo.

Everything about Jejudo is different from the mainland, starting from the sea. It is light turquoise near a sandy beach, and deepens to emerald-green and sapphire-blue farther from the shore. In some places where the black volcanic rock dashes off to a sudden bluff, the indigo waves look like they're reflecting the night sky even when it's sunny and bright. In midwinter the camellia trees with their glossy green leaves were in full bloom, and when the wind blew, their red flowers fell on the black cliffs or tumbled into the sea. The air smelled of salt and ripe tangerines.

Hesoon used to say that Jejudo is the most beautiful place in the world. I haven't seen much of the world to truly know, but she may have been right.

I found an empty hut by the sea. There were a lot of abandoned houses in Jejudo after the unrest and the cholera in the 1940s and 1950s. No one in the village was happy to see me, but no one told me to get out, either. The island people are wary of mainlanders. None of them spoke standard Korean, and I didn't understand them when they whispered and giggled in front of my face.

THE FIRST THING I DID was scatter the ashes. If I had a way to find Hesoon's family, I would have tried—but I was just a child when we met, and I didn't even know her last name. I took them to the top of a cliff near my house and the wind carried them to the sea. "Do you like it here? Isn't it beautiful, Aunt Dani? Are you happy to be back, Hesoon?" No one answered, except for the howling of the wind.

FROM THE CLIFF, I COULD look down and see a cove where the sea-women got changed and rested between dives. After several days of hesitating, I finally went down there. The descent itself sent my head spinning and my legs shaking.

"I would like to learn how to dive," I said to the women, not sure any of them would understand. They talked among themselves in their dialect, laughed a little, and went back to drying themselves over a fire. One of them was nursing a baby, and another one was sharing her tangerines with her mates. They seemed to think I would leave eventually. I turned around, dismayed at the thought of the climb back up to the top.

"What's a mainlander like you doing here?" I heard a voice behind my back and turned around. She was in a pair of black linen diving pants, yet under her white chemise she was heavily pregnant. She was speaking in the thick, lilting Jeolla dialect.

"I was hoping I could become a seawoman," I said.

She laughed heartily. "I never heard such a thing. Auntie, this isn't something you can learn at this age. People drown in these waters. Go take care of yourself, Auntie."

I HAD MORE THAN ENOUGH money after selling the house in Seoul. I didn't have anything to do except walk around all day. One morning I wandered out toward the snowcapped Halla Mountain, which is visible from my part of the island. I thought it would be much closer, but after walking many hours, I was still so far from it. Finally I had to admit that I was lost, and foolish to try to get there without any directions. Somehow I made it back on the path to the village, which I recognized from some familiar trees and shrubs. That's when I heard the moaning and the screams, coming from a fenced-in hut nearby.

I ran inside and found a woman in labor. It was the same seawoman who had told me to go back home. There was no one in the neighborhood; all the men were out at sea on their boats, and all the women were diving.

I tried to remember what the midwife had done with Luna. If it had been a difficult birth, I'm sure I wouldn't have helped. But the woman was young and healthy, and so was the baby. All I really had to do was cut the cord, tie the end, bathe the baby, and put him in his mother's arm.

WATCHING THE SEA MAKES YOU think of things. I spent whole days by the beach, my knees tucked in front of my chest, reminiscing. And a few times at first, I cried thinking of JungHo, the last smile he gave me even as he was being stoned and paraded. But the more I stared at the infinite blue waves, the more my mind was pulled toward the happy memories. Truthfully, it is hard for me to remember in great detail all the terrible things that have happened, save for some images.

I remembered that when HanChol and I broke up, I didn't cry in bed before falling asleep. But I wept so bitterly in my dreams that night that I startled myself awake, and realized my eyes were wet. Nonetheless, I can't remember what we said to each other that last evening—or how exactly he broke my heart. What I can still see with great clarity are only the beautiful parts. Dancing the waltz with Aunt Dani, Luna, and Lotus. The first time I went onstage at Joseon Theatre. Kissing HanChol under the moonlight. The way he looked at me. Being caressed by him. I have to admit—and it is embarrassing, even at this age—that it is HanChol who gave me the most to remember.

I feel sad and guilty about this, on account of JungHo.

"**WHY DO YOU SIT THERE** all day watching the sea, Auntie? Don't you have anyone to look after?"

It was Jindo *daek* in her diving clothes. Because she was from Jindo on the mainland, everyone called her Jindo *daek* or CholSoo's mom, after her baby.

"Where's CholSoo, Jindo *daek*?" I asked her.

"I left him on a rock, over there in the cove." She looked behind her shoulder.

"What? Leave a month-old baby on a rock by the sea?" I jumped up.

"Auntie, that's what we seawomen do. If I don't keep him nearby, how can I give him my breast when he's hungry?" She rolled her eyes.

"I'm always on the beach anyway, why don't you just let me watch him?"

"That's why I came over here, isn't it?" She smiled, already leading the way to the cove. CholSoo was mewling like a kitten inside a bowl-shaped black rock, about a yard up from the ground. His mother quickly opened her chemise and nursed him, and I noticed that there was a large bruise on her shoulder. I asked her about it.

"Oh, this is nothing. The waves were so strong," she said.

THE DAYS BECAME LONGER and CholSoo turned from bright red to light beige. He was such a good-natured little baby. I sat alone in the cove with CholSoo, shielded from the sea spray, the wind, and the sun. The other women came back periodically to empty their bags of abalones and eat a bite of food before heading back out. They were divided by rank and could dive only in their respective areas. CholSoo's mom only went out to the shallow waters by the shore, and when she came back her bag was usually a lot lighter than the others'.

ONE NIGHT I FOUND IT hard to sleep. It was the sound of the waves crashing. As soon as the sky began to lighten, I went for a walk. The sun was just below the sea and the world was awash in orange and pink.

My feet led me to the cliff, and standing there amid the fluttering new grass was a pair of chestnut-colored wild horses. They stared at me for a long time with such calm eyes.

"COME NOW, if you really want to dive, I'll show you," Jindo *daek* said to me, throwing me a pair of diving pants and a white linen chemise.

"What about CholSoo?" I asked.

"He'll be fine. I just fed him and we won't be out long."

I quickly changed into the diver's outfit and put on the circular goggle over my head. She didn't give me a bag, a knife, and a buoy, because I wouldn't even try to dive deep or catch an abalone for months at least.

The water was warmer than I thought. All I learned that day was how to float in the water without sinking. For hours I bobbed in the shallow, turquoise water, the waves carrying me back and forth, rocking me the way I rock CholSoo to sleep.

I FINALLY GAINED SOME RESPECT within the hamlet after I bought a black-and-white television from the mayor of the neighboring town. No one had ever owned a TV in this village, and almost every evening people came over to my house to watch the news—never mind that they barely understood what was being said. Every so often, the screen turned to static and I had to get up and hammer the side of the TV to get it working again. They were even delighted by that. The women started calling me Seoul *halmang*—Seoul granny.

AFTER MONTHS OF BOBBING and doggy-paddling, I was finally allowed to hold my breath and sink down to the sea floor. It was only a little deeper than my height but panic gripped me and I came back to the surface, coughing and gasping. Jindo *daek* gave me her arm so I could hold on to it and regain my breath. I couldn't help but notice that her arm was covered in bruises. Every day her bruises became bigger.

"It's nothing," she said before I could question her.

"You could leave him and come live with me," I offered.

"Auntie, he would break down your entire house and drag me out by my hair," she said.

After some practice, I began collecting sea urchins and oysters near the shore. Instead of going to the cove to relax with the other women, I stayed in the sea and just floated. In the water, I felt the weight of the people I used to be falling down to the seafloor. I no longer felt like the same person who had had all those heartaches and regrets.

ONE NIGHT, the stiff-faced announcer reported that the last tiger to be captured in the wild had died in the ChangGyeong Palace Zoo. It had been discovered as an orphaned cub right after the end of the Korean War. Most scientists believe that the Siberian tiger is now officially extinct in the Korean peninsula. But one scientist who was interviewed said they may still exist in the Demilitarized Zone or the deepest mountains in the northeastern border of North Korea.

I WOKE UP to the sound of mewling outside my door and found CholSoo in a basket. His mom was nowhere to be found in the village, the cove, or the sea. By midday, the word had gotten around that she had left her baby with me and run away back to the mainland. Her husband, a red-faced captain of a fishing boat, soon came lumbering into my house, reeking of alcohol.

"Where's that whore! I will break her in half this time. And where's my son?"

"Jindo *daek* is not here, and I don't know where she is. But it looks like she wanted me to take care of CholSoo," I said as calmly as possible.

"You stupid wench, give me my son back!" He bared his teeth.

"I'm old enough to be your mother, watch your tongue," I snapped. "Do you even know anything about raising an infant? Fine, take him, if you want to see your own flesh and blood starve to death. Because of your stupidity and stubbornness, you're going to kill this innocent baby. Just like you beat up the mother of your own child." I walked into the room and fetched CholSoo in his swaddling clothes.

"Here, take him if you have any idea how to feed and clothe him."

As soon as the man leaned in, the baby started wailing. His father flinched, and I imagined that he had beaten his wife whenever she couldn't quiet the baby quickly enough.

"I can't stand that crying . . ." He grimaced.

"Go away now. If you want what's best for your child, go away in peace."

He turned on his heel and walked out of my gates.

CHOLSOO WAS A GOOD BABY. There were four nursing women in the hamlet and they took turns nursing him once a day. I paid them generously for their milk. For the other meals, I fed CholSoo a gruel made of ground-up rice. He always smiled when I came to pick him up; the top of his head smelled like milk and bread. When I heard his soft breathing at night, I didn't feel lonely anymore. I no longer felt the need to take a walk before sunrise.

IT WAS EARLY SUMMER and the hills and cliffs were covered in pink rhododendron. Something I discovered also is that in Jejudo, the cosmoses bloom even in spring and summer. The sight of wildflowers and the sea made my heart hurt. That was why I sought out the water.

I took the baby to the cove with me and laid him in the bowl-shaped rock. The other women were already hundreds of yards out from the shore. I waded out alone to the shallows with my tools.

The water was so clear that I could see the colorful little fish from above the surface. One orange fish with white stripes, the size of my pinky, nibbled at my toe and then swam away quickly.

I put on my goggle, took a deep breath, and sank down. The

rocks looked promising with their corals, sea anemone, and starfish, but I could only hold my breath for so long. I dove several times before picking up a single sea urchin. Maybe an hour had passed but I was already out of breath and worried about the baby.

I sank down for just one more dive before heading back to the cove. That's when I saw an abalone wedged on a rock, a few yards away from me. I resisted the urge to come up for air and kicked my feet toward the bottom. I slipped my knife under the abalone and sawed it off the rock.

My head broke the surface and I gasped for air, delirious at the sun shining incandescently above the cliff. By the time I came back to the cove, the other women had already left with their morning catches. The best divers caught about twenty abalones a day, and I had only just caught my first one. CholSoo whimpered in his cradle, and I picked him up and rocked him side to side.

After I fed CholSoo his gruel, I sat down on a rock and held up the abalone. Its shell was covered in a thin layer of green seaweed and didn't look particularly appetizing. But I'd seen the seawomen snack on raw abalone many times. I flipped it to its naked underside. When I lifted it up out of its shell, my knife ran into something hard in the slimy flesh. Round, lambent. It was a pearl, glowing pink and gray like a morning moon in my palm.

I stared at it for a long time and I just knew that JungHo was still watching over me. Even from the other side. And I will be the same way, letting go and holding on continuously until only the sea parts of me remain.

Life is only bearable because time makes you forget everything. But life is worthwhile because love makes you remember everything.

I tucked the pearl away in my clothes bag and walked out to the water. I floated weightlessly in the cool azure waves, looking up at the cloudless blue sky. For the first time in my life I felt no wish or yearning for anything. I was finally one with the sea.

ACKNOWLEDGMENTS

This book would not exist without Jody Kahn of Brandt & Hochman, whose integrity, intelligence, and literary stewardship have guided me from the very beginning. An agent extraordinaire and a class act, Jody is one of the great *inyeons* of my life.

After meeting the world's best agent, I somehow lucked out equally in meeting Sara Birmingham as my editor. Her editing was an art in and of itself, and her courage in taking this on made me want to meet her brilliance at least halfway. My deepest thanks go to Sara, amazing editorial assistant TJ Calhoun, and the dream team at Ecco (especially Allison Saltzman for the mythic jacket, Shelly Perron for the awe-inspiring copyediting, and Caitlin Mulrooney-Lyski for the tireless championing). They made this the best book that it could be.

I am grateful to editors of literary journals and magazines who have shown faith in me over the years, especially Luke Neima of *Granta*, who published my first short story, "Body Language," and later, my first translation. I was proud to publish an excerpt of this book in *Shenandoah*, thanks to the warm support of the incredible Beth Staples. Thank you to everyone at Bread Loaf Environmental Writers' Conference, Regional Arts & Culture Commission, and the Virginia C. Piper Writing Center at Arizona State University, especially Ashley Wilkins for her patience and warmth. Olivia Chen,

Hilary Leathem, and James Gruett read drafts and provided keen insights that turned the book from a mere cub to a full-grown beast. My Princeton women authors—especially Keija Parssinen, Alexis Schaitkin, Clare Beams, Eva Hagberg, Kate McQuade, and Amanda Dennis—I've received so much wisdom, joy, and camaraderie from our chats.

More *inyeons* who have touched my life and played a part in turning *Beasts* into a reality: Thank you, Edgard Beckand, for giving me everlasting confidence. Thank you, Max Staedtler, for giving me resolve—I wouldn't have become a writer without you. Thank you Arron Lloyd for giving me optimism. I didn't know it then, but that day when we went running in Fort Tryon Park in a snowstorm was a turning point for the rest of my life. Mareza Larizadeh, your friendship and mentorship mean the world to me. Thank you, Elise Anderson, for the loyalty, bon mots, and memories—the fact that you remember what I remember is one of the miracles of life. Renee Serell, my oldest friend: like the friends in this book, our lives were always meant to be shared.

My warmest gratitude and love go to Mary Hood Luttrell and the rest of my Peaceful Dumpling family. Mary read some of the earliest chapters of the book, and was always just a text away from answering any literary quandary. Support and love from Crystal Chin, Lindsay Frederick, Iga Kazmierczak, Lauren Sacerdote, Imola Toth, Nea Pantry, Kat Kennedy, Lana Stafford, Ema Melanaphy, and other Peaceful Dumpling editors and readers sustained me while writing this book.

I am grateful to Wildlife Conservation Society Russia and the Phoenix Fund for their decades of tirelessly protecting the endangered Siberian tigers and Amur leopards in the Russian Far East. Thank you for allowing me to contribute a portion of the proceeds from this book to your conservation efforts. I'd also like to acknowledge early twentieth-century writers and artists from different countries and ideologies; researching their works was essential to bringing this time and place to the present.

This book isn't meant to declare the triumph of one ideology or country over another, but to reflect and uphold our shared humanity. Suffering knows no borders, and all people deserve and yearn for peace. One day while writing this book, I was passing by Columbus Circle when I saw Japanese activists holding up signs against nuclear weapons. They looked as though they were within a generation of the bombings, yet they were smiling gently. Thank you for the paper crane—the symbol of peace.

My mother, Inja Kim, provided me with her favorite book on literary theory (edited by Kim Hyun), discussions on Korean linguistics and literature, and history lessons—both of the country and of our family. Her stories of her father, Kim TaeHee, his golden-brown eyes, and his mysterious trips to Shanghai during the colonial period became the inspiration for this novel. My father, Hackmoo Kim, mailed me books from Portland to New York, and always picked up any tomes that he thought I might find even slightly inspiring or interesting. But my parents helped write this book long before I even knew I was going to be a writer, passing down their love of the arts and nature, and teaching me how to live as an artist and as a human being. They believed in me before I had any belief in myself. I owe them everything.

And, finally, to David Shaw, the great *inyeon* of my life. We met before we even met, which is how I know everything I wrote in this novel is true.